D1277062

LIVE SHADOWS

LIVE SHADOWS

H. D. Raye

This is a work of fiction. Names, characters, organizations, places, events, and incidents either are products of the author's imagination or are used fictitiously. Any resemblance to actual persons, living or dead, or actually events is purely coincidental.

Text copyright © 2018 by H.D. Raye. All rights reserved.

No part of this book may be reproduced, or stored in a retrieval system, or transmitted in any form or by any means, electronic, mechanical, photocopying, recording, or otherwise, without express written permission from the author.

Amazon and the Amazon logo are trademarks of Amazon.com, Inc., or its affiliates.

Cover design by pro-ebookcovers.

ISBN: 9781795287425

Thank you, Aaron and Alex.

With you, there is always hope.

Chapter One

Madison and Ethan

August 6th, 10:17 p.m.

"If it makes you feel any better, the entire time I was hitting you, I was imagining it was her." I was twelve years old with the back of my shirt around the front of my neck. My exposed back, still stinging from the shower, was towards my father, so he couldn't see the tears welling up in my eyes. It wasn't his confession of his hatred towards my mother that touched me so, but rather it was the terrible pain that radiated from the bloody welts that crisscrossed my back. Each open wound pulsed as his fingertips gently applied ointment. The irony was how gentle he was being when less an hour ago his rage was anything but. The buckled leather belt was still coiled on the floor near the spot where I had wet myself out of sheer fear. From this angle, it resembled a snake; its prong a deadly tooth filled with poison that would leave invisible scars for the rest of my life.

The cursor blinked from a stationary position. It hadn't moved, other than the taunting blinks, in over half an hour. It dared her to type a single word more and Madison longed to take that dare. And then it happened. Words. "This sucks giant moldy monkey balls." Ha! She won the challenge. If only victory came with some sense of satisfaction. The problem was that monkey balls had absolutely nothing to do with reliving her childhood even if it too sucked.

The backspace tapped loudly as she meticulously began removing her true feelings letter by letter, and then stopped at "This sucks..."

with the realization that these were indeed her true feelings. This was supposed to be her passion, when she was supposed to feel the most alive. Madison was supposed to be a writer. She was supposed to be the truth-seeker no matter how difficult or heartbreaking it would be. Unfortunately, everything she was supposed to be was becoming more than what she could be. Here she presented herself with a challenge, to step away from the fantasy of fiction and to write something honest and raw, but she simply couldn't stand up to her memories.

She forcefully turned off the screen assuming it would silence the mocking cursor once and for all, but instead she continued to hear the nagging frustration in her own head. As she stared at the black screen, Madison began to feel the color suck the life right out of her. She strained to look past the darkness and was able to see an outline of herself. It was a struggle to bring herself out of it but she was finally able to see her eyes in the dark mirror. Madison pulled her knees up into the chair with her and sought to find meaning in her own reflection.

The pressure was not something she expected. She expected she would have to write, and not only write, but write well. That was the whole point, after all. It was the reason she left the security of a traditional job. Devoting herself to her art and to her dream meant leaving her steady paycheck and fully throwing herself into writing. She could no longer blame her slow literary progress on lack of time; no more commuting, no more long hours at the office. Her passion had all the time in the world now and now there was nothing. She had turned something she loved to do into a job, and the deeper into it she got, it had also become a time of miserable self-reflection. It was now an expectation to face her greatest fears and hurts and she had created her own roadblock.

Admittedly as the days turned into months, she felt an ever increasing amount of guilt. Her dream had cost half of an income, but Ethan said he believed in her. He said he had faith in her talent and would support her until she could support him. With a smile, he made her promise that when her masterpiece was made into a film, she would buy him a motorcycle to celebrate.

She truly wanted...no...she truly needed to believe in herself tonight the way he believed in her. "I can do this...I can't do this...I can do this. I can do this..."

Her arm felt heavy as she turned the screen back on and prayed for inspiration. Madison reread the last sentence. "This sucks..." and then moved onto the last paragraph. The last page. The last chapter. Again and again. Nothing. All she needed to write was what happened, and yet it evaded her as though she had the task of creating an entire world from scratch.

She should go back to fiction. Creating entire worlds was something she was good at. It was something she used as a coping mechanism to escape her reality as a child, but could she write that? Apparently not. She sighed and dropped her head to the desk harder than she meant to. "Ouch."

"Yeah, that sounded like it hurt. Are you okay?"

She turned to find Ethan leaning against the door jam. He was holding two sweating glasses of ice water in his hands. Madison's smile lacked authenticity as she peeled herself from the sticky leather chair and stretched. Her husband's white work-shirt and boxers were not doing a very good job of absorbing the sweat coming off of her back. "Yes and no." He handed her a glass and before she took a drink she held it against her forehead. "It is so hot tonight. We should get an air conditioner."

"I didn't know the weather frustrated you enough to cause personal bodily damage. Do you want go out and get one tonight? Apparently it is a matter of life and death here. I can't have you going around hurting yourself because you are hot."

"Very funny. I'm just frustrated. I lost it. I have nothing. I thought I would take a break and see if something comes to me."

Ethan sat down in her chair and read the few words on the current page. "It's not like you to lack words." There was a playful tone to him. "This sucks? Very nice touch."

She sat on his lap and looked at him. "Be nice." Their skin instantly fused together with sticky sweat. "It was just like I was in the middle of a thought and poof! The flow was gone. It is just so much harder than I thought it would be." Her eyes found it difficult to meet his and she looked away. "I feel like I'm disappointing you." The slight tremble in her lip was purely involuntary.

He took her drink and set it on the desk before taking her chin in his fingers to force her to look at him. "Listen." His voice was stern. "Don't ever say that again. You could never disappoint me. You hear me?" He softened his tone, "From what I've read, it is amazing. You are amazing. You are going to touch so many people with your honesty." He pushed her hair behind her ears and then wrapped his arms around her. "It's this heat. It has to be well over a hundred out there. I can't sleep. You can't write. Hell, if I didn't love you so much, I'd probably push you off of me and onto your ass. Your body heat is killing me."

She playfully shoved herself away from him, but he held on tight and pulled her down to kiss her. She could feel him hardening against her. Suddenly writing was forgotten and he was all there was. It had been too long since they had the opportunity to enjoy each other. Between deadlines, swing shift, and life, sometimes being lovers was at the bottom of the list. "Oh this is definitely helping with the flow," she murmured against his lips. Instantly he began to unbutton her shirt and pull it off her shoulder in the glow of the computer screen. From the small stereo in the corner of her office, Chris Isaac's "Wicked Game" was playing. She was definitely in the mood.

Ethan was nibbling on her neck and caressing her thighs when suddenly Chris stopped singing and the computer glow faded. He put his hands up, "I wasn't touching anything but you, I promise."

Madison reluctantly pulled herself away from him and straightened her clothes. "I think the power went out."

"Uh oh. Did you save your work?" He stood up and looked at the screen.

"Yeah, as soon as I lost my thought." She walked to the window looking over town and while the moon was full and bright, it was the only light she could see.

He stood behind her and pulled her to him. She could tell that he still wanted her, but she could not take her eyes off of town. He cupped her left breast while his other hand creeped between her panties and skin, but his caressing couldn't distract her. "What's the matter? I thought you liked it better in the dark anyway."

She ignored him, and studied the streets. "What time is it?"

He sighed heavily with disappointment and looked down at his watch. "Well, I can't see it very good, but according to me, it is a quarter until eleven. I've got to be up in six hours. Come on. Let's go to bed." He started for the door.

"Ethan. I don't see any lights."

"It is a power outage."

"Yes, I realize that. But the whole town?"

He walked back to her and looked out. "Maybe. I'm sure the lights will be on again soon. Maybe the heat just taxed all the systems. Everyone is running their air conditioners hard."

"But do you even see any cars? A power outage wouldn't make the cars go dark too."

He paused. She could see even in the dark that he was thinking of a logical explanation. "It is just too hot to go out. It's a quiet Tuesday night in small town Montana." From their vantage point they could see Interstate 15 run north and south right through the middle of Helena, but there wasn't a single headlight out there. "Come on. We'll go to bed and get a fresh start in the morning."

She raised her eyebrows, "And you think we are going to sleep without any air conditioning?" She allowed him to lead her away from the window.

There was a mischievous twinkle in his eyes that lit up in the dark, "Who said anything about sleeping?" Despite a nagging feeling of something being very wrong, she smiled as they headed to the bedroom.

Chapter Two

Summer is the worst season. And trying to sleep in it only confirms it. There is only so many covers a person can kick off, and only so many clothes than can be removed before it won, leaving its victims in a puddle of hot, sticky sweat. While most of her friends loved summer, Madison had no use for swimming suits (didn't look right), or flip flops (couldn't walk in them). They didn't own a boat or a motorcycle or any other toy that required sauna-like air. While summer might be celebrated and enjoyed by most, Madison thought it was miserable and pointless.

Oh yes, she would take a cool, crisp fall day any time. It carried the kind of air that encouraged cozy fires, warm drinks, captivating novels, and snuggles. As she rolled over for the hundredth time in the relentless clutches of summer, she fantasized about stepping out in the morning and seeing her breath in frosty air while feeling a slight comforting warmth of the sun on her back. She envisioned the beautiful change of the leaves to yellow, orange, and crimson and the clean smell of an approaching winter in the air, although the snow she could do without. The sensation of a bead of sweat trickling down her shoulders brought her back to reality, and she sighed miserably.

Only the fitted sheet remained on the bed and even though she only wore her panties, she felt as though she was wearing several layers. The air was saturated and heavy with moisture. She glanced at the clock beside the bed, it was still blank and dark. She sighed again heavily.

"I need air," she whispered more to herself than anyone else and quietly slipped out of bed.

"Don't bother trying to be quiet, I'm wide awake."

She went to the open window and looked out over the dark town. "Power is still out. What time is it now?"

"Like you said, power is out, and I can't see my watch."

Madison found a candle and searched for the lighter on the dresser, knocking down a pile of folded laundry she hadn't gotten around to putting away. "Crap."

"What's the matter?"

"Nothing. I will just have to fold them again in the morning." She found the lighter where the laundry had been and lit the candle. Instantly the light penetrated the deep darkness and the sweet smell of French vanilla floated up to her. She handed the candle to him and he brought it close to his watch. "It says it is a quarter until eleven."

"That's what you said last time. I know I've been trying to sleep for at least a couple of hours."

"That's just great. I just replaced this battery yesterday."

"Hmmmmmm." She slipped her shorts back on and pulled on a clean t-shirt. She held her hand out. "Give me the candle."

He hesitated. "Where are you going?"

"I am going to go look at the clock in the living room. I know the battery is new. I replaced it two days ago."

"I just told you this one was new too."

Madison put her hands on her hips impatiently. "What is the likelihood of two new batteries not working? Now please give me the candle."

*****

Ten forty-five. The clock's arms produced shadows that stretched across the wall in the candle light. Madison sat on the couch and watched time. Time had stopped. It didn't take long before Ethan came into the living room in his boxers and sat beside her. "What are you doing?"

"This clock stopped too. It hasn't moved the entire time I have been out here."

"And you just changed the batteries? Now that is a little strange; about as strange as my watch battery not working. What about the dining room? Our cell phone?"

"Your sarcasm is unnecessary. Anyways, the dining room stopped at ten forty-five, our cell phones are dead, as is the house phone."

Ethan stood up quickly and walked to the phone.

"You don't believe me?"

"Relax, I'm just checking. You never know..." He picked up the receiver, and she knew what he was hearing. Nothing. "You've got to be kidding." He slowly put the phone back on the cradle.

Madison hugged herself despite the heat of the night. "Ethan, I've got a really bad feeling..."

He sat down and took her in her arms and kissed her forehead. "Yeah, it just doesn't feel right, does it? But we both know everything is going to be fine. We are going to be fine. They just had some kind of major electrical surge. Terrorist or something...you know? We are going to be fine."

"Yeah, you said that already." She pushed herself as close to him as possible. "But what about the cars? Why don't we see any cars on the roads? And what about the batteries?"

He paused. "Come on, honey. I'm just trying to look at this in the glass is half full kind of way. I have no idea what is going on, but we are going to be fine. Just fine. You'll see. In the morning, we will have some answers."

"What if we don't like the answers?"

"It can't be that bad. It isn't going to be anything that we aren't going to be able to figure out."

She laid down and used his lap for a pillow. He began to run his fingers through her long brown hair, knowing that it always relaxed her. It seemed to be working until she broke the silence. "Can't it?"

"What?"

"You said it can't be that bad. What if it is that bad?"

He was quiet for a moment. As much as she hated to admit it, she knew that she had created a sense of doubt in him but despite that he finally replied "It won't be." He leaned his head back into the green couch cushion. Madison looked up, but he was looking at the ceiling. His eyes were darting back and forth, deep in thought. She knew him well enough to know that he was trying to convince himself of something. Knowing that about him only worried her.

Chapter Three

Kathy and Justin

August 6ᵗʰ, 10:17 p.m.

I t was getting late, and she didn't want to be there anymore, "Justin?"

He quietly grunted in response. She wasn't sure if it was because he was trying to be quiet for the sake of Wyatt, or if it was because he was feeling the same tension she was in the confines of an SUV that was shrinking in size by the minute.

Kathy hesitated before she spoke, unsure that she wanted to say what was on the tip of her tongue. But it needed to be said. "Ummm...this isn't working."

There. She admitted it.

He sighed heavily. "I know."

Despite feeling the SUV was too small for the two of them, and despite the fact that he was less than an arm's reach across the console, she knew that Justin was miles away from her. There was no way to reach him now. It was a hard thing for her to accept. In fact, six months ago when he came to her, she refused to accept it. He told her he just didn't feel the same way about her, that they were different people now, and he wasn't sure if staying together was the right thing.

At that moment, their life movie started playing in her mind, and it had been on continuous replay ever since. It had the makings of a legendary love story, and she wasn't about to accept that he was going to just cut out all the great moments still to come. Their story was not over. "We can fix this," she had told him through tears. Now staring out of the window, into the woods of nowhere Montana, she knew she should have just listened to him. All he was being was honest, and she dismissed it like it was some silly opinion.

9

This trip was her last desperate effort to convince him that their little family was worth sticking around for. He had moved into the den, and they were barely speaking at all and the only logical solution was to run away from it all. She told him that they would pack everything and just leave for a while and focus on each other and Wyatt. Kathy thought that if they could just be together, without distractions, that he would see what he would be giving up if he left.

The trip was her ultimate failure. As the miles passed, the rift between them grew. She began to realize the only thing that was keeping them together in the first place was space, and she took that away when she insisted that he do this for her and confined him to her.

His cell phone buzzed in the dark. She looked just in time to see him silence it without even so much as a glance at it. Kathy frowned. She quickly checked to see that Wyatt was still asleep in the backseat. He stirred some, dropping is favorite teddy bear, Boo, onto the floor but remained asleep. She turned her attention back to her soon to be ex-husband. "Who was that?" She tried to sound like she was just making conversation but it ended up sounding slightly accusing.

Even though the lights on the dashboard barely lit the cabin, she could see him squirm. He was nervous. "No one."

It probably wasn't even her place to know at this point, but as far as she was concerned she was still married. "How do you know? I mean, you didn't even look."

"Kathy. It isn't important. Just drop it."

"Not important?" It was as though she was slowing stepping out of a thick fog and into clarity...well as clear as a secret can be, and she knew there was definitely a secret here. "If it isn't important, why not just tell me who that was...unless you are hiding something from me?"

She heard him tighten his grip on the steering wheel. "Don't do this. Not right now."

"You've got to be kidding me!" She slammed her fist down on the console.

Her sudden outburst surprised him, and he braked reflexively, "Calm down, Wyatt is sleeping. He shouldn't have to hear this."

She did lower her voice...some. "Well, maybe he should hear what a lying bastard his father is. Jesus, Justin! I specifically asked you if you had found someone else, and damn it, I believed you when you said no!"

"I didn't plan for this happen. I didn't go out looking for it. Kathy...I never wanted to hurt you or Wyatt, but it just happened. It just happened."

"Oh, you are unbelievable! You are going to leave me, and your son for some piece of ass?"

"Shut up, Kathy. I'm not leaving my son, and Amanda is not some..."

"Oh, she has a name! Why couldn't you have just told me? Why have you been stringing me along for six months?" A new breed of tear formed in her eyes and immediately fell with such a force that it even startled her. She had never felt such a conflict of emotions raging from within her soul, everything from hot hate for him to a piercing devastation.

"I tried to tell you, but you wouldn't listen to me. You never listen to me!"

"How long has this been going on?"

"It doesn't matter."

"Damn it, it does matter and I deserve to know!"

"Fine. About a year."

Suddenly Kathy found it hard to breathe. She could feel her lungs gasping for air that seemed to have disappeared from the atmosphere. She could feel her heart beating like she had just run a marathon. She felt Justin brake hard and throw the SUV into park. She heard him open the door, but didn't hear it close, and it seemed like an eternity had passed between that and when her own door was thrown open. Justin reached around, undid her seatbelt and pulled her out of the SUV. He held onto her, he knew that if he let her go, she would crumble to the ground.

"Kathy?! Come on, Kath, calm down! Breathe!"

Slowly, she was becoming more aware. Wyatt was crying in the backseat. The crickets were chirping in some tall grass. It was hot. She was missing the air conditioning. And Justin had his arms around her. She looked up into his strong handsome face, and his gentle eyes. At first she was comforted by the familiarity, but then she remembered they were the same eyes that stared into her when he assured her that he had not found someone else. She was again filled with rage. She brought up her arms and pushed away from him hard. "You're an asshole!"

He let his arms fall heavily to his side. "What do you want me to say?"

"There is nothing you can say. You are finally going to get your wish. It is over!" She looked around and only saw a narrow dirt road and tall evergreens lining the sides. "Where the hell are we?"

"I never wished for this!"

"Where the hell are we?"

"About ten miles from Helena."

"Why are we even on this road? Why did you leave the interstate?"

"I was taking the scenic route. Was that wrong, too?"

"Oh, don't you even..." She clenched her fists and walked over to the closed off backseat and threw the door open. She reached in and started unbuckling Wyatt from his seat. Even at five, he could feel the tension and the anger in the air. He knew the seriousness of the situation, and he cried hard into her shoulder as she lifted him out. "Shhh! Baby, it is okay." She saw Boo laying on the floor and reached in, "Look, here's Boo!"

"Kathy, what are you doing? Get back in the car."

"I'm not going anywhere with you. And I sure am not letting you take my son."

"Our son, Kathy, our son. Just get back into the car and I will take you to town and then you can do whatever your heart desires. But I'm not leaving you out here in the dark."

"You don't really have a choice."

He was trying to keep his composure in front of Wyatt, but she could see that his patience was wearing thin. He threw his arms out wide, "Look around, there is nothing out here!"

"I'll find someone to give me a ride to town, and I will find my own way back from there." She started walking down the road with Wyatt on her hip. "Hopefully Amanda has enough room for all your shit! It will be waiting on the lawn when you get home!" She called back.

"Kathy! Seriously? Be reasonable!"

She pretended not to hear him as she kept walking. She could hear him swearing up a storm before shouting, "Fine! Have a great hike! Wyatt, Daddy loves you, and I will see you soon!"

Kathy had to admit to herself that she did feel a small sense of bittersweet victory as she walked away from their marriage, but at the same time her heart was crushed. It was never supposed to be like this. Their marriage was special, meant to last. It was incredibly hard to let go of the idea of forever. But she was determined to stand firm and to make sure he saw what life he had just walked out on him.

Her lower back was starting to ache under the extra weight of Wyatt so she readjusted him to the front of her. Immediately he tightened his grip around her neck as he looked back at his father. The heat from the air coupled with his body heat suddenly made the simple act of carrying her son more than she could bear. She was becoming more and more aware of how heavy he was becoming. Her attempt to peel him away from her failed as he only tightened his grip.

"Wyatt, honey, I've got to put you down for a bit. You are choking mommy to death. Can you walk for a while?" They had always avoided arguing in front of him and now she was carrying him away from his daddy into some very dark, unknown woods in the middle of nowhere. She was sure it was traumatizing and she felt terrible, and wanted to be able to carry him all the way home. But still, she had to be able to breathe.

She set him down and she could see his little body slump. His bottom lip trembled as he looked up at her and he absently let go of Boo. Kathy kneeled down and dusted the teddy bear off. "I'm sorry you saw that, sweetie. But we are going to be just fine."

He looked down at her offering of Boo and ignored it. Instead he looked her hard in the eyes. "What about dad?" His voice was cold and accusing.

She couldn't help herself and she looked back. Even with a hundred yards separating them, she could see Justin still standing next to the SUV, watching them. She sighed and turned back to her little boy, "He is going to be fine, too. He is going to drive into town and..."

"Why can't we just go together?"

Ahhh. The hard questions. She knew they would come but she wasn't expecting them so soon. Kathy wasn't prepared to answer them. She had not yet even begun to process everything that has happened. How could she even begin explaining it to a five year old? "Well...you see...it is complicated."

"I want daddy to come with us!" He stomped his feet. She looked at him, trying to justify that he was just frustrated with what was going on. He was angry because he was confused. But it was just so strange to see him so angry with her. He was normally a very mild-mannered child, especially towards her. Yet, Kathy could recognize that he was about to throw the type of tantrum he last threw when he was about three years old. Only now, she felt the familiar storm take shape with a whole new intensity.

Kathy took him by his small shoulders and forced him to look at her. "Wyatt, listen to me. Daddy cannot come with us now." Just what she needed, a reluctant co-escapee. She straightened herself. "Let's just find a phone and get to town where we can talk about it." She attempted to take hold of his hand, but he pulled away from her. "Take my hand, Wyatt." He did not offer his hand, but instead stared at her with defiance and anger in his eyes. "Wyatt..."

"NO!"

The sheer force in his voice caused her to take a step back. Never before had she seen her little boy so angry, and it seemed directed very much towards her.

Suddenly she was very aware that Justin was close to her. Kathy felt the same magnetism that initially attracted her to him years before. Before she even set eyes on him, she knew he was in the room and that she had to be close to him. However, unlike before, she no longer welcomed that pull and resisted it with all her senses.

"Is everything okay?"

Kathy turned on her heels and faced him. He could see even in the dark how hot her eyes were, full of mistrust and anger. "No. Everything is not okay! Look at what you've done to Wyatt!"

"What I've done to Wyatt? Would you just stop with the dramatics? I mean...seriously! What were you thinking? Who the hell knows who or what is out here? He just doesn't want to go prancing off into the dark in the middle of nowhere!"

"Well, I sure wasn't going to leave him with you!"

"You know what? I'm driving to Helena, and I'm taking Wyatt with me."

She took a step towards him with her fists clenched. "The hell you are."

He pretended not to notice. "What you do is up to you. You can ride back with me if you want but I'm not going to let you put our son in danger because you are pissed off at me."

"Oh now you are worried about him? You didn't seem all that concerned about him when you had to 'work' all those late nights!"

Justin sighed. "That is different, and you know it. I knew he was safe at home with you."

"And he is safe with me now!" She was screaming at him now.

"I understand why you are so angry, but you had to have seen this coming, Kathy. I've known our marriage was over for years, how could you not?" His words caused her to wince. Years? Minus the last six months, she thought they were happy all those years. "But despite everything, I still care about you and I'm not about to leave you and Wyatt out here alone."

She crossed her arms in front of her chest and looked away from him.

"Kathy. Please. Just come back to the car. I will take you to Helena, and then both of you can fly home or whatever you want."

She was shaking her head. Her rage was now being expressed through tears and they shined bright in the moonlight. Silver rivers flowing down her cheeks. "I can't."

"For God sake. You will never make it. It is blistering hot out here...and you have no money. You left your purse in the car." He could see the realization of truth hit her. Although it pained her, he was making progress; she hadn't thought of that. However, she wasn't about to admit that to him. "Just, please, will you think of Wyatt? Just for a minute..."

For a moment she bowed her head in defeat, but then she looked at him straight on. Her blue eyes glowed with emotion as she searched his face. "I hate you." That was a stab and he flinched. But he knew he deserved it. "Just so you know, it was you who destroyed this family. After we get to Helena, I never want to see you again."

"I understand." He looked over her shoulder, "Wyatt...Wyatt!"

Kathy swung around. "Oh my God! Where is he?"

"I don't know! Wyatt!"

"Wyatt!" Kathy's voice was borderline shrill as she called out to him.

"Shhhh! Listen!" But all they heard was a gentle breeze, a hot breath disturbing the upper limbs and the normal orchestra of a night in the woods. "Damn it, Kathy! You were supposed to be watching him!"

"I was! He was right here!"

Justin looked up and down the road, but the headlights only illuminated so much. Then he faced the trees. There was something very foreboding about them. The way they swayed in the wind, beckoning them, almost daring them to step among them.

Kathy must have felt it too because he heard her intake a sharp breath. "You don't think he went in there, do you?"

"I really hope not. Wyatt!"

Kathy followed his lead and called out into the night. But just standing there discouraged her quickly and she stepped off the road into the tall grass. A strong hand grabbed her upper arm and pulled her back. "I don't think we should leave the road yet. He might come back, and we aren't even sure he went this way. It isn't going to help him any if we get lost too."

She jerked her arm out of his hand. "Don't touch me! We cannot just stand here and wait! We have to do something, we have to find him!"

"Kathy, just listen..."

"No! You listen. We have to find him now!"

This time he took her by both of her shoulders and he shook her as he spoke. "We will find him, but you have to calm the fuck down. We just need to..."

Instantly their world went dark and silent. The lights from the car had simultaneously died. The wind, the crickets...all silenced like they were controlled by a switch. The darkness surrounded them and caressed their skin, but the night air suddenly felt dirty and it made Kathy's skin crawl.

"Justin...what just happened?" In this kind of silence, even her whisper seemed too loud.

"Ummm...yeah. I don't know. That was really weird, huh?"

Kathy shrugged his hands off of her shoulders, "Weird?" She shook her head, almost in amazement that he could understate the situation by so much. If she didn't know better, if she couldn't at least hear her own breathing, she would have thought she instantly went deaf. "You think?"

"Shhh! Listen!"

"Justin, I don't hear anything, that is the problem."

"I do, so shut up!"

He didn't give her enough time to be shocked by his tone, or to even ask questions. But when he took off sprinting into the trees, calling Wyatt's name, she had all the answers she needed. It didn't matter that these trees suddenly terrified her, it didn't matter that the world suddenly seemed too dark, too quiet, and too eerie. What mattered was that she thought she could suddenly hear Wyatt somewhere in the trees.

Kathy raced in, trying to follow the sound of Justin crashing into the underbrush all while keeping communication with Wyatt going. But Kathy couldn't hear Wyatt anymore, and she was running blind. Dark shapes of trees seemed to merge into giant shadows. Kathy dodged and ducked to avoid branches that seemed to reach for her like skeletal arms. "Justin? Wyatt! Justin, wait!"

"Come on!" Judging by his voice, he was getting impatient with her.

"I can't see you!"

"Jesus, Kathy! We are going to lose him again!"

She thought that he was just to her left, so she changed her direction, driven to run faster by guilt. How could she have lost track of him? He was right there! But she had let Justin distract her so easily. What was she thinking? How did her life come to this? How...

Kathy felt something hard against her right ankle and watched as the ground rushed toward her face. She struggled to put her hands out to catch herself, but the sheer force of the fall caused her elbows to buckle. For an instant she thought about yelling out, and maybe she did, but she wasn't sure if a sound got out in time. She hit something hard and the pain flashed white and hot. And from somewhere deep in her subconscious she thought of herself only half an hour ago when she didn't think this night could get any worse. She was wrong. The thought of dying alone in the woods made it so much more terrifying than imagining a life without Justin. The thought of dying without making sure her little boy was okay was out of the question. And just then all her thoughts stopped and everything went black.

Chapter Four

He was sure she was right behind him as he chased down their son. But he didn't have time to worry about that. He could hear Wyatt calling out for them but he could never pinpoint the exact direction. He had never heard sounds bounce off of trees the way they did here. He stopped, hoping to be close enough now to locate him. "Wyatt?" Sweat was coming down his forehead in rivers and he used his sleeve to wipe it away as he listened for a response. And as the seconds of silence continued to pass, he began to panic. "Wyatt! Answer me! Please! Where are you?"

The seconds turned into what seemed like hours. He could hear Kathy calling out for him, but at this point he couldn't bring himself to answer. He was disoriented and terrified. The thought of losing Wyatt made him want to fall to his knees. He could have easily been on his way down to the ground when a flicker of light caught his eye.

He narrowed his eyes, trying to focus on it between the trees. It was warm and welcoming. It kind of reminded him of a fireplace glowing softly in a dark room. It had to be a house. There had to be a phone and they could call for help. Send out the biggest damn search party in the history of the state. They were going to find their son. Justin took a step towards it but froze when he heard Kathy give a quick scream. He only briefly hesitated as he weighed the importance of her and their son. It struck him deeply and painfully to realize they were equal. They were his world, and he royally fucked it up. Amanda was excitement, but Kathy was home. He quickly turned on his heels and started toward her the best he could. Suddenly, he was very scared of losing her too.

"Kathy?" He didn't get a verbal answer but he found her just the same when he practically tripped over her. He steadied himself and looked down at her. She was on her stomach and she wasn't moving. "Kath?" He whispered so quietly that one would think he was afraid to wake her. He hesitated, and then slowly turned her over. Even in the dark he could see the thick blood coming from her forehead. "Oh, Jesus! Kathy! Kathy, wake up. Damn it!" He put his fingers to her neck and quickly found a strong pulse. He stripped off his shirt, wadded it into a ball and pressed it to her head.

The pressure to it caused her to frown and moan. "Okay, Okay. Good sign. Come on, baby, just wake up."

Her bright blue eyes fluttered open. "Oh thank God! Are you okay? Does anything feel broken?"

"Besides my head?"

Justin smiled and she started to prop herself up. "No, no, I don't think you should get up yet."

"No, I need to."

Justin helped her sit up while still applying hard pressure to her head. He hoped her injury was much more superficial than it looked. She waved his hands away and started her own pressure hold. "I got it. Did you find him?"

He leaned back until he was sitting down and bowed his head, feeling like the ultimate failure. "No. But there is a little good news. I found a house. At the very least we can get some help."

"Okay then." She got herself to her feet, but with visible pain. "Let's get going."

Justin had to admire her at the moment. What she needed was a doctor but he knew that she would go anywhere, do anything for the sake of Wyatt regardless of what kind of shape she was in. He watched as she staggered forward and jumped up to catch her as her knees began to buckle. She looked up with apologetic but mistrusting eyes. "Can you help me? I'm a little dizzy..."

"Of course. You never have to ask me for help."

She looked away. After what had happened tonight, he didn't blame her for not believing him but he meant every word. Despite everything, he did love her and would do anything for her. The reality of it hit him like a ton of bricks, but he would take each and every one of them to help rebuild the foundation of their relationship. He had made a huge mistake and had forgotten how valuable she was to him until he thought he lost her. Never again. He would make it up to her every day for the rest of her life.

They stumbled their way through the dark until Justin was able to relocate the source of the flicker. She had been using him as a steady crutch, but once the light was seen and beckoned them, it renewed her energy and she let go of him. She moved as quickly as she could through the tall grass surrounding the house until she stopped dead in her tracks. He came up behind her and put his hand on her shoulder. "Are you okay?"

"Shhh...I think there is something in the grass." She pointed to a dark twisted shape on the ground.

"Oh wow! That's a good size snake." It wasn't moving but suddenly the light caught its eyes in a very unnatural way as it stared at them.

"Is it poisonous?"

Justin knew that Montana had snakes, but only one was considered poisonous. The thing was, the Western Rattlesnake always gave a warning when threatened with a distinctive rattling noise. This one was silent, but within its silence came a loud and clear warning. Something about it seemed more dangerous and more lethal than the venom of a rattler. It was better to be safe than sorry. "I don't know."

"Whatever. We are wasting time!" Kathy made a wide circle around the snake and then raced through the yard. Justin hesitated, memorized by the light in the serpent's eyes. The light began to resemble an angry flame, until the eyes themselves seemed to glow red. Justin shook his head and whipped the sweat out of his eyes. He had to be imagining it. The snake opened its jaw. Initially he thought it was in preparation to strike, but as it began to resemble a mocking grin, he really started to worry.

Kathy must have reached the door because she was pounding on the hard wood. "Hello? Hello! Please help us!" Justin was shaken from his trance and then he too made a wide arch around the snake. He kept his eyes on it while it stared him down with its angry eyes and menacing grin. Really weird snake. As soon as he felt that there was a reasonable distance between them, he raced to join Kathy who was still knocking urgently on the door. Even then, he struggled with having his back to the tall grass and the things that lurked within it.

Justin swallowed hard as he heard a creak from behind the door as someone approached it and then the door squeaked open. Images of cheesy old vampire and werewolf movies popped into his head and wasn't surprised that Kathy took a step back to join him on the grass. If it wasn't for the possibility of a phone being inside that house, he would have turned and ran himself. Something was wrong. Something beyond his son missing.

The woman who answered only cracked the door, but it was enough to see that she was looking straight past them. Her pale grey eyes scanned the dark trees. "There is a lot of hate out there tonight," she whispered.

Justin glanced at Kathy quickly and could tell that they shared the same thought. It was just a bizarre thing to say to people who were pounding at her door in the middle of the night. He cleared his throat and took a small step forward, "We know it is late, we are very sorry, but..."

At the sound of his voice, the woman's bright eyes darted to him. It was odd how bright they were when the only light around was coming from behind her. But the whites of her eyes were clearly visible in the dark. It reminded him of the snake in the grass. "Are you here for the boy?"

Justin heard Kathy intake her breath but he didn't hear her exhale. Still she managed a whisper. "Oh my God. Wyatt?"

The woman standing at the door smiled. But it seemed forced to Justin. He was sure it was because of the poor lighting that it came across so unpleasantly. She moved aside and opened the door wide. She motioned him in with her hands, "Come inside. Quickly."

He didn't really like the idea of going inside. It felt like once there, everything would change. He sensed dread and bad news, but if Wyatt was really in there, he would be in there too. Nothing could stop him.

22

He jumped when Kathy's hand grasped his shoulder for comfort. If only she knew how comforting it was for him as they stepped over the threshold. And as the door thudded closed behind them, she pressed her body against his back. She was afraid. He knew it and he took a sick pleasure from knowing that she needed him after all. In a small way, it seemed like a gesture of forgiveness.

The room thankfully wasn't lit by a fireplace because it would have been insanely hot if it had been heated by a fire. But even so, the many candles in the room gave off an unpleasant warmth. But now in this light, he could see the woman wasn't nearly as terrifying as she appeared in the doorway. Out there she appeared to be an ominous witch. Here in her living room she was simply a sixty-something woman. Her long flowing nightgown modestly covered her fail, thin body, and her long silver hair hung loosely to the middle of her back. Justin even noticed her toenails were painted bright pink. How dangerous could a woman who painted her toenails pink be?

"Where's my son?" Kathy was still clinging to him.

The woman sat down on a long couch covered with a crocheted blanket. She sighed, "He is safe for now...sleeping. My husband is guarding him."

Justin stiffened. "Guarding him from what?" He didn't wait for her to answer him. "You know what, just take me to him."

She ignored him. "You know...hate is such a powerful thing. It brings out the demon in us all. Couple that with anger...fear...then you've got yourself a real monster."

Kathy stepped away from him. "Why are you saying these things?" She turned back to Justin. "Why is she telling us this?"

"I'm telling you this because your son told me he hated you both." She paused and then looked directly at Kathy. "Especially you. That is why he ran."

Kathy looked stunned and Justin could see the tears well up in her eyes. "What? My son does not hate me! He loves me!"

The old woman did not look sympathetic. "We don't get a lot of those ugly things around here. It needed to be that way. There is a reason why we are so isolated, and then the three of you come along and well shit, you really stirred up a hornet's nest."

Justin was getting very uncomfortable. "What the hell are you talking about? I want to see Wyatt!"

She looked hard at him. "It only takes one to start. And your little boy in all his hurt and anger at the two of you woke it up."

Kathy glanced at Justin nervously and then back at their creepy hostess. "What are you talking about? Woke what up? Just take us to Wyatt, please!"

The woman studied them and then took a breath. She opened her mouth, perhaps to tell them what it was, perhaps to spout off more riddles, but they were interrupted by a gun shot and a little boy...their little boy... screaming.

Justin and Kathy sprinted down the hallway toward the back of the house. They found a man standing in the hall taking aim into an unseen room.

Wyatt was now screaming in agony, and Kathy could feel her son's pain deep down in her soul. It twisted her insides, and made her instantly ill. "Oh, Jesus! Justin, he shot our baby!"

Justin rushed at the overweight elderly man, who was wearing nothing more than boxers with red hearts printed all over them. "You bastard! What have you done?"

The man's eyes widened and he brought the gun up defensively, "No! Wait! There is still time!"

Kathy fell against the wall and sobbed as she watched them struggle for the possession of the rifle, even as Wyatt grew silent. And she watched as Justin caught his first glimpse into the room. Instantly he grew silent and still. He let go of the gun and stepped forward. "What the hell is that?" he whispered.

Kathy was confused. While she couldn't bring herself to look at the room, and what may remain of her son, she knew it would break her, she hardly expected this kind of reaction from Justin. Rage? Yes. Grief? Yes. Whispers? "What is going on?"

Behind her the surprisingly strong hand of the long forgotten old woman grabbed on to her arm. "You don't want to know." She was whispering too. "I'm so sorry."

Kathy gently pulled her arm away, and the woman let her slip through her fingers. Just as she reached her frozen like, soon to be ex-husband, the old man took another shot. Something other than their son screamed at them in rage.

Kathy closed her eyes before she could turn and face the room. She didn't want to see it. If she didn't see it, it wouldn't be real. It couldn't be real. The scream itself told her that whatever was in that room was not the usual dreaded night time intruder. This was something else. This was worse.

Justin's voice brought her eyes open... "Wyatt?" She tried to focus in the dark room, but all she could see was just a darker shape directly over the bed. She might have even said it was just part of the dark, but it moved; it pulsed as it worked on her son. She was transfixed, and barely flinched when the old woman pushed past them with a lit candle in each hand.

"Ernie! Where's the light?"

Ernie lowered the gun, defeated. He knew that being shot at was a mere annoyance to it and he knew that bullets could do no real harm to it. "It waited until the candle burned itself out. I fell asleep and it...it was too late. I....I'm...I'm so sorry."

"Jesus, help us all." The woman thrust her arm into the room and Kathy could finally see some finer details. Wyatt lay motionless on a twin bed covered in a patch-work quilt. By the dim candle light, she could see his beautiful blue eyes staring at the ceiling lifeless and cold. His mouth gaped open in a silent scream.

The shapeless dark thing was huddled in the darkest corner. She knew it was there only by the burning glare from hot red, hate filled eyes. It hissed and spat at them. "What is that?" she whispered.

The man she knew only as Ernie took a candle from his wife and stood next to Kathy. He sighed heavily, "We own this whole mountain. I've lived here my entire life. We all hoped and prayed this would never happen." His voice cracked with emotion. "Why did you all choose my road? Now there isn't any hope! Because of you, we are all going to die!"

Tears started streaming down Kathy's face and Justin put his arm around her. "But what is it?"

The woman stepped further into the room and the dark thing slipped further back, just out of reach of the light. "You all brought your problems up to our mountain. You brought all your anger and fears and mistrust here and now...here it is! And there is no stopping it!"

Kathy sobbed. "You aren't making any sense!"

The woman snapped her head towards Kathy. "Calm down. Don't you understand? It takes all the energy...feeds off of it. It is only getting stronger!"

"Alice, we don't have much time." The old woman looked sadly at her husband and nodded.

Alice took Kathy's hand in hers. They were warm and even in the heat they brought Kathy so much comfort. "Listen, honey. I know you are scared but it is so important for you to control it."

"Alice....the candle."

"Ernie, I know!" She looked Kathy squarely in the eyes. "Right now there is only one, but soon there will be more than you can imagine. If you don't want your little boy to be one, you will take him and this candle and lock yourself in a room. Whatever you do, don't let the light go out."

Justin shook his head. "I don't understand."

Alice let go of Kathy's hand and she felt an instant emptiness. "Young man....save what is left of your son. Take him and go now."

Justin looked over at the bed, at his little boy and his heart shattered into a billion little pieces. The most selfish of thoughts raced through his mind. Who was he going to play catch with now? Who was going to look up to him as though he was a superhero? Who was going to laugh at his dumbest jokes?

"GO! NOW!"

Ernie's command shook him out of his thoughts. With tears streaming down his face, he ran to the bed and scooped up his child's lifeless body. He returned to the trio at the door and finally looked at Kathy's face. She was still staring hate straight in the eyes. "Kathy?"

Alice grabbed her arm and pulled her into the hall. Only then did Kathy acknowledge that Wyatt was dead in her husband's arms. Instantly, she began to wail. "Oh my God! Please, Jesus! No! No!" She took Wyatt out of Justin's arms and cradled him like a newborn. "Wyatt? Baby? Baby, please, please wake up!"

Alice was at the end of the hall and called out to them. Justin tried to push Kathy along. He could barely move himself now with his whole reason for living gone. "Come on Kath...almost there."

From back at the bedroom another gunshot shook the house, followed by a cry from Ernie. He screamed his wife's name in such an agonizing way, Justin could see Alice instantly sag, but she still stepped forward and pulled them into a bathroom. She handed Justin the candle. "Lock the door. Stay in the light. Always stay in the light."

Justin stared into her clear blue eyes. "What about you?"

She looked down the hall where Ernie sounded like he was being pushed through a meat grinder alive. He was pleading for her. She looked back at Justin and bowed her head. She aged a hundred years in a few brief moments. Even her eyes appeared to pale. "My place is with him, no matter in what form." With that she grabbed the door handle, "Stay in the light. Lock it," and she closed it behind her.

Justin stood there staring at the door, speechless. He felt like he fell into the white rabbit's hole and instead of safely arriving in a place called Wonderland, he found himself locked in the bathroom of Hell.

Behind the wooden panels were the screams of tortured souls. Justin never thought of himself as a religious man, and now he felt like they were in a place where God couldn't touch them. If He could, He surely would put a stop to this by now.

He felt helpless. He wondered what kind of man hides while two elderly people are screaming like that? But Alice told them to stay. She made her choice. There was nothing they could do...if they didn't want their son to be mutilated like them; they need to take him...

His son. His beautiful baby boy. Justin dared to turn his back on the door and looked down. He watched Kathy stroke Wyatt's blonde head knowing exactly the texture of each strand her finger touched. Thank God she had closed his eye lids and now he appeared to be merely sleeping. She rocked him as steady silent tears rolled down her face. Justin sank to the floor next to Kathy. Her eyes were blank as she stared at the flickering light against the shower curtain. He wanted to say comforting words; to tell her that everything was going to be alright, but he didn't want to lie to her. Honestly, he believed without Wyatt, nothing was going to be right again.

Without realizing it, his own tears began to fall and he closed his eyes as the agonizing screams of two from down the hall became the pleas of one. Alice seemed so strong, and now she was whimpering. He admired her, and thought of her as brave and noble. She is going through unimaginable pain and he was sitting there just listening. And she did it because she couldn't spend a day without Ernie. That was love. What did he know of love? God, if only he hadn't cheated on Kathy, they never would have taken this fucking trip. They never would have been on that God forsaken road. Wyatt never would have run off...

He kept his eyes closed even as the house grew silent. He was thankful for that much, but now he waited for it to find them, and when it did, he didn't want to see it coming.

And as he drifted off to sleep, he was thankful that he was even able to. Because maybe, just maybe, he would wake up to find this had all been a dream. A really, really bad dream.

Chapter Five

Sam

August 6th, 10:17 p.m.

The asphalt in front of him weaved its way through the hilly landscape like a giant black serpent. Even though it was a little past ten at night, he could see the mountains in the distance due to a very large bright moon that seemed to be chasing him through most of the state. He was sure that if he did turn off the lights of the Neon he would be able to navigate just fine.

Ahead of him he could see the lights of what looked like a decent sized town. Finally. Sam wasn't accustomed to the remoteness of Montana. Ever since he left Lisa in Dallas, and after going through Colorado, with the exception of a few places, he had only passed through small towns where people stared at him like he was a freak show exhibit.

It wasn't that these northern states completely lacked racial diversity, but he found that his dark skin stood out. It probably didn't help that he was 6'4 and pushing two-forty of mostly muscle. He kept his head shaved and his eyes were overly intense. Women had told him he appeared to be looking into people's souls. If he was sleeping with them, it was intimate. If he wasn't, it apparently made people uncomfortable. These days he was making a lot of people uncomfortable. Intentionally or not, they were doing the same to him.

Especially now. People noticed him wherever he went. But being noticed was the last thing a man who needed to be invisible wanted.

So he made his stops quick, only for gas and cheap fast food. His plan was to drive straight through to Washington. Occasionally he would pull off at quiet country roads to sleep, but he couldn't really sleep. He was always waiting and watching for an overly curious HP officer or local sheriff to investigate the 'abandoned' car. Besides, the faster he could put distance between himself and that bitch, the better off he would be. Apparently he was still angry at her. A few days ago, he thought he was past all that, and even agreed to help her when she begged him to drive her and her shit down to Dallas. He thought he could handle it. Time supposedly heals all pains.

Wrong. Wrong. Wrong! Time is a rug that covers up pain. Just because you can't see it, doesn't make it any less filthy. And in his case, she came in, snatched his rug up, and exposed all of his unresolved messes and then blew it all over the place.

Sam was hot. He wanted to blame the weather, but be was pretty sure a lot of it had to do with guilt too. He went to turn up the air conditioning, but found it already to be maxed out, so he started to roll down the window. Instantly a blast of furnace air entered the car. "Shit." He quickly cranked the window back up. "Isn't it supposed to be cold in Montana? Where did all this damn heat come from?"

There wasn't anyone in car with him, and yet he half expected her to answer him. He glanced at the passenger seat hoping to see her. If she was there, then the nightmare of the last few days would be just that, a nightmare. He could go back to starting over and she well…she would still be alive.

The details of her were so familiar to Sam he was sure that he could see her there. She would be smiling at him, or twirling her silky black hair with her fingers while she was deep in thought. Then those legs. Those long, shapely legs in her tiny jean shorts. She would cross, and uncross them, over and over again, absolutely driving him insane with lust. And every day she would wear these tight t-shirts that left nothing to his imagination. But she wasn't there and Sam sighed heavily. God he hated her.

It is funny, in a not ha-ha way, how differently he felt about her now. Two days ago he thought he loved her. Two years ago he absolutely, without a doubt, loved her. They were engaged, they had a fantastic apartment in Seattle, and they were happy. At least he thought they were. Then out of nowhere, she tells him that she doesn't want to be with him, she met someone else, and she was moving out to be with that guy.

The day she left him was the day Sam turned into a new man. That first year alone, he lost his job at the firm, had to move into a tiny one bedroom basement apartment, and turned into a cold, heartless bastard. He hated her, he hated women, and he hated life. His job as a short-order cook supported his drinking problem more than anything else.

Then he woke up. He literally woke up in a dark, dingy alley. The previous night's memories evaded him, but somehow he ended up sleeping amongst rats and maggots. Someone was kind enough to beat the shit out of him and throw him in a dumpster like the trash he had become.

It truly was a wakeup call for him. He started working to get his life back on track. He cleaned up, went through the academy and was hired on the department, and moved into a better neighborhood. Then there was Sandra at the coffee shop. She always was kind to him as she poured his coffee and served him pie, but lately she lingered in conversation. She would bless him with a sweet smile that turned even his darkest days into hope, and then last week, she touched him. It was innocent enough, just a brief squeeze of his forearm as she laughed at his joke, but for him it was the all clear he had been waiting for. He was more than close to asking her to dinner. She was everything that Lisa wasn't; down to earth, calm, and beautiful in a very natural way.

His career.

Sandra.

His whole life.

There was no hope for any of that now.

Chapter Six

He was pacing. He felt like he was sixteen, trying to gather the courage to ask a popular girl to the prom, even though he didn't recall even being this nervous then. Things were different now though. For the first time in his life, he doubted he was good enough for even the average woman, and Sandra was anything but average. She was his salvation. For the first time in a long time, he cared. He cared about her. He cared about tomorrow.

Sam looked in the mirror and attempted a pep talk. "Okay, you got this, man. You turned it all around..." He shook his head, chuckled, slightly embarrassed that a one-time ladies' man has come to this and then reached for the door. "It is now or never."

And then his phone rang. He stared at it with consideration but dismissed it from being a bad omen and reached for it. The number wasn't recognized and he almost walked away. It might be someone from work asking him to cover their shift. On most days, he would have no problem working for someone, he needed the money, but not today. He had been putting off asking Sandra out long enough.

He almost walked away, but he didn't.

"Hello?"

"Sammy? Baby is that you?" Her voice was deep and sultry, and oozed with the promise of sex.

"Lisa." Just saying her name painfully pierced his heart and the air escaped his body harshly. Despite her inability to see him, he stiffened the muscles in his back, and quickly built up his defenses. "What do you want?" His voice came out steady enough, but it was cold and stained with resentment.

"Now, Sammy, is that any way to talk to an old friend?"

"You are kidding, right?"

"Okay... so obviously you're still mad at me."

"No Lisa, I'm not mad. I was enraged, but I don't care anymore. Hope you're happy with What's-His-Name, but I've got to be somewhere, so thanks for calling, have a nice life." His was rambling; anxious to get off the phone and ease the tension her voice created in his soul.

"Now hold up, Sammy..."

"Stop calling me that. You don't get to call me that."

"Okay, I'm sorry...for everything. Especially for hurting you the way I did."

Her voice had softened, and he started to feel a familiar longing for her bubble to the surface. He liked himself so much more when he was with her. People stopped conversations to watch them when they entered a room together. They were attractive and powerful together. She still was attractive and powerful, and now he was a recovering alcoholic with a cheap apartment and a bus pass. No one noticed him now. She destroyed him. He reminded himself to remember that.

"Okay, whatever. Why are you calling me?"

"I need your help."

"Seriously? You are unbelievable."

She ignored him. "I got this once-in-a-lifetime opportunity waiting for me in Dallas."

"Two questions. One: what's his name, and two: did you tell Malcolm you are screwing around on him."

There was a long pause on the other line, "That was low, Sam. Real low. It isn't anything like that. Not before and not now."

Her tone revealed her hurt and for a moment he felt guilty for what he had said, "Lisa, I'm sorry, but why can't you get your boyfriend to help you. You and I aren't even friends anymore. I haven't heard a word from you in over two years, and now you want my help? It just doesn't work that way."

"Sam, I don't have anyone else. Malcolm and I aren't together anymore."

"What about the guy in Dallas?"

"I never said anything about a guy in Dallas. For your information, it's a job. A great job at one of the largest firms in the southwest."

She used all of her experience in arguing to convince him that it was the only neighborly thing to do, and he ended up loading up a U-Haul, hooking her car on a tow trailer and embarking on a long ass drive with her sitting in the passenger seat.

Most of the first day was spent with long pauses between awkward conversations, but he found that he couldn't take his eyes off of her. Sandra suddenly became the furthest thing from his mind. The two years away from Lisa had fogged his memory, because she was more beautiful and more exotic than he remembered.

"You look great, Lisa, you really do."

She gave him a brilliant smile, "Thank you, Sam. You obviously have been working out. I don't remember you being so strong. Just look at these arms." She started rubbing his bare shoulders. And despite the heat, she made goose bumps rise all over his body.

So then began the friendly flirting. It was like they were in high school again, teasing each other, and laughing over sheer silliness. On the third day she gave him a blow job while they sat in traffic in Denver, and later that night they had long overdue make up sex.

It was like nothing had changed between them and Sam found that he was happy. He was the happiest that he had been in a long time. Having Lisa back in his life was the best thing that could have happened to him. And it seemed to have been mutual. She worshiped his every move. The next couple of days were bliss. Pure bliss.

When they got to Dallas, he helped her unload the truck, carried everything into her new apartment on the third floor, and together they set up the bed. He then spent time rediscovering every curve of her body, and then fucked her brains out. He made her scream, she scratched his back up and the neighbors banged on the wall and told them to shut the hell up. Best night ever.

Afterwards she laid her head on his stomach and he smiled contently. "You know, Lis, this week with you has been great."

"Yeah, like old times."

'"So, I've been thinking...."

Lisa snuggled up closer to him and started to fondle his crotch, "Hmmmm, I was thinking the same thing."

Sam squirmed away, "Yeah that's a good idea, but wait a minute. Come on now, this is serious."

Lisa lifted her head and fluttered her lovely long eye lashes. "What's the matter, baby?"

He sat up, and took her hands in his. "Lis, you know I still love you."

She dropped her eyes and turned to face the window.

"And, I was thinking of maybe joining you here in Dallas. You know, get on with the department down here. That way we could work on things, give it another shot. You know?"

She pulled her hands away from his grasp and sat on the edge of the bed. The moonlight was streaming through the window and reflected off of her bare skin. She looked like a goddess. "Ummm, Sam, I don't think that is such a good idea."

No way did he hear her correctly. "What? What are you talking about?" He came up behind her and started to rub her shoulders. "It will be great...the two of us again."

She stood and picked her shirt off the floor. "Don't go do anything foolish like quitting your job in Washington, Sam."

He looked at her dumbfoundly, "Why not? What are you trying to say?"

She pulled on her shorts and looked at him. He could see, even in the dim light that she had pity in her eyes. Pity. "Look, Sam, don't make this out to be more than it was. This week has been fun, but that is all it was...fun. There is not going to be any rekindling of our relationship. It is really time that you move on."

Sam stood up, "Move on? What are you talking about? Lisa, you can't be serious after what we've been doing this week. You acted like you wanted to be with me."

"It was just sex."

He swallowed hard. "I see. Just sex. Well that is just fucked up. You actually stooped low enough to use me."

She went to the bathroom and flipped on the light. Lisa began to brush her long hair, letting the paddle brush glide through her silky strands. Everything was in slow motion for him. "Okay, yeah, maybe I did. We both had fun. But Sam, really, you didn't honestly think we were going to get back together, did you?" She giggled.

She was laughing at him. He could feel the blood rushing to his face. He was not only angry, but now also embarrassed beyond words. Sam yanked on his jeans and stalked to the bathroom doorway. "Well, actually, yeah, I did. You let me think we were. You knew exactly what you were doing. Bitch..."

She swung around to face him. "Excuse me?"

"Why the hell did you have to involve me? Why couldn't you just hire some movers or something and stay out of my life?"

She shrugged nonchalantly. "You were cheaper."

"You're a God damn whore."

She shook her head and rolled her eyes, "Oh whatever." She pushed her way past him. "I'm going out to get some food, and when I get back, I hope you are gone."

"Yeah? I feel sorry for the poor bastard you screw in exchange for your meal, but I will be sure to wave as I pass you on the corner."

She smiled, but Sam knew her well enough to know that she was fuming. "I never imagined you would take this so hard. You are acting like a wounded puppy." She paused, "How can I put this in a way your simple mind will understand; I do not want to be with you. You are a loser now. Just a lousy, broke cop."

He sat on the corner and began pulling on his shoes, "You know, Lisa, that's fine. I don't want a woman that sells herself so cheaply. I'm sure I could have done a lot less for just as much. Fucking slut."

She didn't hesitate. She walked right over to him and slapped him hard across the cheek. Sam would never forget the seconds that followed that. It was almost as if time had stopped as they stood there staring at each other. It was in those brief moments that Sam lost himself in rage, and decided to make her pay. She had hurt him for the last time.

He took one last look at her face, her beautiful, flawless face; her eyes so wide with fear, he could see the details of her irises. She took a step backwards, obviously realizing she had made a mistake. "I'm sorry I hit you, Sam..."

Her words fell on deaf ears. Frankly the rage drowned out everything; he never even hear her. He closed his fist and hit her hard on the side of her face. She swung around and fell face first onto the bed. He immediately and roughly yanked her shorts down, and pulled his own pants down. "You want to be a whore? Fine! I'll treat you like one!"

Lisa didn't say anything. She must have lost consciousness. He pulled her body down so that she was virtually bent over the bed and he thrust himself into her hard. It must have hurt like hell because it was enough to wake her. "Oh my God, Sam! What are you doing? No! No! Stop it!"

She tried to crawl away, her fingernails digging sharply into the bedding, much the same way they did an hour ago. However, instead of her grip being fueled by intense pleasure, she was in the throws of brutalizing terror. But he held her firmly down and continued to assault her body so hard the bed was scooting across the floor, scratching the finish. She started to scream. "Shut up!" He turned her head into the mattress and pushed it down hard. The neighbor pounded on the wall again.

Lisa was failing her arms around. Lisa tried to lift her head. Lisa went still, but he continued to hold her down until he was finished. Then he stepped away from her and slid down the wall, his pants still around his ankles. The realization that he just raped a person flooded into his soul and the shame pieced him like a hot poker. He put his face in his hands and breathed the warm air. He expected her to get up, or cry, or something, but she didn't move. He childishly peeked through his fingers. "Lisa?" She didn't respond.

"Lisa, are you okay?"

"Fuck." He jumped up and hesitated to touch her, but he forced himself to turn her around. Her mouth was frozen in a silent scream and her eyes were slightly foggy; the details no longer obvious. "Fuck. Fuck. Fuck."

"Jesus Christ!" Her felt her neck for a pulse but couldn't even locate a faint one. Sam attempted to give her mouth to mouth, but it was too little too late. He had killed her. She probably suffocated when he pressed her face into the mattress.

37

Sam fell back into a corner and started to cry. Through his blurred vision, he could see her still body on the bed. He never intended to kill her, he just want to scare her, make her feel a fraction of the pain that she was causing him. Now there was no fixing things. She was feeling no pain now, and he had created a whole shit more for himself.

"I've got to get out of here." He wasted no time trying to wipe down his prints. His fingerprints would be on every single box. Hair would probably be everywhere from the car to the bed, and his semen was inside her. His skin under her fingernails. He was screwed. His only hope was to disappear, but first he had to get back to Washington.

Before everything happened, his intention was to rent a car and drive back home, but instead he took Lisa's car. Her little Dodge Neon was pretty small for his large frame, but at the time he felt it was his only option.

Now that he had spent the last few days in it, he almost wished he could go back and take the time to rent a bigger car. Not only for the comfort factor, but also because it was pretty stupid to have taken her car. If Lisa has been discovered, they would be looking for her missing car.

Sam barely noticed the slow moving station wagon in front of him, and he braked hard. He was so lost in his memories that he didn't realize that he was entering into Helena city limits and traffic had increased. Helena came just in time because the gas light just came on.

He pulled into the first gas station he came across and while the car was gassing up he went inside for some coffee and food. He had basically been running on fear and adrenaline for the past few days, rarely stopping to rest on back roads, but it was starting to catch up to him. He was tired.

The elderly attendant was reading the paper, and barely looked up as he entered the store. He went to the bathroom and came back for an extra-large coffee and a couple of hot dogs. Sam set his purchases on the counter and reached for his wallet. The attendant was shaking his head, "What is this world coming to?"

Sam noticed his small rectangle name tag said Earl. "Excuse me?"

Earl glanced at him and set his paper down. He slid off his stool and started to scan the food. "Do you have gas out there, son?"

"Yes, sir. Pump four."

"Yeah, I was just reading in the paper. They found the body of a promising young attorney down in Dallas. Apparently she was beaten and raped. Just moved there too; boxes weren't even unpacked. I just think it is so sad."

Sam's heart stopped beating, and his lungs seemed to have tightened up. He glanced at the paper on the counter, only to see Lisa's smiling professional photo. But her eyes were accusing him right through the newspaper ink.

"Are you okay, son?"

He swallowed hard, "Umm, yeah. It is just too bad. Did they catch the guy who did it?"

"No. Not yet. But apparently he left it messy. They'll have lots of evidence when they do catch up with the s.o.b. Excuse my French. What kind of person could kill a pretty young thing like that? It is just sick, I tell you. Just sick."

Sam handed him a couple of twenties, and received his change. "Thank you, Earl."

"Thank you. Have a nice night."

Sam snorted. Thank God Earl was either too old or too distracted to notice. His friendly good-bye irritated Sam to no end. Intentionally or not, it felt like Earl was mocking him. Sam doubted that it would be a very long time before he would have another good night. He grabbed his purchases off the counter and practically ran out of the store. It probably didn't help his mission of keeping a low profile, especially as he pushed past someone coming into the store. He could feel their accusational eyes pierce his back as he raced back to his car.

Sam got into the sweltering car and sat for a moment shaking his head. His eyes stared into his own imploding future. "Shit. Shit. Shit." There was no way he could go back to Washington now. The paper was right. He did leave Lisa and the whole thing messy. He should have known better. He was a cop for Christ's sake. There were options. He could have disposed of her body, and attempted to clean up a little. It would have at least bought him some time. But instead he panicked. He also could have just gone down to Mexico. It was a hell of a lot closer to Texas than Canada. But for some reason he felt like he had to get back to Washington.

The reason suddenly hit him. He had to see Sandra one more time, and apologize for not making a move months ago. He knew she was interested, and if they had gotten together, he never would have left with Lisa. None of this would have happened. But what difference did it make now? She would never want to be with him if she knew the truth about him. It wasn't like he was going to get away with it. The truth always comes out.

Sam sighed heavily as he negotiated his way through Malfunction Junction, which was an intersection of five streets. He could have gone straight and made his way back to Interstate 15. Instead he found himself veering off to the left, staying on the path to Highway 12. Apparently he was still on his way back to Washington. It almost felt like he hadn't even made the decision to do it. Somewhere deep inside, he knew he wasn't thinking straight and was hoping that he would be able to convince himself to make his way to Canada by the time he got to Idaho. Three hours to go.

The traffic was starting to taper off as he approached the end of town. It went by fast. Sam knew there was a small, private Catholic college in town with a pretty successful football team. Nonetheless, it was awfully small and quiet even for Catholic kids.

Sam was just finishing his second hot dog when the speed increased to fifty-five miles an hour and Helena suddenly ended. He knew from before that he would enter into a canyon area with some private drive-ways and dirt roads intersecting with it, and then he would go over McDonald Pass before intersecting with Interstate 90.

The moonlight couldn't reach into the depths of the canyon. The tall rock walls and steep mountain sides blocked every opportunity for any illumination. Even the Neon's lights struggled to penetrate the darkness. As far as he could see, he was the only car on the road.

The radio, which had been playing the closest thing he could find to alternative music, suddenly went to static. Sam took his eyes off the road long enough to find the search button. It began its cycle through the numbers, and it just kept going.

At first he barely saw it as he shifted his eyes from the radio to the road and back again. But something clicked in his brain that something wasn't right. He wasn't exactly familiar with the twist and turns of the canyon, but he was pretty sure there was something in the road. He squinted some, and could make out two bright red objects. He didn't know what they were, but he knew they weren't brake lights. "What the...."

The objects suddenly moved. It was a simultaneous individual movement. It had to be an animal. But what kind of animal eyes gave off such a fiery glow? In any case, Sam slowed the car. You usually could count on if there was one, there was going to be another and the last thing he needed to do was hit something.

The closer the car came to it, the larger it seemed to be. Maybe a bear? "No, not a bear," he advised himself. He knew he wasn't seeing anything like a bear, or like anything he'd ever seen before. By now he was sure he was staring right into a pair of bright red eyes. And as if it was aware he was looking straight into them, the eyes narrowed.

In that moment, Sam's heart seemed to seize. He couldn't breathe. He was deathly afraid of whatever was in the road, now only about a hundred yards away. "Jesus Christ, what is that?"

It was then that he decided he didn't really want to find out. He was pretty sure that if he did, it would be the last thing he did in his life. Sam sharply turned the wheel to the left and the tires screamed in protest. The steering wheel slipped roughly out of his hands and the car spun out of control. Sam fought to grab hold of the rotating steering wheel and bring the car under his power. The speed of the turns made him dizzy as the headlights slashed through the dark canyon.

Suddenly the car bounced and the sound of metal against metal pierced the night air as the car crashed into something and dragged it behind it. Not even a second later, Sam was thrown forward as the car came to a abrupt stop. The seat belt tightened and cut into his shoulder.

It wasn't until he opened his eyes that he realized that they had been closed. Sam took a deep breath, thankful to still be alive. The car was quiet, and the lights were gone, but he could still see that it was a hillside that had stopped the car. The front right side was buried.

Sam realized that his back was turned towards the thing in the road. He whipped his head around and looked for the red eyes, but the night was dark and still. However, he still wasn't able to shake the feeling that he wasn't alone. Sam wasn't about to wait around and meet whatever it was. He straightened himself in the seat and turned the key to restart the car. The car remained lifeless. "Come on. Come one." Nothing happened.

Sam checked his surroundings, looking for it, but it remained out of sight. He tried the car again. The car disappointed him. It didn't even try to start. "No way." Sam couldn't imagine that the Neon got that damaged when it hit the hill; at least not to the point that it wouldn't even start.

The silent night was suddenly alive with noise. Sam could hear what sounded like a war zone coming from the direction of town. Tires screeching, horns, collisions, and small explosions, but he wasn't able to see anything past his bumper. Although he watched in a mix of terror and awe the glow of city lights above town was swallowed into darkness.

The inside of the car was turning into a sauna. Sweat was dripping down his forehead and cheeks. The windows were crank so the lack of power wasn't an issue, but Sam couldn't put the windows down. The thin glass gave him a sense of some security. The way town was sounding, he needed all the security he could get. He was willing to live with heat if it meant he got to live.

Silence returned. At least at first. All the chaos from town seemed to have ended at once, and the only thing that Sam could hear was his own heavy breathing. Then he heard a weird clicking noise. Sam visualized incredibly long claws clicking against polished tile, and whatever was making the noise was close.

He slowly turned his head back and forth, and determined that it was just across the road. Or maybe it was in front of the car, but it also seemed to be from behind him. He felt as though he was surrounded by it. His hands tightened around the steering wheel and strained to see through the gloom.

The clicking noise was getting closer and his eyes widened as he could distinctly see hundreds of the red objects coming around the corner. "Oh damn..." Movement in the rear view mirror caught his attention, and he could see another red-eyed army coming from that direction. Without a doubt, the thin glass of Lisa's little blue Dodge Neon no longer made him feel very secure. He was very close to panicking. He briefly considered just closing his eyes, sinking down into the seat, and letting whatever was going to happen to happen.

However, the moment he closed his eyes, he could see those imagined long claws tearing into his flesh. That just wasn't the way he wanted to die. He had to get away. He started to just open the driver's door, but doing so would put him right in the middle of the two approaching evil-eyed groups. He decided then to just slip out of the passenger side, and try to make his way up the steep hillside.

Sam pushed himself across to the passenger seat. He quickly opened the door and slid out to the ground. The sound coming from them must have been muffled by the car, because the sound he was now hearing was almost overwhelming. It had the force of a thousand jackhammers that felt like they were pressed hard against his ear drums.

Sam started up the hillside by staying low, and trying to blend in the grass. Several times the sand and dirt gave way under his weight and he would slip. Halfway to the tree line he stopped, and looked back. From where he sat he still couldn't see anything but the glowing eyes, but he knew that they were now at the car. They were fast, whatever they were. But that fact only inspired him to go faster before they discovered where he went.

As soon as he reached the first tree he stood up and hid behind the trunk. Above him, a slight breeze rustled the leaves. However, Sam's imagination took him somewhere beyond thinking it was the wind. He nearly yelled out as he jumped away from the tree. A quick glance down the hill revealed that they had already started up the hill.

Sam couldn't remember ever being so afraid. Looking into those hundreds of angry red eyes filled him with a terror that made him want to curl up in a fetal position. Any other situation and it could have been funny; a big, strong man like himself, curled up and crying like a baby. But no one was laughing right now, certainly not him.

Instead, Sam took off in a dead run through the dense trees and bushes. He leapt over fallen trees and clawed his way through undergrowth. Dead tree limbs seemed to be reaching for him like skeletal fingers. But Sam kept going, despite tripping several times and scratching all of his uncovered skin.

No matter which direction he went, he felt like they were right behind him. The clicks followed him everywhere. They surrounded him. He searched the dark forest for any signs of the red eyes, but he could only make out the outlines of trees. From somewhere to the east, a twig snapped and Sam spun around, but still couldn't see anything.

Sam fell backwards and was caught by tree trunk before hitting the ground. He tried to catch his breath, but it evaded him. His lungs burned, his cuts stung, and his muscles ached. He knew if the time came, and he was forced to run again, he would be screwed for sure. Sam knew he didn't have that much left in him.

Sam pushed away from the tree that was supporting him. It had kept him from completely collapsing to the mossy floor of the forest. He looked up at the sheer height of the tree and its strong thick limbs. He studied and attempted to calculate if they would support his weight. "It has to work."

The nearest branch was about two feet overhead, and he normally would have no problem getting to it. However, on this night it might has well have been task only Superman could have taken. The way he was feeling now, it seemed to be at least three stories up.

With his initial attempt he jumped from where he stood. The roughness of bark scrapped the pads of his fingertips, but that was the closest he got to grabbing hold of the branch. He was still breathing too hard. It wasn't only because he exhausted himself on the assent of the steep hillside, but also because he was experiencing a fear that he had never known. When he was a small child, the dark shadows of his bedroom terrified him to the point of covering his head with his Spiderman sheets and trembling. He was way beyond that now. At least when he was a child, the shadows that taunted him stayed where they were, but that didn't seem to be the case anymore. These creatures were so dark, they were like live shadows. He put his hands on his knees and dropped his head, trying to muster up the strength to reach what could save his life.

The clicking sound, which had been so constant, suddenly stopped, and Sam shot up straight. The forest was an eerie silent, very possibly more disturbing than the clatter from the red-eyed things. Sam peered around the thick tree trunk and watched for any movement, but even the breeze seemed to freeze up in fear. The dark was still and quiet, but it made Sam uneasy just the same.

He suddenly realized that he had been holding his breath. Just as he exhaled, something started screaming. But it wasn't just something...it was them. And from the sound of it, it was all of them screaming at once. It was unlike anything Sam had ever heard before. Taken straight out of the scariest of horror films, it was the sound of a million and one tortured souls, finger nails on a chalkboard, and teeth grinding all rolled into one horrifying song.

His hands spontaneously shot up to cover his ears, but he forced them down. The screaming seemed to be coming from only yards away, but in every direction. He was already hampered by the darkness so he needed all of his other senses to work even harder.

Just as abruptly as it began, it ended. Sam was startled to hear heavy breathing when the screaming stopped, but then he realized it was his own. Again the forest seemed too still. The silence seemed heavy and toxic. But as quiet as it was, Sam heard it as a warning, loud and clear. It was the calm before the storm. He knew he didn't have much longer to figure out whether he was going to run, hide, or lie down and wait to die.

He rested his forehead against the rough bark of his supportive tree and briefly considered the last of his options. It would be so easy to relieve the red hot fatigue in his legs by simply sliding down the trunk and wait for the red eyed hunters. He searched his soul for a reason to live, and for a moment he came up empty-handed. Murdering Lisa destroyed everything for him, but then Sandra's angelic face surfaced.

He sighed heavily and started to walk away from his tree. He winced as dry pine needles crunched under his weight. In the silence, the simple, quiet sound seemed as loud as a gunshot. They would have no problem locating him with him sounding off his location. He started to take extra precaution, almost tiptoeing through the trees like he was the star of a morbid ballet.

Sam had no idea where he was going, but he knew he couldn't stay there, and he knew he couldn't die. Not tonight. He hoped that he was wrong about his suspicions, but as far as he knew, the creatures were not an isolated occurrence in small town Montana. For all he knew, they were popping up all over the place. Sam had to make sure that Sandra was okay before he could lie down and wait to die. He had to find a car.

She was his reason for living now. His only reason. And she was his for the taking, at least for the moment, at least until she found out about his secret. Then he would be the monster in her eyes. But it didn't matter if she knew or not. If she was in trouble, he wanted to be there to help her; to protect her, even if he didn't know how to protect himself.

He stopped and listened to the night. Silence greeted him. Nothing was rushing up on him, and nothing seemed to be stalking him. But he doubted his senses. He looked around and suddenly he felt so small and insignificant as he stood among the forest of ancient trees. The feeling came with the gut wrenching realization that he was more or less lost. Of course he could just start walking downhill and return to the highway, but he felt that was a sure guarantee that he would encounter them again. A lot of good he was going to be to Sandra if he couldn't even find his way out of a populated forest.

And as if God had heard his desperate thoughts, and had granted him a little hope, Sam came across someone's back yard. The large log home loomed over him like a prehistoric animal ready to pounce. None of the windows held a welcoming glow of light. It was foreboding, and Sam almost stepped back into the trees. Here the moonlight illuminated the yard, but every corner held deep shadows. Just as he advanced towards the house he saw movement. Sam couldn't believe his eyes as he watched pockets of darkness step away from the house. He dropped himself behind a nearby decorative bush, confused and frightened.

Just to the left of the back door a pair of glowing red eyes appeared. Sam strained to see past the eyes, and to see what actually possessed them, but whatever it was blended so well into the dark that it seemed to be a part of it. Sam didn't think that he had been seen, and he was content to stay hidden like a coward, rather than risk being spotted as he tried to escape back into safe cover of the trees.

As more red eyes appeared, Sam pressed himself into the ground. The earth smelled rich and clean and the grass tickled his nose. He took comfort from the pure smell of it, and was even able to slow his breathing close to normal.

That is until he heard a scream. At first he thought it was the shadows again, but this was all too human sounding. He shot himself to all fours and peered around the corner of the bush. Sam could tell it was coming from within the house. Suddenly the back door burst open and a woman...no a girl, maybe nineteen, sprinted out. Her long blond hair was luminous in the moonlight as it streamed behind her almost as a surrender flag would fly behind a defeated warrior.

The girl made the mistake of looking back. "No! Don't look back, girl, keep going!" Sam begged under his breath. She must have seen the swarm of eyes coming for her because she stopped and put her hands up in defense. It did no good. The shadow things were on top of her even as she started screaming.

Sam wanted to be a hero. He wanted to stand up and run to her rescue with his fists flying. But he didn't move. He couldn't. And as her screams of fear turned into cries of agony he started to cry. Nothing in this world could have prepared him for her cries for mercy. She was begging them, and she was begging God to end her pain and she was crying for her mom. But whatever they were, they were heartless. From the sounds of it, they were ripping her apart, so Sam started to talk to God himself. He thanked God he couldn't actually see through them to see what they were doing to her, and he asked God to take away his imagination.

Finally, after several minutes, the girl went quiet. God finally helped her, or maybe the shadows just decided to finish her off. Whatever the case, Sam prayed for her soul.

He lifted his head and watched as the shadows moved away from the scene of mauling, and what he expected...a torn and mutilated body, pools of blood, body parts, things that would have been easy to see in the bright moonlight...were nowhere to be seen. "Jesus." They must have eaten her whole. There was no other explanation.

He briefly panicked again as he became aware that he hadn't been keeping track of the shadows. For all he knew they were coming up behind him, so he searched for dark movement. He sighed with relief as he found a dark mass moving into the trees on the opposite end of the house. They were leaving, on the search for more victims.

He watched as they disappeared into the trees, but he hesitated to get up from the ground. Even though he saw them go, it didn't mean they all went. How many more were lurking in or around the house. There was no way to see them unless they opened their eyes. Sam resigned himself to stay there, partially covered by a decorative bush, at least until the morning, still some seven hours away. He figured at this point it would be better to be a coward than a victim like the girl with luminous blonde hair.

Chapter Seven

Madison and Ethan

August 7ᵗʰ, 6:24 a.m.

The early morning sun was breaking through the living room blinds creating a stripped pattern of light and shadow on the wall. Madison slowly sat up and saw that she had fallen asleep on Ethan's lap. Ethan had his head cocked to one side and was snoring softly. He was going to have one hell of a crick in his neck if he's been in that position long.

She glanced up at the clock. Ten forty-five. Then the events of the night before flooded into her memory. She hesitantly walked to the phone on the wall, not wanting to hear what was on the other side. Silence. The plastic ear piece felt strangely cold as she was greeted by no one; not even a dial tone. The pit of dread in her stomach grew and forced her to swallow hard. Something was wrong. She hit the button a few times, hoping to beat in a dial tone, or even just that recording that told her to try her number again. Still nothing.

She slammed the phone back down on the cradle and went back to the couch, feeling slightly lost. She saw the remote to the television wedged under Ethan's butt and pulled it out. That was enough to wake him and he stretched hard. "What time is it?" he said in the middle of a yawn.

"You tell me." She was hitting the power button repeatedly. Ironically she thought people who continuously hit the elevator button, or cross-walk buttons over and over again were foolish and impatient. As if hitting it more than once was going to make things work faster. It suddenly occurred to her that she was starting to panic. She was becoming one of those people.

She stood up and walked to the television to manually turn on the set. Hitting the button over and over again produced the same results. "Madison, the power is still out. Calm down. I would estimate that it is probably about six; so we overslept by half an hour. If I'm wrong, I'll either be early to work, or I'll be late. I'm sure no one is going to be too upset if I am considering the circumstances." He walked over to her and kissed her on the forehead. "Go take a shower, and I'll find something for us to eat that doesn't require a toaster. Okay?"

She closed her eyes and nodded. "You're right. I'm overreacting. It is just a typical power outage. The clocks and cars...just coincidences."

It was obvious that he had forgotten about those when his face paled slightly. But to his credit, he put on a smile for her. "Right. Coincidences."

*****

In the pale morning light her reflection looked more ghostly than real. The small window above the toilet wasn't giving off enough light for her to do any real beauty treatments, but she was looking forward to washing off the salty residue of the night's sweat. She pulled off the shirt and resolved to forgo the hot shower and settle for lukewarm. She realized there would only be so much hot water in the electric hot water tank. Besides, in the heat, lukewarm would probably feel better anyway. Ethan however always wanted a hot shower, even when it was hot out. He was weird like that.

She remembered their trip to Phoenix last August. They thought she was in remission, but a simple gallbladder procedure discovered an aggressive return of the disease. They drove seventeen hours to attend their thirty-three year old sister-in-law's funeral and turned around to drive back the following day. But for some reason, it was Phoenix's water that really made a lasting impression on her. Cold water was lukewarm, which meant lukewarm water in 117 degree weather rather disappointing was when all you wanted was cold water. It sucked and she would never take nice cold water on a summer day for granted again.

Madison finished undressing and looked at her reflection. In the upper left hand corner was a sticky note that Ethan had written the week before. "Good morning, beautiful." A tease of a smile started at her lips but instead she turned sideways and held up her breasts up to get a really good measure of her stomach. No matter how much she examined her reflection, she couldn't see what he saw to write that note. She even turned to the other side, hoping for something different. Being only 5'2", she was too short in her opinion. Her breasts, which were heavy in her hands were too big for her stumpy body. She didn't even have any visible ankles. Instead her calves seemed to start right from the top of her foot. She had her father to thank for that.

Maybe after another twenty or thirty pounds that note would describe her. In the meantime, people can keep telling her she has such a pretty face with her easy smile and bright green eyes. She rolled her eyes, convinced that was a polite way of people saying someone needed to lose weight.

Well, at least she had personality too, right? And creative talent! Yeah, that too....at least until last night. Nope, as of last night, the lights and her creative talent went dark.

She turned away from her reflection and turned the shower knob, but no silvery liquid came out. The shower head was dry, and apparently it would remain so. "Oh no..." She tried the separate bath-tub, and the two sinks, and still no water. She thought better of trying the toilet, thinking that they may need that before everything was up and running again.

Looking back at her reflection she shrugged to her silent companion, who simply shrugged along with her. "Okay. So it's a Wednesday that thinks it is a Monday. I shouldn't expect anything less than this." She quickly brushed out her hair and put it into a low pony tail and applied extra deodorant to hopefully cover the stink of heat.

In the bedroom she pulled on a pair of jean shorts and a white tank top. The great thing about her office was that it was at home and there were some clear advantages. The dress code was pretty lenient, and she could keep with Ethan's work-schedule, taking the same days off. She tried to treat it like a real job though, making sure to be in by eight and trying not to quit for the day before five. Unfortunately lately that meant spending a lot of time staring at a screen with no progress. So she walked away, only to force herself back to stare more for several hours, sometimes days. If she were still working for a traditional job, they would have fired her by now. Hell, she was pretty close to firing herself.

Madison walked down the hallway and watched Ethan from the kitchen doorway. He was singing "Baby Got Back" as he was pouring milk onto some cereal, and this time she couldn't help but smile. "Is the milk still cold?"

He looked up and grinned. "That was fast."

She stepped into the kitchen and sat at the bar. He handed her a bowl and spoon. "Well, yeah, since the water isn't running."

Ethan swallowed his mouthful of Captain Crunch and looked at her. "No water at all?"

"Nope. Try the sink though."

He walked the few steps and lifted the handle. "Not a single drop. You would think there would be at least something. But you know a lot of these wells run on electric pumps." He sighed and looked out the window. She could tell that despite all of the optimistic talk, he was starting to get a little worried. She knew that he could feel the strangeness in the air as well as she could. "Well this stinks." He sighed with such an air of drama, she laughed out loud. "We all stink. I stink like gym shorts. You stink like Secret for women."

She gave him a friendly punch in the arm. "Haha...very funny."

"Hey, you laughed for real! We all heard you!"

"Yeah, yeah. Go get dressed, goofball."

He kissed the top of her head and disappeared down the hall.

Chapter Eight

Sam

August 7th, 6:33 a.m.

His eyes fluttered open. Above him was a brilliant sky. Purple, pink, and orange cloud fingers stretched across a light blue background. He smiled contently. God was an artist and this was one of his masterpieces. His next thoughts were those of confusion; where was the roof? Sam frowned. And why was an unfamiliar heaviness on his chest? It was already warm out, but the weight on him was uncomfortably cold.

The memories of the night before tsunamied into his mind and he started to get up. But the thing on his chest was moving. He glanced down and stopped breathing when his eyes met a pair of slanted red eyes staring back at him. The thick, black snake was coiled on his chest and was swaying side to side as it studied him with interest. He didn't know if snakes had the emotional intelligence to be interested, but this snake almost seemed to be smiling with it, proudly displaying fangs. He watched as the fiery red in its eyes changed to a brilliant purple and then to a golden yellow. This was no ordinary snake. He wanted to yell out, but couldn't decide if the snake or the dark creatures from the night before were more threatening. Sam absolutely did not want to get their attention, so he watched the snake watch him.

Time seemed to stop as the serpent and he engaged in a staring contest. Sam didn't want to move in case its venom was as paralyzing as its stare, and it seemed to be sizing him up. But then it started to move away. It took its time though, and Sam was frozen in fear as it began to caress his arm. Caress? What a strange word came to his mind, but the way the snake moved, it almost seemed to be stroking his flesh in the way a lover would; the way Lisa did. And he knew he imagined hearing it hiss his name.

He waited until he couldn't see it move through the grass before he shot up to his feet. He tried to brush away the feeling of violation. He felt unclean and knew only a shower would be able to wash it away.

The early morning sun streamed through the limbs of the tall ponderosas. He wasn't sure if it was just his imagination or not, but he was sure that the forest smelled more of decaying flesh than of life, but then maybe it was just the lingering stench of horny lizards without legs. Just thinking about it made him want to throw up.

Sam was in a bad state. His clothes were soaked from night sweats and his body was smeared with earth and blood. He was shocked that he even had the ability to fall asleep after witnessing the blond haired girl. Maybe it was the silence of the night after the shadows marched into the trees, or maybe it was sheer exhaustion. That could explain color changing snakes eyes too. Hallucinations caused by exhaustion. That made sense.

It wasn't only his body that was a mess. It was in his head too. He felt like crying. He wondered how long he would be able to hold out until tears began to fall again. He already knew his face was stained with streaks of dried tears. There wasn't a time in his life that he had ever cried as much as he had in just the past evening. Not even when his father died.

If his father were to see him crying like a child...Sam could almost picture the shame and embarrassment cross the old man's face. He would have told Sam to act like a man and suck it up. He knew he would be letting his father down if he just sat there and cried. Instead, he turned and examined the log home. He could already see heat radiating off the shingles on the roof and the sun had barely risen.

He then turned his attention to the exterior walls and watched for any shadows shifting. For all he knew, those creatures could blend in as well in day as they could at night. The house stood still.

His first steps were those of a baby trying out walking for the first time...hesitant and cautious. He felt vulnerable as he walked away from his bush and he was suddenly aware of how many directions surrounded him. He couldn't turn his head, and he couldn't turn his body fast enough to keep track of them all, so he found himself darting to the house. With the smooth logs of the home pressed firmly to his back...they couldn't walk through things, could they?...he inched his way towards the back door of the house.

The first thing he wanted to do was find a phone and call the police. He knew they would be busy in the city with all the commotion he heard last night, but they had to know what he saw. Would they necessarily believe him? Probably not. For all he knew, this was an isolated event, and whatever happened in town was purely coincidental in timing.

Sam also resigned to turning himself in. If he was lucky, after they hear his tale, they might just toss him in a loony bin and throw away the key and chalk up his murdering ways to insanity.

After he was done talking to the police and as he waited for them to come, he was going to search for the family of the house, minus the girl, if any of them indeed survived the night. If they were smart, they would have hid somewhere in the house...under beds, closets, cupboards. Shit...if he could hide under a bush and escape the murdering shadows, surely they would have been safe somewhere in the house.

And then he was going to raid their fridge, and get something incredibly cold to drink.

Sam reached for the door handle, and slowly cracked the screen door. The heavy wood door was propped open, not thrown open. That actually didn't surprise him much, considering the hot temperatures. Inside were plenty of windows that lit up the kitchen adequately, but still Sam slowly entered the room, checking every corner for movement or glowing red eyes. He wished he had his revolver with him.

His room scan stopped as he spied a phone against the far wall. He threw all caution to the wind and darted across the room. In his excitement he knocked the phone off the receiver and it dropped to the floor with a heavy thud. "Shit!" His curse came out louder than he had hoped and he stopped to listen to the sounds of the house. Sam was met with a silence he didn't know existed. How strange not to hear anything. No wind. No birds. No barking dogs.

He quietly placed the phone back on its base, and picked it up again. It was dead. He must have damaged it in the drop. But what house didn't have at least a couple of phones? He would just have to find one. That meant going into the darker corners of the house. Thank God for lights. It was just as well, he needed to search for the family anyway. But since he was in the kitchen...

He walked to the sink to wash the bloody dirt that was caked on his body away. But lifting the faucet handle produced no results. Sam frowned. "What the..." Maybe if he was lucky, they kept some cold water in the fridge and he'd use that to at least wash his hands before he started in on the food. However, opening the fridge brought only more disappointment and confusion. While there was a pitcher of water, there wasn't a light, so either the bulb blew out or the electricity was off. He touched the gallon of milk in the door. Ahhhhh, still cold. So at least he knew he'd eat and drink.

After he washed his hands with chilled water, he helped himself to the makings of a ham and cheese sandwich. He located the bread in the pantry and a knife in the drawer next to the sink. For good measure, he added a butcher knife. It would be a suitable substitute for his revolver if it came down to it.

After devouring two sandwiches, a can of Coke, and after discovering a bag of Oreos and enjoying several of them, he politely placed his cup and plate next to the sink, and then firmly grasping the butcher knife in his hand, he headed towards the next room.

Thankfully he covered most of the rooms at once. The kitchen, dining room, and family room were just one big open space. But he took the time to look under all the tables and behind all the larger furniture. The smallest of family members could hide in any one of these areas.

As the early morning rays began reaching far into the family room, Sam began noticing family photos. The blonde haired girl from the night before truly had been a beautiful teenager. Looking at her close up, she seemed so young and innocent. As he studied the long line of photos stretched along the fireplace mantle, he saw she probably had one little sister and her parents. But he stopped at a photo of her alone. Blonde girl was a cheerleader for her local high school. Her maroon and white uniform was clean and crisp, but it was her smile that radiated. She was absolutely stunning, and he couldn't take his eyes off of her.

It wasn't that he was having impure thoughts of one so young, but he couldn't accept that someone so beautiful, pure and so happy looking could have been taken so ruthlessly from this earth. He mourned for her deeply, as if she was his own daughter, and a sob escaped him. He bowed his head to the mantle and cried.

He had seen some crazy, disgusting things since becoming an officer, and not once did he ever shed a tear for any of the victims. He had created a cold stone barrier between them and his emotions. Somehow blond girl penetrated that, but he knew that if he wanted to make it through this, if he was going to survive, it was time for him to suck it up, and get the job done. Sam straightened his shoulders and took once last glance at the picture of the pretty teenager. He vowed to himself that those would be his last tears.

For the next twenty minutes he thoroughly searched the two bedroom house. He looked under beds, in closets and the shower, but the house was empty. Either blond girl was home alone, or no one survived the night. Sam shuddered as he remembered the way the creatures devoured the girl. It had to be the worst death handed down to a person.

He found himself standing in the middle of the family room again. A beautiful, carved grandfather clock stood tall but still against the wall. Ten forty-five. Sam frowned. He knew it was much earlier than that. He could feel it in his bones. Maybe the damn thing didn't work anyway. But looking at the hanging clock in the dining room and another in the kitchen meant that none of the clocks worked. Maybe time just stopped.

No people. No water. No power. No time. "Shit. Those things must have been hungry to eat all that." He tried to laugh at his own joke, but it seemed too possible to be funny.

Sam noticed several sets of keys hanging on some hooks next to the front door. He started towards them. He would have to borrow one of their vehicles to get back to town to report what happened. Half way there, he glanced at her pictures again. He couldn't help himself. Sam decided that blond haired girl was going to be his guardian angel. God knew he needed one because he was scared. She was going to be the one to get him through this. He would live in her honor.

He lifted the frame off the mantle and weighed it in his hands for a few moments, just staring at her smile. Then he turned it over and removed the backing of the frame. The back of the picture revealed "Abby, Sept. 2017" in neat handwriting.

"Abby," he whispered. The name itself seemed to hold some magic in it. A subtle calm washed over his frayed nerves. "Abby."

Chapter Nine

Madison and Ethan

Madison placed their dirty cereal bowls in the sink and was instantly hit with the pungent smell of day old tuna. "Why oh why did we have to have tuna casserole for dinner last night?" The universe responded with maybe a better question of why did they put off washing the dishes? The involuntary gag of disgust was her consequence for being lazy.

Ethan had left five minutes ago to head over to the jail where he worked twelve hour shifts as a detention officer, smelling mostly of deodorant himself. With him gone and without water to do dishes, or electricity to work on her book or vacuum with, she wasn't quite sure what to do with herself. But then out of the corner of her eye she noticed the ever increasing mound of laundry waiting to be folded, and she remembered she had to refold the clothes in the bedroom too. She could try to tackle that while she waited for the power, and try to think of where to go with her story in the meantime. Multitasking at its finest.

She grabbed the overfull basket and dropped it in the middle of the living room floor. She sat down and stared at the pile. Folding laundry was one thing she really hated to do. She could go without folding altogether in her life, but it was a pet peeve of Ethan's to have to wear wrinkled clothes. Her argument was that anything could be thrown back into the dryer to get out wrinkles, but he never accepted that when clothes could just be folded. It was an ongoing debate. She started praying that the power would come on so that she could do anything but fold socks, knowing that once she started, she would have to finish it.

She had the first shirt in her hand when Ethan walked through the front door. He always took her breath away whenever he came into a room. They had been married for over two years and he still gave her butterflies. He wasn't tall by any means, only four inches taller than her, but still dark and handsome, and when he gave an honest smile, he could light up a room. But he wasn't smiling when he came into the house. "Hey, I thought you left."

"I tried. Honey, we've got a problem. Where are your keys?"

Madison got off the floor and followed him into the kitchen. "They are on the counter. Why? What's wrong?"

"The truck won't start. It won't... god damn thing won't even turn over. She's dead." She could tell that he was frustrated. It wasn't often that Ethan swore in front of her.

"What the hell is going on, Ethan?"

He didn't answer her. Instead he swiped the keys off the counter and strode over to the door. Madison followed closely behind him in her bare feet onto the hot pavement of their drive-way. The initial heat was enough to cause her to wince, but Ethan kept going so she kept on, knowing her feet would eventually get used to the temperature.

At the front of her brand new Chevy Impala he stopped and looked at the car thoughtfully. She stood beside him and alternated her glance from him to the car. He looked at her and shrugged. "Something tells me this isn't going to start either." Just the same he walked around the side and unlocked the driver's door and got in. She watched as he put the key in the ignition and she waited for the car to roar to life, but she didn't hear anything.

She didn't hear anything. That realization made her hold her breath, as if her breathing could cover up any noise that was supposed to be there. There wasn't the sound of the early birds, or the insects buzzing in the summer sun. She couldn't hear the yapping of that stupid poodle a few houses down that barked at leaves. There weren't any far away car alarms or sirens. There wasn't even a breeze.

The click of the hood being opening caused her to exhale. Ethan stood looking at the brand new engine. "I'm no expert, Madison, but isn't this supposed to run? It ran yesterday, didn't it? Nothing was wrong with my truck, nothing was wrong with your car. This is way fucked up."

There's that swearing again. She had no answers for him. Nothing was making sense. No electricity for almost twelve hours, no phone, no water, and now the cars. "Maybe the battery operated radio will work. Maybe there is some kind of public announcement we should hear."

"Well, it is worth a try, but all indications say those batteries won't work either."

*****

He was right of course. Even as they replaced the batteries in the radio with brand new ones, directly from the package, they knew it was pointless. It was like the whole world disappeared. Static didn't even exist. They sat on the living room floor amidst a mountain of unfolded laundry. Neither one of them spoke or even looked at each other for about five minutes. They were both deep in thought, trying to make sense of everything.

Madison looked over to Ethan and reached for his hand. "Ethan?"

He broke out of his trance and squeezed her hand. "Yeah?"

"Are you okay, sweetie?"

He slowly shook his head. "Don't you think this is all too…weird? I can understand the power being out, maybe even the phones and water. But batteries and the cars? Why don't they work?"

She sighed. "Well what do you think we should do?"

He stood up and looked down at her. "I think maybe you should put on some shoes, and maybe we should walk down the road to the neighbors and see what they've got going."

They walked hand in hand down their long driveway. There was a house about a quarter of a mile down the pine tree lined road. They hadn't officially met their neighbors yet, even though they had moved in over three months ago. Madison and Ethan thought that seclusion and privacy were the main reasons that people moved away from town anyway. They were the reasons they had.

Madison looked back at their small ranch style home. It wasn't her dream home by any means, but it was home. Their first. It blended in well with the large boulders and looming pine trees that filled their property. They were planning on covering the chipped and cracked brown paint with siding, redoing the roof, and replacing most of the windows. The interior was mostly brown as well. Brown wallpaper, brown cabinets, brown carpet. Madison hated brown, but she loved her home. By the time they were done, it would be perfect enough.

"You know what's funny?" Ethan spoke but didn't look at her. "I've been listening for a while, but I haven't heard anything. Only us walking. Nothing else."

"Yeah, I know. I was noticing that back at the car. Maybe God accidentally pushed the mute button." She was hoping the joke would lighten the air around them, but it remained heavy with anxiety. He did humor her with a fake smile though.

They turned up the first long driveway they came across. Around a small bend there was a mid-sized two story log home. Several vehicles were parked in front of a small porch, including an F-150 and an older Ford Taurus sat in the open garage. "Looks like they're home." Ethan led her up the four steps to the front door and rang the bell. They stood there for a few moments and looked at each other.

"Try knocking." They could hear the knocks echo through the house, but no one came to the door. "Maybe they aren't home after all."

Ethan studied the door, and then headed down the stairs. "Come on, let's go around back."

They followed a stone path to the rear of the house, and trekked through a well maintained lawn with several lawn chairs strung about. Summer flowers were planted throughout the yard, and a pretty gazebo sat in the center of all the color. There was a small concrete slab with a gas barbeque and a picnic table. On top of the table were tipped over plastic cups with their contents staining the concrete blow. There were also four plates; including a knife and fork piercing a piece of steak as if all it was waiting for were the hands to mobilize it. And there was a spoon full of corn, waiting for a mouth to devour it. And there were a couple more lawn chairs outside of a sliding glass door, knocked over carelessly.

Madison put her hands on her hips. "Looks like they were having a party last night. Maybe they were just too tired to clean up?"

Ethan walked up to the door and pressed his face to the glass, leaving a sweaty smudge.

"Hmmmm." He reached for the handle and pushed the door open.

Madison grabbed his bicep. "What are you doing? You can't go in there!" She kept her voice down, sure that any minute the family would find them breaking into their house.

Ethan pulled away from her and stepped into the house. "Just look."

She peered inside the open door and found the eat-in kitchen. She stepped in and examined the table. A game of Monopoly was set up. There were half drank glasses of milk and what looked like ice tea. Paper money decorated the floor. Most of the chairs were tipped over. A high-chair sat on one end, smeared with mashed potatoes, the bib lying in the seat. On the stove sat leftover food, most of which had developed a cold crust during the night.

Ethan stood there looking at the scene with his hands on his hips. "Either they left in a big hurry…without their cars…or…"

Madison narrowed her eyes, and walked into an adjoining family room. There was a small toy bin in the corner, and besides a cloth doll with red yarn for hair, and buttons for eyes in the middle of the floor, the room was very tidy. Family photo's showed the smiling faces of a couple in their mid-thirties and three children; a girl of about eleven, a boy of around eight, and the baby couldn't have been two yet.

Upon further examination, the house was completely empty. There were still clothes in the washer, which didn't have a chance to drain before the power went out, and damp clothes in the dryer. In the girl's room was a math book open to an algebra lesson, and the pencil laid on neatly printed notebook paper. In a boy's room there was a video game controller waiting for him to return from the party. The baby's room had a pair of pajamas laid out, and the parent's room was practical and clean.

Ethan was still in the kitchen when she made her way back. "Find anything?"

Madison frown deepened. "No."

He sat down in a still standing chair. "Well I found that their phone, electricity, and water don't work either."

"What about the cars? Those must be their keys by the door." She pointed to a group of small hooks next to the door.

He just shook his head.

Madison was nervously chewing on her bottom lip as she surveyed the abandoned kitchen. The scene was very unsettling. But it went so far beyond how it looked; it simply felt wrong. She relied on Ethan to be her voice of reason when her writer's imagination took off with her, so she baited him for reassurance. "Earlier you said that they either left in a big hurry or they... what?"

Ethan shrugged. "Or they disappeared."

No, no. That wasn't reassuring at all. Try again. "People don't just disappear."

He shook his head and gestured to the room. "Well then you explain it."

So much for that idea. Mission Reassurance disastrously failed.

Chapter Ten

Kathy and Justin

August 7th, 6:42

He was awake. His head hurt. His back hurt. But most of all his heart hurt. He delayed opening his eyes for as long as he could. As long as they were closed he could deny the gnawing reality of what had happened last night. As long as his eyes were closed, he could pretend he was at home, in his bed. Safe. And Wyatt was just down the hall, huddled under his SpongeBob sheets.

Justin could feel sunlight on his face through what must have been a skylight, but he pretended that it was light streaming through his east facing window. It was going to be another hot day. Hot or not, he knew he needed to get out in the yard and mow the lawn. It was overdue for a cut. But somewhere in his mind, he remembered a woman named Alice who had told them to stay in the light. That he could manage. He could stay right there, bathing in yellow warmth, with his eyes closed, and he could prevent ever experiencing a nightmare like that again. As long as his eyes were closed.

Not that it was really possible to go through that kind of pain again. He only had one son. And Wyatt was gone. Death itself probably felt better to a soul than watching some shapeless thing with red eyes steal the very life from a child...his child. As long as his eyes were closed he could pretend that it was all just a bad dream. The worst dream of his entire life.

Suddenly it occurred to him that his bladder hurt too. He had to take a piss...badly. Instead he concentrated on his breathing to continue prolonging opening his eyes. None of this has to be real as long as he doesn't open them only to find himself on a stranger's bathroom floor.

He wondered if Kathy was ever able to fall asleep. She never made a sound, even as Ernie and Alice screamed for their lives. Normally a restless sleeper, he never felt her move against him during the night in search of a comfortable position. He strained his ears to concentrate on her breathing instead of his own, but he couldn't find it. It was almost as if she wasn't even there.

"Kath?" His voice was barely a whisper, but he could hear the roughness in it; kind of like someone had poured gravel down his throat. It now occurred to him that he was incredibly parched on top of having to pee. Pee first, then take a drink from the sink. But his priorities changed when the seconds ticked by and she still hadn't answered him. "Kath? Are you okay?"

He waited. But he couldn't hear anything past his own breathing. He reached out and could feel her sitting up next to him so he gave her a small shake. "Kathy. Please. Wake up."

The body next to his shook with ease, but still didn't stir beyond that. Damn it. He was going to have to open his eyes. Check on Kathy, then pee, and then drink some water.

It took actual willpower to open his eyes. They were heavy with a cement mixture of tears and sleep. But with effort, he was able to pry them open. He instantly shut them again to the brightness of the room and took the next opening effort a bit more slowly.

Across from him the candle had burned itself down and he looked at it with much despair and much gratitude at the same time. On one hand it had shined its protective light for a better part of the night. On the other hand it was completely worthless in case they came back in the coming darkness.

Kathy's foot caught his eye and he followed it up until he saw his son, sleeping peacefully on his wife's lap. Justin found comfort in his denial. As long as he kept believing that none of that really happened last night, and his son really was just sleeping, he could keep on going...keep on living.

She was still stroking his head. So he followed her hand to her arm and up to her neck. From there his eyes easily met her eyes. But she didn't return the stare. Instead she was staring at the shower curtain...just as she was last night. Her eyes were empty, almost dead.

Dead? No. No. No. There will be no death. Her eyes were not dead. Just like Wyatt was not dead. He was just sleeping.

"Kathy?" Nothing in her posture revealed to him that she had even heard him. The only thing that moved on her was her hand as it glided through thick blonde hair. So he repositioned himself to his knees. He grunted and groaned at the stiffness of his body, but leaned into her line of sight. He thought that if she could just see him that maybe she would snap out of it. But even as he looked directly into her eyes she continued to look straight through him.

Justin's bladder continued to scream for attention. So he stood up and walked over to the toilet. So he was taking care of task number two. After all, he did what he said he was going to do. He made sure Kathy was okay. In a matter of speaking, she was okay. She was alive...just dead to the world. And when he was finished he probably would go ahead and take care of getting a drink of water too. Then he would go back and tend to her. Get her up and moving around. She probably would be thirsty too. Maybe he'll just take some cold water and splash her face. No doubt that would wake her senses up.

An involuntary sigh of relief escaped him as he drained himself. He zipped up and walked over to the sink and turned the faucet on to get it really cold. The room was getting hot and stuffy and nothing sounded better than a freezing glass of water. But the knobs just turned and turned, but no ice cold water was to be found. Justin kneeled down and looked under the sink. He found the main water valve and adjusted it. But it was already where it should be. "Huh. That's interesting."

He tried the sink again and then moved onto the shower. Moving the shower curtain didn't cause Kathy to react, so apparently she was not really even focused on that. She was seeing something only she could see, in a world that was known only to her. He had to get her to come back. The ways things were going, they would not be able to stay there in the sauna-like room for long.

After trying out the shower with disappointing results, he slid down the wall next to Kathy. He grasped her one free hand and held onto it for dear life. Being even in partial denial was not going to allow them to survive another night. He needed to face reality. Wyatt was gone, taken ruthlessly away from them, and their poor excuse for a sanctuary was in no condition to sustain them. They may die if they leave the confines of the bathroom, but they were surely going to die if the stayed there.

For all he knew the nightmare of last night was over. Erased by the promise of a new day, and there was no way in hell he was going to let those things deny his right to live. There was no way he was going to let them convince him to not go on simply out fear of the unknown. Justin suddenly, and with a certain degree of relief found himself sobbing. He knew he had to deal with everything in order to move on....to be smart. And he knew that Wyatt would have wanted that. Wyatt would take the very same principle that Kathy and himself had used since the day he was born for him now. If you fall, you need to get back up. Fall forward. True. Never in his worst dreams would Justin imagine how far he would fall, but he knew he had to get back up. Even if only for the sake of Kathy now.

He waited until he knew he could speak through his tears, and then he gave Kathy's hand a little extra squeeze. "Kathy? Listen, babe. I know how devastated you are. I'm there too. Really. Wyatt....ahhh, Jesus. Kathy, Wyatt is gone. He...He's dead. He is not coming back to us." He watched her eyes as he spoke, waiting for some kind of acknowledgement from her, and was rewarded with a flash of life, although subtle. It was something.

"Kathy? We can't stay here. There isn't any water, and God knows we have been through hell already, but now we've reached the heat of it. We are probably already dehydrated, and it is only going to get worse. I need you to come back to me. To help me. So we can get out of this. I don't think Wyatt would have wanted us to just sit here and wait to die."

Her eyes finally moved away from the shower curtain and down to their son. She shook her head slowly and touched his cheek. And silently Justin rejoiced. No matter how deeply pained she was, she was back.

He stood up and lifted Wyatt off of her lap. His little boy was stiff and heavier than he remembered but he cradled him and kissed the top of his head. Kathy sat there and stared at her empty lap. "Come on Kathy, stay with me."

She looked up at his eyes and nodded. Slowly she stood up and reached for him to help with her balance. Between her injury the night before, being dehydrated, and staying in the same position all night, she would probably need his assistance. He offered her his shoulder and carried the weight of their son to the door.

Justin hesitated before unlocking the door. He thought better of rushing out and put his ear to the wood to listen for anything that might jump out at them once he opened it, but it was in vain. If anything was indeed waiting for them on the other side, it was very quiet. It was a chance they would have to take.

He looked at Kathy and she nodded at him as her only means of assurance. "Do you think you can hold him?" And she nodded again.

Once he had his hands completely free, he cracked open the door and peered through the small gap. It didn't offer much, but he could at least see that the hallway was brightly lit. As long as they stayed in the light...

He pulled the door open and jumped out with fists gathered...just in case. The hallway was deserted, so he pulled Kathy by the elbow to join him. Slowly they walked down Alice's and Ernie's long hallway. They paused at each doorway with caution, but passed by without incident. However, as they neared the room where Wyatt was sleeping only hours before they stopped all together. The sounds of Alice and Ernie being eaten or tortured or whatever those things did to them made Justin's imagination spin out of control. He could vividly picture the gore of that room and it instantly sickened him.

"Kathy, you may want to close your eyes. I don't think this is going to be anything you want to see."

To her credit, she didn't question him but instantly shut her eyes tight. Maybe she wasn't completely there last night, but her subconscious was well aware of what went down and she was just as prepared for the worst as he was. The only problem was that he couldn't just close his eyes. They were well past that point.

He took her by the elbow again and took a step forward. He wished that the square of sun light in the hallway wasn't nearly as bright. With all this natural light, the blood would be all that more vibrant. He tensed when they physically entered the light, but quickly relaxed with confusion.

There, just past the doorway, laid Ernie's abandoned gun. And besides that and a slightly messed up bed and wounded plaster on the walls from bullets, nothing was out of place. This wasn't the massacre scene that he had imagined, and it made absolutely no sense. Their screams would haunt him for the rest of his life. They had to have been ripped open to have made sounds like that. It wasn't as if the creature was causing that kind of agony with a simply glance or word. It was physically hurting them. But now, standing in the doorway, there was no indication of that. And Justin just couldn't bring himself to believe that someone or something had cleaned up the mess.

"I....I don't understand." Did he dream it after all? No...looking in his wife's arms confirmed that he didn't dream the attack. Looking at the gun on the carpet confirmed he didn't imagine it. He shook his head violently as he tried to force common sense into his head. "We've got to get out of here."

He looked Kathy in the face and saw that she still had her eyes closed. "It is okay, Kathy. You can open your eyes." She complied but would not look into the room. It was just as well. In her condition, it might force her to shut down even more. He put his hand behind her shoulder and led her quickly down the hall, no longer wondering if they were being stalked. He knew they were alone, completely alone in the house; not even accompanied by the corpses of the homeowners.

When they reached the main living area, he quickly made his way to the kitchen. He tried the faucet and wasn't all that surprised by the lack of water, so his next stop was the fridge. He noticed right away that the light didn't come on when he opened the door, but he was confident as he grabbed the gallon of orange juice that it was still safe to drink. He put the jug to his mouth and let the cold fluid sooth his dry throat. He felt the chill move all the way down to his stomach. It was pleasure in its purest form. He finally pulled the jug away and saw that he had nearly finished it off. Slightly ashamed he looked back at Kathy still standing in the same place he had left her. He knew he had to get some fluid in her.

Justin walked back to her and led her to the couch. He took Wyatt from her arms and gently laid him down. He then sat her down at Wyatt's feet, and brought the jug to her lips, and although she almost seemed to be slipping from him again, to her credit, she took a sip. It wasn't nearly enough, but it was a start.

"We've got to get out of here." She needed a doctor. They had to know what had happened here. He tried the phone next to the couch, and it was silent. And then he started searching for keys. Once he found them, he headed for the front door. He quickly glanced back at Kathy, and being confident that she was going to be fine, in a matter of speaking, he stepped out directly into the blinding sun.

He walked around the side of the house to an older model Ford truck. He doubted Alice and Ernie were going to be needing it any more. He put the key in the ignition expecting salvation, but a vile sense of panic rose to his heart as the turn of the key produced the same results as the faucets, lights, and phones had produced. Nothing. "Damn it! Damn it!" He was so angry and frustrated and admittedly scared enough that he barely noticed the pain that shot up his forearm as he took it all out on the steering wheel.

Once he was satisfied with the beating he rested his head against his hands as he leaned against the battered steering wheel. The sweat moved from his forehead to his hand and he finally noticed how hot the interior of the truck was. It was early in the day, he knew that much because he watched the sun come up through the skylight, but the sun hung high in the air, blazing down unsympathetically on Montana.

Justin stepped out of the useless truck and slammed the door shut. He paced its length several times trying to decide what to do. They could stay at the house where there was no running water, electricity, or telephone hoping that the utilities would return or a neighbor would stop by. But he also thought it would be likely for those things to return and he didn't want to be there when they did.

No. The best thing for them to do would be to walk away from this place. Find a neighbor, find a phone or car and get some help. He doubted anyone would believe a shadow murdered their son or dragged the homeowners kicking and screaming...literally...away. But he saw what he saw. He heard what he heard, and sooner or later the truth would come out. He would make sure of it.

Justin returned to the house and walked in on Kathy covering Wyatt with the crocheted blanket from the couch. He thought that maybe she would pull the blanket up over his head, but instead she tucked it up around his chin like she was putting him to bed for the night. Justin's heart sank when he realized they would have to leave Wyatt there until they could bring back help. He gently touched Kathy on the shoulder and he felt her jump before she realized it was him. He smiled at her gently, "Sorry. I didn't mean to scare you." She looked at him for just a moment before returning her attention to Wyatt and began to lightly stroke his hair.

Justin sighed. It wasn't going to be easy to take her away without taking Wyatt with them. "Kath. Listen to me. Their truck isn't working. And I'm worried that those...those...monsters are going to come back. I think we would have a chance if their phone at least worked...but it doesn't."

Kathy started humming a lullaby.

"Do you understand what I am trying to say? We need to go get help ourselves."

She didn't acknowledge him.

He finally took her by both shoulders and made her face him and she gave him a startled look and took a few clearing blinks. "Kathy, we are going to have to walk until we find someone. But we can't carry Wyatt so we are going to have to come back for him. He can stay here on the couch. He'll be safe." At least he hoped he would be. They wouldn't mess with something that was already dead would they?

She nodded and looked back to the couch. Boo was in her hand and she pulled it close to her heart as if she was contemplating leaving it with Wyatt or to take with them simply out of the need to be holding onto something. She decided the latter and leaned down to kiss Wyatt's forehead and then stepped back. Justin kneeled down beside the couch and looked at his little boy. He fought back the denial that tried to tell him that Wyatt was just sleeping and that by the time they came back he would be awake and ready to get back on the road...ready to go home. No. By the time they came back they would be ready to bury him. He had to face that reality if he was going to get them through this.

He took his own steps backwards, all the way to the front door, feeling guilty that he was abandoning his son, even in death. Leaving him in an empty home of strangers. But when he stepped out onto the porch, Kathy silently pulled the door behind them. Justin sighed quietly with a sense of relief. In the moment he didn't think he would be strong enough, she pulled through for him. She did what he knew he couldn't do and he was so thankful for it. And she slowly took the first painful steps away from Wyatt with Boo clutched in her left hand.

Chapter Eleven

Madison and Ethan

They walked back to their house in an uncomfortable silence. A warm breeze finally came up and stirred the leaves on the trees. Madison was thankful for a little noise. The absolute silence was very unnerving for her. She would occasionally glance at Ethan and was tempted to talk to him just to break the quiet, but he seemed so deep in thought. If he could come to some kind of conclusion she would give him the time to do it. She needed answers.

But once they reached the house and he simply sat on front steps without a word, she found that she couldn't take it anymore. "Ethan, do you really think they just disappeared?"

"I don't know. I mean, doesn't it seem like that's what happened?" He paused. "Kind of crazy sounding, huh?"

She smiled. "Honestly? Yeah, a little. People don't just vanish. Do they?"

"I don't want to admit to believing it, but the only thing that is really going to convince me otherwise is if we head down to town."

It was over ten miles to town. Madison groaned when she thought about walking there in the heat. But if it would make Ethan feel better, she would do it. She also wanted to go to town. It would make her feel a lot better about things if they could just run into someone on the street, or see a moving car. However there was a small part of her that thought it would be wiser just to stay home and wait for things to be fixed...if they ever were. "It's going to be a long walk."

"Naaa. It won't be that bad." He stood up and started walking to their garage. "Besides, who said anything about walking? I figured that we could air up the tires to the bikes and ride them down the hill. I knew that they would come in handy someday. Three years is a long time to wait though if you know what I mean." He gave her a knowing glare and disappeared into the garage.

It was true. They did buy the bikes at Madison's request. She was convinced that she would go for a ride every day, and be skinny in no time. It was after the first ride, and a very sore ass, that she gave up on that.

Ethan poked his head out of the garage door, and frowned slightly when he saw that she hadn't moved from her post on the front steps. "Uh, hey, Sexy, being that it is so hot out, maybe we should grab a couple of bottled waters?"

She knew she was being dramatic, but visions of someone stumbling across their dried out bodies popped into her head. No doubt they would shake their head and say to each other, "If only they hadn't taken those couple bottles of water they'd still be here. Such a shame."

"Are you sure? What if it takes a few days before they get the water running again?"

"Just in case, grab a couple. We might need it."

It felt like she was walking in slow motion as she made her way to the pantry. There was a heavy sense of dread with every step, and each step seemed like it was bringing her closer to answers she may not necessarily want to know. Nonetheless, she reached in and grabbed four bottles and put them on the dining room table. She then walked back to the bedroom and habitually flipped on the light switch to the large walk-in closet. However, the room remained black. The light from the bedroom window couldn't bend into the closet. Somewhere in the darkness, she knew there would be a backpack. She almost walked away from the task of finding one but knew that it would be a lot easier to carry water and whatever else they may take with it, so she stepped into the dark.

The spontaneous shiver exploded from her core and she held her breath. Darkness never really was a friend to Madison. The child in her still feared the dark in many ways, and the adult in her always chastised the child for being foolish. It was an ongoing battle. She wasn't sure if it was because her father let her watch the eighties horror movies when she was too young, or if there was a legit reason to be afraid of the dark, but she never truly felt alone while standing in it. Her mind always made the shadows out to be more.

But this time she was determined to chase away her demons and get what she came for. She felt along the wall and found the first area of hanging clothes. She knew that they kept most of their bags and luggage on the floor, so she dropped to her knees and felt around for the draw-sting backpack that she has been holding onto since college. It wasn't until she felt her way past their travel luggage that she heard the quiet clicking noise in the corner. She froze and listened.

It was coming for the other side of the closet, from the darkest corner. It was like someone was tapping their long fingernails on the tile floor. The hair on the back of her neck instantly stood on end. "No, no, Madison. It is only your imagination. Nothing is there. Stop it." The adult Madison sounded calm and reassuring. The child in her called bullshit.

The sound of her voice made the imaginary noise cease. Even so, her inner child was trembling. She wanted to run from the closet and outside where it was bright and sunny. She started to leave. "Remember the backpack...remember the backpack" she reminded herself in barely a whisper. She reached past the luggage and froze as she felt movement across her fingertips. It was cold as ice and rough, but smooth at the same time. Her first thought was snake. Madison's instinct was the pull her hand away as quickly as possible, but she found the chill from the serpent paralyzing. However, as a forked tongue flicked her skin, and then seemed to linger as though it was relishing the taste of her, she pulled her hand away so briskly, she stumbled back into the hanging clothes. She couldn't see it and her eyes darted to the darkest corners, searching for movement.

Wait...was she hearing a snake before? Madison reached past her common knowledge of snakes to high school biology class and reminded herself that snakes don't have nails. Snakes hiss. Snakes rattle. Snakes slither, but snakes do not tap. No, there was something else in here with her and the snake. She could feel it, and it was so much worse than a mere serpent. Although grown-up Madison had told her it was all in her head, she was convinced that whatever it was, was looking right at her. She could feel a hateful stare burning right into her. She even imagined she could see the color red. "It's not real. It's not real."

"Madison, you okay? Who are you taking to?"

The sound of Ethan's voice made her cry out, "Oh my God! You scared the shit out of me!"

Ethan laughed. He always appreciated the reactions she gave, and took pride in his abilities to get a rise out of her. He was also boastful about his abilities to deny her any reaction when she retaliated, making her revenge so unsatisfying. "I'm sorry, gorgeous." The smirk on his face made her doubt his sincerity.

"It's not funny! Ethan, there is a snake in the closet! It was huge...and I touched it!

"A snake? Are you sure?" He looked into the darkness with skepticism in his eyes.

"Yes! It...." She shivered with revolution. "...slithered across my hand! And licked me!"

Madison watched as Ethan tried to fight the laughter that was building up inside of him, but it was all in vain; be burst with loud amusement, "Licked you?!" Madison frowned. "Okay! Okay! Well without flashlights or anything, I don't think I'm going to be able to look for it. What were you doing in there anyway?"

"Getting a bag for the water bottles." She had backed herself up into the bed.

He glanced at her empty hands and then studied her face. He shrugged. "Don't worry about it, I'll get it."

"Oh my God, just be careful! Maybe it is poisonous!"

"Relax. I'll be alright." She watched as he stood at the edge of the closet and studied the darkness. He apparently didn't feel the threat that she did, nor did he indicate that he saw a snake let alone something terrifying with red eyes because he stepped in and emerged a moment later with a backpack. He smiled at her as he handed her the bag, "Phew! I lived!"

An involuntary sign of relief escaped her lips but she forced a smile anyway. "Are the bikes ready?" She decided not to tell him about the "imaginary" thing in the corner, simply for the fact that she was pretty sure that it was truly imaginary. She knew the look he would give her well. She would say that she kind of thought that in addition to a snake, there was probably also a monster in the closet. He would just cock his head and look at her like she was crazy, intentional or not. Then he would blame it on her over-active writer's imagination.

"All set." He had changed into a pair of shorts and a t-shirt he found on the living room floor.

"Okay. I'll get the bag packed." She found herself backing away from the closet, instead of walking away, afraid to turn her back on the darkness.

"Are you okay? You look a little pale. Are you sure it was just a snake..."

She gave him a sarcastic smile. "You would be pale too if you just survived a heart attack."

"Well, if it makes you feel any better, I didn't mean to scare you that bad." He walked with her while she backed down the hallway.

"I'm sure you didn't." But she was sure that the "imaginary" thing in the closet did want her that scared, and then some.

Chapter Twelve

They had been riding for an hour. The breeze was making the sun dance with the shadow leaves on the gravel in front of her bike tire. If it wasn't for the heaviness in the air, and the heat, and all the weirdness, it would have been a perfect day for a ride. However, after the first ten minutes on the hard seat, Madison was reminded of why she stopped riding in the first place. She was just thankful that she didn't have to do too much pedaling; gravity was helping them go down the hill very efficiently. The ride back was going to suck.

Ethan was riding circles around her. "You know if you let go of the brake, you'll go faster."

"I don't want to go faster. The hill is too steep; I know I'll lose control and wreck."

"You will not. Just let go."

"No. I'm fine. We'll get there soon enough."

They were nearing Highway 12. Madison could see a small section of the asphalt at the bottom of the hill. From there it was only going to be a matter of ten minutes for them to reach city limits. She had been watching the road, hoping to see a car speed past, but so far nothing. She was starting to get nervous butterflies in her stomach.

Ethan was staring at the highway as well. When he noticed her looking at him he gave her a quick smile but turned his attention back to the approaching road.

"Ethan? What do you think we are going to find down there?"

"Hopefully people."

"Yeah, but what if we don't? Or what if we find something else?"

He looked back at her and frowned. "What do you mean?"

Madison looked away and shrugged. "I don't know. I just have a bad feeling. I actually had it back at the house in the closet."

"And you think there is what, a snake monster, in town? Something came and ate everyone?"

"Ethan, don't be mean. I'm just saying something doesn't feel right. It hasn't really since last night."

"I don't mean to sound mean, Madi. If it makes you feel any better I don't feel too good about it either. I don't know about monsters, but..."

"I never said monsters." But in truth, she was thinking it. It was there with her in the closet and it was watching her. Its hateful stare left an impression on her that she didn't think she would ever forget.

"Look, I'm sorry. I'm just a little freaked out with everything. I don't mean to be sarcastic."

They slowed the bikes down to a near creep. Despite their mission, it seemed like neither one of them were in a big hurry to reach the road, which was now only twenty feet away. The heat radiated off the pavement and gave the illusion of moving water, and as the tires of their bikes left the gravel, it was like they rolled into the heart of the devil himself; the slight coolness of the forest now gone with modern man's advancements in transportation.

Ethan had stopped his bike all together and was looking up and down the highway. About half a mile up the road, there was car stopped at an angle in the ditch, but otherwise the highway was deserted. Across the street was a white colonial style home with a run-down picket fence and a large weeping willow in the front yard. It had a rusty station wagon parked in the driveway. Ethan started crossing the road to the house, but Madison stopped him. "Let's just go to town, I don't want to go into that house."

"I just want to look. We won't go into any others if it is the same as before. Okay?"

"Can't we just go into town and look there for someone? The stores, or a house there? Just not this one?"

Ethan looked at her thoughtfully. "What's so different about this house?"

She looked down at her feet to avoid his eyes. He always could read her like an open book and by looking away she felt that she still could hide some of her fears from him. It wasn't this house in particular that she didn't want to see. She actually wanted to go home and to board up the doors and windows, and surround herself with candles and lanterns, and anything else that produced light. But she knew that her imaginary creature would still be in the closet for her to fear, so going home was out of the question right now. But her irrational instincts were telling her that there were more creatures, and that town would be full of them. "It is an abandoned house, can't you tell?"

"Madison, what's up?"

She met his stare and started to tell him that they needed to get away from Helena, but thought better of it. He would never believe her anyway. Maybe they could find somewhere in the city that would be safe. "Nothing, sweetie. I just think that if we were looking for people, which we are, we would have better odds in town. We are sure to run into someone there."

He studied her for a moment before he nodded. "You're right. We'll skip the house search. Okay?"

"Yes. Thank you."

"Are you okay though? Maybe a little scared?"

"Yeah, a little. I just don't know what to expect."

Ethan leaned over and gave her a hug. "I'm scared too, sexy. But I'm sure we are over reacting."

She closed her eyes and laid her head on his shoulder and took comfort in his warmth. "You think so?"

"Sure." He grabbed her chin and tilted her head to make her look at him. "I know so. Let's just go and get it over with instead of standing here in the middle of the road wondering what we are going to find."

"Okay."

Chapter Thirteen

Sam

The sun was too high in the sky for early morning. And it burned hot. Heat was coming off of every surface, giving the world a strange shimmer. It reminded Sam of the visual effects movies had when a stranger in the desert came across an oasis. But this was no paradise. There was no chance for relief. Even in the shade, Sam felt like he had a thick wool sweater wrapped around his face. It was smothering him.

Sam sat on bench under the covered porch. He retreated there after discovering that neither of the vehicles in the driveway started. Confusion set in and Sam was very uncomfortable with the unfamiliar feeling. He always had a plan, but since there wasn't any logic to the situation, he had no idea what to do.

Granted, that rusty old work truck may have had engine problems but it was parked closest to the front door and so it was the first one he tried. He wasn't terribly surprised when nothing happened as he turned the key. But that Dodge Durango was new. The dealer's name was plastered where a license plate should have been. He was surprised when that turned out to have a dead engine too.

He looked under the hood. Sam was hardly an expert, but he prided himself on his ability to handle simple repairs himself. He knew what he must have looked like; standing there in front of an open hood, literally scratching his head. The engine was new, clean...perfect.

So there he sat, trying unsuccessfully to escape the heat of a sun that was just too high for the hour of the day, trying to gather his thoughts. But Sam was tired, and he couldn't even scratch the surface of what was happening to him. Instead, he reached into his pocket and touched the now folded picture of Abby. "What am I going to do?" He said it out loud. Not really expecting an answer, but was not all that shocked when he got one anyway.

"You walk." It came out of his mouth. He knew it did, but in his mind it was her voice. It was soft and as musical as rain. Abby's voice was that of an angel's. His angel. And she brought him much needed peace.

"But, what about them? I can't run anymore. I'm tired."

He saw her standing at the end of the steps. She was flowing. Her beautiful blonde hair flowed, the long blue dress flowed. Even if there wasn't a whisper of a breeze to cause it. Sam swallowed hard and wiped his brow. He knew he was teetering on the edge of something he wasn't sure he could come back from. If he could only will himself to take a step back and grasp onto facts, he might be able to save his sanity. However, it was just too hard to do when the facts seemed so unrealistic. The angelic hallucination in front of him seemed more probable. Here goes nothing. "Are you real?"

She smiled. That beautiful radiating smile that seemed to make the day all that much warmer, and shook her head. "No, I'm not."

Well, shit. That confirms it. But the conversation was going so well, and Sam didn't think he could spend another day hour alone. So what if his best friend right now was himself pretending to be a teenage girl? "Okay."

"Sam, start walking. You don't have much time. You know that."

"Yeah, I do."

"The day is going to be short."

"I know."

"They'll come back."

"I know that, too."

"Get up, now, Sam," she persisted.

"Okay, Abby." Sam stood up. And she was gone. "Wait! Don't go!"

"I'll be here whenever you need me."

"Okay."

"Go! Now!"

Sam stepped off the porch and walked between the two dead giants on wheels.

Chapter Fourteen

Madison and Ethan

The car was a pretty blue Dodge Neon from Washington. The closer they got to the car they could tell that the driver hadn't simply pulled over. The skid marks told a story that the car was heading west, towards home, when for whatever reason, the driver slammed on the brakes. The driver then swerved to the left and lost control, doing a couple of doughnuts in the middle of the highway before taking out the city limits sign. It was now lodged underneath the rear passenger tire. The front of the car was pushed into the hillside, and the passenger door was wide open.

Ethan got off his bike and put the kickstand down. He walked over to the open door and peered inside.

"Do you think their battery died while they were driving?"

"No. I think they were avoiding something in the road."

Madison set her bike next to his and joined him at the open door. He was kneeling down and looked to be deep in thought. In front of him on the seat were registration papers. The car belonged to Lisa Glenn. She wasn't sure if she should interrupt his internal examination, but she didn't want to be left out either. "What are you thinking?"

"You don't want to know."

She raised her eyebrows, almost offended. He saw her react and sighed. He then stood up and brushed the gravel from his knees. "What is it, Ethan? I do want to know."

"Okay. The way I see it, something scared her. Whatever it was, it was in the road."

"Why do you say that?"

He pointed to the footprints on the side of the hill, leading away from the car. "Well, I would think if it was a simple deer, or car and they wrecked, they would start walking back to town, not up the side of the mountain. There aren't any houses on this side of the road, not right here anyway." He climbed up the hill a little to where it started getting steep, and pointed to some lines in soft dirt, "And if you look closely, you can see fingernail claw marks in the dirt. Baby, she was trying to get up here fast."

Madison started scanning the pines that started about hundred feet away and felt herself shiver. She didn't see any reason to doubt him, but she so much wanted to believe he was wrong. What could scare someone so bad that they would run away from the safety of the city? But then she realized that around a quarter to eleven last night, town disappeared. And her neighbors this morning. And not a single car has passed them since they had set out. She realized that she suddenly felt vulnerable in the warm sun. She hugged herself. "Ethan, let's go, I don't like it out here."

"Yeah... I know how you feel." He stood up and slid down the little ways to the road. He stopped to look one last time into the dark trees, where somewhere the footprints probably entered...and disappeared. "How about some water before we continue?" He slid the backpack off and opened up the large compartment to hand her a bottle. Besides water, they had brought some matches, a lighter, and some candles in place of the flashlight that they discovered stopped working with everything else battery operated. They had also brought some apples and crackers in case they got hungry, but they both sensed that their appetites had left them.

Madison took a long drink from the bottle and handed it to Ethan. He tilted the bottle back and chugged down the rest. He was infamous for being able to drink down entire glasses of water without taking a break, and she had to smile as he took the bottom of his shirt to wipe his chin. He stopped when he saw her staring. "What?"

She shook her head, but kept smiling. "Nothing."

He grinned. "Well it must be something for you to be smiling like that in a place like this."

Her smile faded, and she looked away. He had brought her back to reality. He saw her anxiety and hugged her. "Hey, Sexy, I'm sure there are some answers, we're just not there yet."

"I know, I mean, I hope you are right. Let's just get out of here, and get it over with."

"Okay, we'll go." He put the empty water bottle in the bag and pulled the drawstring closed. He slid it back on and straddled his bike. Then he waited for her to situate herself before they pushed off onto the road again. After the curve, a mile away, they would be dumped right into town, and hopefully into some answers.

Chapter Fifteen

"Hello?! HELLO?!" Ethan threw his bike down into the grass of Memorial Park, and continued to try to get someone's attention. Madison slowly lowered herself to the cool lawn, too stunned to speak. And the only response Ethan received was the rustling leaves of the park trees, and the Old Glory American Flag flapping in the wind, which definitely had picked up speed. Somewhere nearby a pop can was being tossed across the road.

They hadn't gone into any buildings yet. They didn't need to. They didn't want to. Not after what they had seen.

Madison surveyed the biggest public park in Helena. Normally on a hot day like this, there wouldn't be any parking. The public pool would be crowded, couples would have blankets spread across the grass, families would be enjoying a lunch picnic at this hour, and children would be playing in the fort. But the pool was empty, and the park was deserted other than the two of them. The swings swung empty, either powered by the wind, or ghosts of children. Across the street a car had rolled down the small embankment into the nearest soccer field.

She pulled her knees up and buried her face. But nothing she did could block out the images in her memory. When they got into town, it was like they had arrived into a war zone. She wasn't sure what she expected to find, but it wasn't that.

Ethan was still yelling for only her and the wind to hear, but his voice had grown hoarse. Madison knew that he was panicking, but she also knew that she couldn't do or say anything to help him.

At first it seemed that Lyndale Avenue was deserted until they came across the first car stalled in the middle of the road. Another car had driven into Pizza Hut and another into the Clean and Coin Laundromat. There were also countless vehicular collisions. Some of the abandoned cars and trucks even appeared as though they were attacked. Roofs were caved in, paint jobs were scared by scratch marks, stuffing ripped out of seats, windows shattered, doors ripped off. A police cruiser was even missing its steering wheel. They had tried to start of few of the cars that were still intact, but all batteries continued to be dead. And all the people were gone. There weren't any signs of them.

Ethan fell to the ground next to her. "Jesus Christ, Madison...I don't even know what to think!"

A stop sign on the corner started to shake in the wind. Madison could see dark storm clouds in the North. She also noticed how it was not nearly as hot as it had been earlier in the day. There was actually a slight coolness to the wind. "So what now?"

"How the hell would I know?"

Madison took no offense to his tone. She realized that he was scared, even though he wasn't about to admit it to her at this time. "Should we go home, you know, barricade ourselves in there?"

He rubbed his face with his hands and shook his head. "No. We don't have enough supplies. Who knows how long until...well...until we find someone, or someone finds us."

"So where should we go?"

Ethan stood up and started to pace. "Well, maybe we should go to one of the stores, you know? Maybe like SuperMart. Maybe there will be some people there, and if not, we could you know, check it out, make sure it is safe, and board up the door. There will be food, and blankets, and tampons...and Jesus, Madi, what the fuck happened here?"

Madison stood up and brushed off her shorts. "I don't know, but whatever we need to do, we should go now, I don't like it out here at all. And on top of everything, there is a storm coming."

He stopped and listened for a minute. He still held onto a glimmer of hope that someone would be answering his calls, but silence greeted him. "Yeah, yeah let's go to SuperMart."

*****

They spent the early afternoon hours by periodically weaving in and out of wrecked or stalled cars, trucks, and semis. They took turns calling out, but they both knew they were alone.

A mile away from SuperMart, the sun disappeared. Madison looked up to see that the dark clouds now covered the sky. A combination of fear and the absence of warm sunlight made her skin instantly cool. She started to pedal faster.

Ethan didn't ask her why as she quickly passed him. She assumed he knew why. Despite everything, they felt like the sun kept them safe, and with it gone, they felt more vulnerable than ever. They just had to get to other side of the interstate.

From behind them came a flash of light that was followed by a roar of thunder that made Madison cry out. She always liked the idea that thunder was the sound of angels bowling, but now she knew otherwise. Heaven had nothing to do with it; thunder came from the bowels of Hell.

Ethan had caught up with her. He was breathless. "We better hurry! That storm is right over us!"

Madison could see their sanctuary just ahead of them. Like an oasis, Helena's SuperMart sat alone in an ocean of fields. A farmer had finally sold out to the corporation, and Madison knew that he was paid handsomely for his sacrifice. He built a house shortly after the sale that was the envy of most of Helena. Madison wondered if he survived the night or if his modern day castle became his tomb.

By the time they reached the barely full parking lot, the clouds had swelled to capacity and the rain began to pour. It fell so hard that it stung their skin, and puddles were instantly formed.

Ethan reached the automatic door first, but the store was dark and the door had no power. He started pounding on the glass with his fist. "GOD DAMN IT!"

Madison jumped off her bike and let it fall to the fast running river that formed in the street. "Ethan! The side door!"

He couldn't seem to hear her over the howl of the rain and wind. She suddenly felt the hair on the back of her neck and arms rise. "Oh no! Oh, God, no!" The electricity in the air had changed and Madison could feel the warning. She couldn't wait for him to hear her. She grabbed his shirt with a strength she didn't know she had and pulled him. They rounded the corner and she yanked the door open and pushed Ethan in. "Get down!"

They fell to the concrete floor and covered their heads just in time for a bright light to fill up the foyer and then the glass front imploded. Madison's screams mingled with the crash of glass, but all sound was muffled by the booming thunder. She could feel shards of glass hit her, and she cried out in pain as some pierced her skin. She opened her eyes to see the remainder of the glass mixed with the rain now spraying into the decimated foyer. Every sliver of glass seemed to have captured the power and light of the lightning bolt.

Ethan grabbed her by her shoulders and pulled her up to a standing position. He started to shake her and she wasn't sure why until she realized that she was still screaming. She looked at his face and saw that he had a large cut above his left eye, and a worried look on his face. For a moment she could see his mouth moving, but she couldn't hear what he was saying. All she could hear was a loud buzzing, but then his voice started breaking in, and he was asking her if she was alright. She threw her arms around him and held onto him as tight as she could. The tears started to fall. "Oh my God! What is happening?!"

He was pulling shards of glass out of her hair, and then he gently pulled away from her. He took her chin in his hands and after wiping her wet hair away from her eyes, he forced her to look at him. "We're alright. Just a little scratched up is all." He forced a smile. "Let's just get inside and have a look around. I know they say lightning never strikes twice in the same place, but I'm not about to test the theory." He was obviously faking his calmness.

He took her hand and pulled her behind him. Broken glass crunched under their feet as they stepped over several stuffed animals. Madison saw that the Plexiglass front of the Claw Machine was destroyed and pink elephants and ballerina teddy bears were scattered on the concrete floor. The claw itself dangled like a hideous dead limb stripped of flesh.

Another flash of light and the boom that followed made them both jump. Ethan looked at her sheepishly, "Some storm, huh?"

"Yeah, it's like the end of the world." She said under her breath.

They were standing in front of the second set of electric doors that led into the interior of the store. While the doors were damaged by the lightning, they were still intact. Large cracks stretched from top to bottom. Ethan shook his head. "Damn."

"Do you think we could kick them in?"

"Hmmmmm, well it's worth a shot. It shouldn't be that hard with these cracks. Stand back, okay?"

Madison stepped back into the rain and shivered. The warmth of the morning went down the gutters with the dirty rain water. The sky was dark and threatening, and every minute or so there would be a flash of light followed by an explosion of sound. She couldn't even hear Ethan kicking at the door over the noise of the thunder.

By the looks of the sky, it would seem that it was approaching dusk, but Madison estimated that it was about three o'clock in the afternoon. Daylight seemed to have fled with the coming of the storm. Before long it would be dark.

She had to admit to herself that she had been scared most of the day. But with the realization that darkness may be near, she became terrified. Something wasn't right, she knew it the moment she stepped into the lightless closet earlier and felt...it. She didn't know if being in the store would help, but she definitely would feel better if they were.

She turned back to Ethan, and saw that he was making little progress on the door. It obviously was reinforced for security purposes. She looked down in defeat, and saw a garbage can on its side. "Maybe..." She picked it up off of its side and tried to lift it up. It was heavy, but it needed to be. "Ethan! Help me!"

He didn't ask her questions; instead he came over and lifted the bottom portion of the can. Together, they walked close to the door and they started swinging their arms. "Okay! On three! One! Two!...Three!" They let go as they hurled with all their might and the can shattered the glass as it passed through. It bounced once before it crashed into a row of grocery carts leaving a trail of fast food wrappers and pop bottles.

They hugged in celebration, and stepped into the store. However, their joy was short lived as they turned and looked at what remained of the doors. They were so busy worrying about how to get into the store that they never considered how they were going to barricade the doors. Now the rain, wind, and whatever else was out there could get in.

Madison slumped down into a small wooden bench that was usually occupied by elderly men waiting for their shop-o-holic wives. Outside the rain was coming down harder than ever, and the parking lot was turning into a small black lake. She laid her head back against the wall and closed her eyes. Without some kind of door, they might as well have been out in the open. She started to make her peace with God.

"Maybe we could stack the carts up?"

As she considered the option, she opened her eyes. A long metal bar above the shattered doors caught her eye. She cocked her head. It was actually three long metal bars; two thicker bars straddled a thinner bar that had small hooks on it. She pointed to it, "What's that?"

Ethan looked up and smiled. "It's the gate. We just pull that down and there we go...instant door. It will be a little airy, but at least it will keep the animals out."

"It's not the animals I'm so worried about."

"Are we talking about your monsters again?"

"Damn it, Ethan! How can you make fun of me after ever thing we've seen?"

"Wait a minute, wait a minute, don't do that. Yeah, earlier, when it was just us up at the house, I did tease you, but now...that it is still just us, I'm starting to reconsider my opinion, as illogical as it may seem." He sighed heavily. "But then again, we haven't exactly seen any...creatures yet either."

"That's because they only like the darkness." She knew how ridiculous she sounded.

He crossed his arms in front of him. "I see, and how do you know this?"

She stood up and walk away from him. "Look, I don't, for sure. It is just a feeling. When I was in the closet..."

"Okay, Madi, I don't want you to get upset."

"Let's just get the gate down. I will feel a whole lot better when it is down."

"I don't really want to put it down until we have a look around. It would be in the way if we had to get out fast. We'll seal up the other doors as we go by them."

Madison stared out into the darkening day, and knew that they would be cutting it close. "Okay, let's just hurry."

Chapter Sixteen

Sam

The gravel crunched under his feet, announcing his precise location with every step, but he wasn't worried. Abby wouldn't have sent him out if he was in danger. Besides, Sam thought he had those red eyed things figured out. Abby helped clear his head.

At first he walked the narrow dirt road terrified. It was slow going. At every sound he would stop and listen, turn, and look as far between the dense columns of trees as he could. He was sure they were in there. He was sure walking out in the open would be asking for death. But he never saw anything. And with time, he put his trust in Abby and his confidence in his safety began to return.

Time. That still puzzled him. The sun's location in the sky said it was late afternoon, but he knew, he felt it was only lunch time. But he couldn't focus on time right now. He was on a mission to get back to town, and out of the woods. Earlier he noticed there were some clouds in the north that didn't look to friendly, and he wanted to make sure there was cover in the event they decided to come to Helena. Sam chucked at the thought about just shortening the town's name to Hell.

With the clouds came a strong wind that Sam was thankful for. It possessed a coolness that finally began to dry his skin of the constant river of sweat. And it was noise. The sound of him walking was his only company for the longest time, and he welcomed the change. He didn't feel nearly so alone. He wished the Abby ghost would have stayed with him a little while longer. She may have replied no when he asked her if she was real, but she was real enough to him. Some people back home would probably say he was certifiable, but he knew the truth. She was just an angel in denial. Of course she was real! And she was the voice of reason. He was really close to losing it back at the house, and he was thanking God that she came when she did.

The smell of rain made its way to Sam. He noticed that the forest had indeed dimmed. The sun was gone. Sam frowned. Those dark clouds from the north were moving quickly into the area. It was going to be a bad storm. Sam had a sudden urgency to find shelter. He knew he would need it, but he didn't imagine the need would arise so quickly.

He surveyed the area around him. He was about a hundred yards away from the highway. He could see the black road, and just on the other side an old house in desperate need of repair. Then there was the forest. But there was no way in hell he was going back into that mess. He looked at the old house again. It had a shitty white fence that needed to be replaced all together, and an old weeping willow with branches that acted like arms beckoning him into a forbidden place. The station wagon parked in front was rusty, and the weeds had grown up to the door. This was the house of childhood nightmares. The kind of house that cocky teenagers snuck into for shits and giggles just to run out with wet spots on the crotches of their pants. Every town had them, and he was tempted by the spooky house allure when he was a kid too, and as an adult thought it was all stupid superstitions. But after last night, he wouldn't doubt that the place had plenty of resident ghosts or at least dark places for red-eyed demons to hide.

No way. There have to be other choices.

He now stood at the edge of the highway trying to figure out exactly where he was. It wasn't until he looked right that he saw Lisa's car with the front still buried in the side of hill. He smiled. Town was just around the corner. He would be there in no time. But as he took his first step, the world shook with the first boom of thunder. "Jesus!"

"Time to go, Sam!" Abby's voice urged him to make a decision.

"The car, Abby! I'll sit the storm out in the car." He started sprinting towards the car as the sky opened up. The rain fell hard and he was back to having rivers running down his skin. The road was suddenly very slick, and he slipped and fell hard into the black-top. He was on his hands and knees making his way back up when he was blinded by a flash of light directly in front of him. Sam covered his eyes with his dirty hands, but he heard the lightning bolt connect with something and then a crash. He was afraid to look, but he took his hand away from his eyes and through the driving rain could see that a massive tree from the opposite side of the road was hit and it fell across the road and directly into Lisa's car. The car's roof was completely caved in.

Sam stood up and threw his hands up in the air. "You've got to be kidding me," he screamed. He was answered by the loud crash of thunder and Abby telling him that he needed to take cover.

Forest or house. Forest or house. Sam's confidence in his safety dropped again, but it had to be the house. If trees were going to start falling, he wasn't going to be under them. Unless of course, one happened to fall on the fucking house. In the distance another bolt hit something and thunder that followed filled his head. He took one last look at the house. And as he felt the electrical energy increase around him, he decided to take his chances with the ghost or whatever else may be lurking in the darkness of the house.

The door was either really swollen or locked. Sam didn't waste any time taking a rock from the weeds and throwing it threw the closest window. If by chance the hillbillies were home, he hoped they would be a little sympathetic and allow him to stay with a promise of reimbursement. But as he stood dripping in the dim front room he knew no one but mice...and maybe ghosts lived in this house.

The only piece of furniture in this room was an old dusty wooden chair, propped up against the door. The wallpaper was faded and coming off the wall, and the carpets were worn and stained. There was a pile of wood next to stone fireplace and now there was a broken window to add to the effect.

Too many shadows. From what he could see, all the light fixtures had been stripped of bulbs. He wished he would have thought of a flashlight or matches...

"Maybe there are some matches in the kitchen." She was nowhere to be seen, but Abby's voice brought life to the house.

Sam smiled, "Yeah, yeah. That's a good idea. Let's go check it out."

He crept along the dirty walls with such stealth no one would know he was there. Not that it mattered. If the demon-eyes were in the house, the broken window and talking to Abby probably would have alerted them to his presence. But out of habit he moved quietly through the rounded archway into the antique kitchen. The stove and refrigerator had long been hauled away. There once was spring-time green tile behind the sink, but pieces had been smashed away from the wall by vandals. Graffiti covered the cabinets. He disturbed the urban art by opening up the cupboards one by one looking for a source of light. He didn't really take any notice of the details but in the corner of the last on the wall, one word caught his attention as he started opening the thin door. Abby. It was small, and carved out of the wood. Abby loves Ty.

"He was my boyfriend." She was standing next to him. Still flowing. "He's gone now."

"How can you be sure?"

Abby looked at him with a look only a woman could give, wordlessly telling him to use the brain God gave him.

Sam looked away and down. "I'm sorry...for everything."

Abby herself looked down. If angels could cry, Sam was sure she was about to. She shrugged her shoulders trying to shake off emotion and faded away. Sam felt a deep sympathy for her. But he was also assured that she was in a better place with Ty and her family. He opened the cupboard bearing her name and there, the only thing in there, was a packet of matches from "Lucky's Bar." Even though it was half used, it would have to do. Lucky indeed.

Something fell in the house. Sam jumped back and pressed himself against the counter and listened beyond the pounding rain on the roof. After a minute he thought it was nothing, but then there was another bump into a wall. Something much bigger and heavier than a mouse was in the building. All at once, Sam broke out into a sweat despite the chill he was feeling from being wet. His heart beat hard against his strong chest. He was sure if he took his shirt off, a person would be able to see the fierceness of the beats. He had left the knife at Abby's house and now he was missing it.

He considered just bolting out and braving the rain, but he knew he would never be able to face himself in the mirror. Especially after being such a coward the night before. Abby had died a horrible and tragic death because of him, and Sam didn't know if he would ever be able to forgive himself. He would have to investigate. For all he knew it was just a cat or dog, and he couldn't allow something so simple chase him out. He located the dark hallway just off the living room, and studied it for a moment...watching for the demon-eyes before slowly walking through the darkness. His fists were clenched, ready for a fight if it came down to it.

The first room he came to was an empty bedroom. But there was a closed closet door. The thud he heard seemed pretty close, so Sam thought it could have easily come from this room. He stood there in the center of the room, just watching the door and listening. He wasn't sure he wanted to open the door. He wasn't sure he wanted to face anything scarier than a cat or dog and that really limited his options. He started to shake and bolting seemed more and more appealing to him.

"No," he whispered, and began to back away from the door. He was almost back into the hallway when bolting no longer became an option. The closet door flew open, and a wild-eyed woman threw herself at him. Her fingers bent into claws. Sam fell backwards out of surprise. He didn't know what he expected to be in the closet, but she wasn't it. She was on him before he even knew what was happening, screaming and trying to scratch his eyes out. Sam did everything in his power to defend himself, but for a small petite woman, she had a strength that rivaled even his own.

He was about to hit her when she was suddenly picked off of him. A man held her against his chest as she struggled against him. She wanted Sam's blood.

Sam scampered to his feet and eyed his attacker and her keeper. He knew that a blue flame burned hotter than an orange, and her clear blue eyes were no exception. They were hot with fury. Her long red hair kept falling in her face but it didn't hide her gaze well enough to make Sam feel any better. She was about 5'10", and maybe...maybe 130 lbs. She was wearing shorts that accented her long, shapely legs, and even though the man's arm covered her chest, Sam was very aware they were fantastic. He knew there was a model-worthy woman underneath the animal.

Though not as big as Sam, the man was built. He would have to be to hold onto her. He was also in shorts and hiking boots. He was shirtless and he held her to his chest with a decent set of arms. His veins were bulging as he struggled to hold her. His face was square and hard. The close-cut hair gave Sam the impression of a military man...maybe a marine. Sam addressed him, he thought the woman was too far gone, "Holy shit, man!"

The guy ignored Sam, and just kept holding onto the woman as she kicked and try to claw away from him. "Kathy, calm down, baby."

"Yeah! Calm down, Kathy!"

The man holding her looked at Sam hard, "Shut up!" He turned his attention back to Kathy and put his mouth near her ear. "He didn't do it, baby. He's not the one. He isn't one of them." Kathy suddenly went limp in his arms and sobbed.

Sam took a step towards her, "I didn't do what?" he whispered.

The man's look softened and then he nodded towards the closet. Sitting on the floor was a child's teddy bear, but no child. All at once Sam understood. Kathy was an avenging mother.

Chapter Seventeen

Madison and Ethan

The skylights dimly lit the store, but there were enough of them and they were spaced in a way that there weren't many shadows. Every few moments the store would light up brilliantly from the electricity of the storm. The store music was no longer that of Kenny G, or Barbara Streisand, but that of giant rain drops hitting the roof and glass skylights. But there was comfort in the noise. At least it wasn't as deathly silent as the morning had been.

Ethan found a baseball bat for protection. Madison would have preferred a gun, but he didn't want to break into the glass case and let anyone or anything know that they were there. "Isn't it a little late for that?" She asked as he took a couple of practice swings. "I mean, we shattered a door."

"That could have been the lightning for all they know. Let's just not push our luck."

As they passed the hardware department they grabbed a hammer, some nails, a utility knife, and some rope. Madison looked up at the sky light and knew they didn't have much time. "I think we should split up."

"You're kidding, right? There is no way in hell I'm going to let you go anywhere alone until this place is checked out."

"I just think you should go work on the doors and I'll walk the aisles. Ethan, I seriously don't want this place to be open when it gets dark." She knew her voice shook when she spoke. She also knew it came out more like a whisper.

He studied her for a moment before he too examined the overhead skylight and sighed. "Why is it getting so dark already? It feels like it is still early."

"I know." She shivered. The cold and dampness of her clothes had indeed chilled her to the bone, but her shiver came more from fear than weather.

Ethan held out the bat for her to take. "Okay. I see your point. I'll start in the back room where they keep all the extra inventory, you know, the storage area and seal up all the doors. I'll check any of the closets and other rooms and you walk the store." She took the bat from him and held it close to her. "If you come across anything you just start swinging and yell for me. Ask questions later. Okay?"

She nodded rapidly, "Okay."

He reached for her and pulled her close to him. As custom, he pressed his forehead to hers and looked deep into her eyes. It was something she always felt connected them on such a deep level. She couldn't help but melt into him. The warmth of his embrace started to seep into her. "I love you, gorgeous, even if you do look like a drowned rat."

"Very funny," she said into his shoulder as she sighed with content. "Can we please just stay here like this?"

His arms went tight around her. "Just as soon as we make sure it is safe to stay here." He smoothed her hair. "You know we are going to be alright, right? I can feel it." He pulled himself away from her. "We'll do this fast. Okay?" He started to walk away from her.

"Okay."

"Be safe, Madi. I love you"

She swallowed hard. "I love you more." It wasn't a competition, and she knew that he knew it. It was a statement about loving him more than any trial or tribulation, or anything that that could come between them. It was about loving him more than herself.

He was standing at the end of the aisle, and she could see him smile. He would walk over to the layaway and go through the employees' only door and out of her sight in a matter of moments. "See you soon?"

She forced a smile, "Yeah. See you soon."

He disappeared around the corner. She could hear his wet sneakers squeak against the floor as he jogged away. She started to shiver again.

*****

The shadows were growing darker and deeper faster than she had hoped for. It was all happening too fast. She had to remind herself several times the pounding noise she was hearing was not the rain, but the beating of her heart. Her anxiousness was in overdrive; she was convinced that her heart would be overworked, and any moment there would be an explosion in her chest and she would drop down dead right in the middle of the Barbie aisle.

Madison stopped and looked at the nearest skylight. The rain had softened and she strained to hear the slight tap on the glass. It was too quiet.

The inspection of the store had gone quickly for her, and now she was starting to doubt that she had done a thorough job. She was so concentrated on looking that she had never thought to listen beyond the roar of the rain. And now with its absence, she was more than aware of the silence.

There were only a few more aisles to go. She had looked behind the bakery and deli counters and inspected the kitchens, under the check-out lanes and in the garbages. The salon, game room, Montana souvenir store, and the small Subway restaurant all appeared to be clear. Each of her searches were led by the bat, ready to strike at a moment's notice.

Despite her anxiety, she wasn't prepared to hear the clicking noise. It stopped her right in her tracks. Her mind raced to find an explanation that was harmless: the rain? A leak in the roof? Fingernails? Yes, fingernails. That's exactly what it was. Long, sharp, definitely not harmless fingernails. "Oh my God." Her voice had failed her, and the sound from her throat was barely a dry, hoarse whisper. She would never in a million years forget the sound that she heard when she was in the closet and now it was back.

Madison clutched the bat close to her, seeking some kind of comfort from the cool dead wood, but it didn't help. The clicking noise was nearby; one or two aisles away, right where she had just been only moments before.

She couldn't breathe, and she was sure that whatever it was could hear the drumming of her heart. She looked around for somewhere to hide, but to try to squeeze into a shelf would be pointless. Knocking down boxes of dolls and bins of balls would more than likely give her position away. She knew that she was going to have to defend herself. There was no other choice.

The bat shook as she held it away from her, waiting for it to turn the corner. It wasn't until that moment that she grasped the concept; searching the store alone was worthless. Someone or something could have easily known about her and circled around. She would never have realized until it was ready to make its presence apparent to her. That moment had arrived.

She took a step forward and said a little prayer to herself. "Please, God, please help me. Give me strength." The end of the aisle was only a few feet away and the clicking continued. Sometimes it was fast, and sometimes it was slow and meticulous.

For a brief moment courage found her. Waiting for her destiny was never her style anyway, and she decided to just go ahead and confront whatever was waiting for her now. "Hello?" The clicking stopped. "Is anyone there?" Her body was tense and beads of sweat began to roll down her forehead despite the chill she had been feeling. "Hello? Ethan?" All at once the clicking commenced, like it was shot out of a cannon. The sound surrounded her as it echoed off the walls, and by the time she realized that it was coming up behind her and fast, it was too late. She closed her eyes and braced for impact as a large, wet, hairy creature slammed into her body.

She couldn't open her eyes, she was too terrified of what she would see, but she found her voice and began to scream as she tried to fight off her assailant. Madison expected to feel pain at any moment, knowing that the creature would sink its claws and teeth into her fragile skin, but it never happened. Instead a rough wet tongue continuously lapped at her face.

Madison found herself confused so she forced herself to open her eyes and her screams changed into giggles and squeals of joy. Her creature turned out to be nothing more than a large mutt of a dog, obviously overjoyed at finally finding a person. If only it knew how happy Madison was to see it. Even having its cold black nose repeatedly pressed into her skin was pure bliss.

Before Madison knew what was happening the dog yelped and scampered away. Ethan was standing over her with the bat she must have dropped in the collision. A lot of good that would have done had it been an actual attack. She scrambled to her feet. The dog was at the other end of the aisle, tail between its legs, head dropped low, and shivering.

Ethan took a threatening step towards the dog, "Get out of here!"

It dropped down to its belly and whined.

Ethan raised the bat and started after the poor animal, but Madison grabbed the back of his shirt. "No! Ethan, stop!"

"What? Madison, that dog was going to kill you!"

"No, no he wasn't. He was just excited to see me. Look." She kneeled down on the cold floor and whistled quietly. "Come here. It's okay." The dog raised its head and cocked it to one side. It started to crawl towards her but hesitated. Madison saw that Ethan was still holding the bat in the swinging position. "Ethan, put the bat down. You're scaring it."

He reluctantly lowered the bat and sighed. The dog remained at the other end of the aisle.

"Maybe you should call it, Ethan. After all, you are the one who owes it an apology for hitting it with a freaking bat."

"I owe the dog an apology? Give me a break! Madison, you were screaming! What was I supposed to think?"

"I would think you would maybe notice me laughing as he tried to lick me to death. But never mind, we need him to come back to us." She pat the floor and whistled again. "Come on. It's okay. Come on, baby." The dog slowly inched its way to her and stopped just short of Madison being able to reach it.

Ethan ran his fingers through his hair. "For God's sake, Madi, we've got more important things to do than worry about a damn dog."

"Well, I think this is pretty important. This damn dog happens to be the first living thing we've seen." She slowly moved closer to the animal. She knew the dog was afraid of them and that they would have to earn its trust again. Her hands were close enough for the dog to inspect her hands.

Ethan abruptly pulled her to her feet. The dog again retreated to the far end of the aisle, looking back warily as it trotted off. Madison was more than tempted to slap her husband. "What the hell is your problem, Ethan? That dog was the closest thing to reality that I've all day! I needed to hold onto him."

He started to walk away towards the front of the door. She struggled to keep up with him. "Listen. It's not like the dog is going anywhere, Madi, he's in the store. You can make friends or whatever with him later!"

She caught up with him and grabbed his arm, pulling him to a stop. "What is with you? I would think you would be happy to see him."

"It's not about the stupid dog, Madison! Do you have any idea how scared I was when I heard you screaming?

"I'm...I'm sorry. At first I thought I had reason to scream."

He sighed heavily. "Look. Let's just forget about it. We need to pull down the gates to the front doors and set up a place to sleep for a night while we still have some light left to work by." He started to walk away again. "Why don't you go gather some candles and lighters and meet me back at the souvenir store? I'll get the gates down."

He left her alone standing in front of the cash registers. At first she felt abandoned and hurt, but by glancing up at the nearest skylight, she could also see that it truly was getting dark, maybe only half an hour more of light. A renewed sense of urgency filled her. Behind her was the familiar clicking noise, and she could see the dog peeking from behind a mouthwash display. It was going to be hard to distinguish between what she heard in the closet and her new four legged companion.

She could hear the gate crash down on the grocery side of the store, and she knew that she better hurry in order to meet Ethan. There was an abandoned grocery cart next to her and she started to steer it to the large supply of candles the store had. It was an eerie feeling to walk through the empty store, and she couldn't help but smile at how many times she had wished she could be at SuperMart without the crowds, rude employees, and hassle. "Here's a life lesson to be learned: be careful of what you wish for." The only one listening to her was the dog.

The candle aisle was a melody of summer smells; apples, peaches, pears, cherries, and fresh linen drying in the sun. At least no one could say their little corner of the store would smell bad. But who would they be trying to impress? The wet dog, who was trailing closely behind her? She grabbed a couple of packages of lighters and made her way to the linens for pillows and sleeping bags.

The second gate crashed down.

Madison wondered if she should get some food, but she knew she didn't have an appetite. Besides, they still had what was left in the backpack if Ethan was hungry. The dog was watching her intently. "Oh yeah," and she quickly headed over to the pet area for dog dishes and food.

Chapter Eighteen

Sam, Kathy and Ethan

Sam kept his distance from the mourning parents, still uneasy, still
unsure whether or not "Kathy" would fly into a rage again. He was
sympathetic, of course. He didn't necessarily blame her. If his son had
been murdered, he was sure he would be the same way. Probably even
worse. Unpredictable to say the least. But still, Sam was fond of his
skin, and his eyes, and keeping distance from her was the best way to
make sure he kept both intact.

They had retreated back into the living area of the house. There was
a steady stream of water flowing in the right corner of the kitchen, but
Sam could tell from the tapping on the roof that the rain was starting to
let up. The trio had settled into an uncomfortable silence. Focusing on
the tapping and watching the stream was a good distraction for him,
but every now and again he would glance over to the couple in the
living room to make sure they were keeping their distance too.

It was on one of those glances that he accidently made eye contact
with the man. He still had his arms protectively around his wife, her
face pressed into his shoulder, but he was looking right at Sam. Sam
quickly looked away, but could still feel the glare on him. So he
cleared his throat, "I'm Sam Coldburn." He thought better than to offer
his hand for a customary handshake.

The man didn't seem to mind. "Justin, and Kathy." Justin led Kathy
over to the lone chair and sat her down. "I'm sorry..."

Sam waved the statement away. "No worries, man. I get it. You
know, with circumstances being the way they are. But, I've got to
know, Justin, what the hell were you doing in the closet? You scared
the shit out of me."

Justin quickly glanced at his wife and then walked closer to Sam. He paused when he saw Sam noticeably stiffen, but Justin seemed to want to speak quietly to prevent pushing Kathy further into her detached state. "We were just coming out of the hills when the wind started coming up. I saw the clouds and knew we better get inside. And as appealing as this place looked, it seemed to be the only option at the time. We were looking around when we heard a crash." Justin nodded to the broken glass next to the door. "The door was unlocked."

Sam instantly felt embarrassed. Even with a chair propped up against the door, a big man like himself should have been able to knock it down.

"We thought it was maybe..." Justin looked like he felt embarrassed, too. "...them."

Sam frowned. Almost afraid to ask. Almost afraid to hear that he wasn't insane. That would make them real. "Them?"

"Yeah. Them. I don't know what else to call them. Monsters? Demons? I know this must sound crazy."

"Shadows."

Justin blinked. "Yeah! Shadows...so you've seen one, too?"

Sam grunted, "One? If only. I've seen hundreds of them. That blue car out there is mine. There was one right in the middle of the road. Scared the shit out of me, so I tried to turn around, but crashed instead. Then an entire army of those things came over the hill from town. They chased me up the damn mountain."

Justin glanced out of the dirty kitchen window where the rain had stopped. "On one hand, I am so glad to hear you say that. It means we aren't cray. On the other hand...shit. You know? We seriously need to get out of here." At this point, Sam didn't think he was necessarily speaking to him. But then he turned back and faced him, "You said they came from town?"

"Yeah. So many."

"I saw one take the life out of my boy. Just one. And then it took Alice and Ernie away. Just one. And now you say there are hundreds of these things in town? God help us! Is there even going to be anyone there to help us, let alone believe us?" He started pacing nervously. "Have you noticed the light?"

Sam watched him for a moment. "Yeah...seems like it shortened up. It is just a dark storm, that's all." But honestly, Sam didn't really believe it was just the storm. It was too dark for as early as it was. He knew it was mid-day, but his senses were telling him that the day was drawing to a close.

"No. No. It is going to be dark soon. We need to get out of here. We need to stay in the light." He walked over to Kathy and helped her up. The woman's eyes looked glassed over but she responded to Justin's assistance and stood. But she didn't look at him. She didn't look at Sam either. She didn't really seem to be looking at anything. "We aren't staying here, Sam. There are too many rooms, too many windows, and we need to find a place with light."

Sam frowned. "What does light have to do with anything? I mean, they blend well in the dark...but..." It occurred to him that he didn't see any of them on the way here.

"Alice told us to stay in the light. They don't like it. Even a candle will hold them off." He headed towards the door leading his wife by her hand. "We don't have a lot of time, but I think we can make it to town. It is just up the road, right?"

"Uhhh...yeah. I drove through it last night. Maybe a mile or two." He took a few steps towards them. "Maybe we should stay together until we can find some help?"

Justin paused. He looked Sam up and down and then nodded. "Yeah...it can't hurt to have an extra set of eyes."

"Just as long as they aren't red."

Chapter Nineteen

Outside the air was damp and cool. It was amazing how quickly the day changed, and how quickly it was disappearing. They had trudged through the tall grass and weeds turned swamp, onto what was now a flowing river of run off on the road. At first they walked in silence, but then they started comparing stories. Justin told him of their argument and how their son had run off. He talked about coming across the house and how the weird old lady spoke of hate and anger and waking "it" up. Sam involuntarily teared up when Justin spoke of the shadow hovering over their son and then taking his body into the bathroom with a single flame as their defense.

"Sam. I swear to you. They were screaming in agony. I had to sit there and listen to them scream. But this morning...that room was clean. I mean, even if they were dragged off somewhere, I expected there to be blood just from the way they were screaming. But there was nothing. It was as if they just disappeared."

"I know what you are talking about. I saw a group of them take down Abby."

"Who's Abby?"

"She lived in the house that I found. I only know her name by the pictures I found." He didn't bother to tell him that he had seen her after her death. "Anyway, a group of them swarmed her, and she was screaming like they were eating her alive. I looked away, but just for a second. Not long enough for them to take her anywhere. When they left I thought there would be blood or bones or something...but there was nothing."

"Nothing?"

"Nothing."

Justin stopped in the middle of the road. He was frowning. Sam knew that town was less than five minutes away, and all this talk about staying in the light made him nervous. They needed to find shelter right away, and he wasn't in the mood to stop. He looked over at Kathy realizing he had almost forgotten that she was there. She hadn't made a sound since trying to kill him.

"So...they eat them whole? And you said a swarm of them attacked her. You can't split a....person...between many and not make a mess."

"Man, I don't know. I know how it sounds, but it doesn't make sense to me either. I'm just telling you what I saw."

Justin started walking again. And Sam was thankful for that. "I know. I'm not saying you are lying, Sam. I'm just...I miss Wyatt."

Sam's defenses went down. "I understand. I can't imagine what that must feel like. I guess if there is one thing to be thankful for, it's that they didn't finish him off the way they did the others." He glanced at Kathy again. He was unnerved by her silence. "Is she going to be okay?"

Justin shook his head and then shrugged. "I don't know. When Wyatt died, she kind of shut down. Every now and again, I get little glimpses that she is still with us, but for the most part, she has been like this since yesterday."

Sam didn't like that she wasn't alert. Even though he was in the midst of conversation with her husband he was still very aware of everything that was going on. He knew they didn't have much time before it started getting dark, and Justin was adamant about staying in the light. He knew he was cold, and that the heat of the morning was a distant, if not an almost pleasant, memory in comparison. He was also aware of the feeling in his gut that told him they were being watched and being out in the open gave their watcher so many places to hide. Between that feeling and the comatose-like woman following them around, Sam felt vulnerable, and he didn't like that feeling either. Not at all.

"Justin, I don't mean to be a jerk about this, but we've got to get her moving faster. The sooner we find help, the better, but I've got a feeling that we don't have much time."

Justin looked at the stone gray sky above them and watched a single snowflake fall. "You've got to be kidding me." He gave a nod to Sam before he took Kathy's arm and started to walk, almost jog toward the first buildings in the distance. To her credit, Kathy allowed herself to be pulled at the faster rate and Sam took off after them. He took a moment to scan the trees to his left and almost collided with them when they suddenly stopped dead in their tracks.

"What the hell? Why did you stop?"

They didn't answer him, or even acknowledge him but continued to stare right in front of them. Sam glanced around them and saw a lone woman standing in the road in front of them. Human, thank God, but Sam wasn't relived to see her. She unnerved him worse than Kathy ever did. The woman stood as motionless as them, dressed in a dirty yellow summer dress. The wind wrapped the dress around her legs, plastering itself to her thin pale body. Her stringy brown hair hung in her eyes, and even from this distance, Sam could see she was shivering uncontrollably.

Sam cleared his throat softly and stepped in front of Justin and Kathy. "Stay here." He walked slowly towards her. Fifty feet separated them, then thirty, then less than ten. Up close, she was white as a ghost and filthy beyond just the dress. Her legs and arms were streaked with grime. She was a dirty skeleton. Perhaps all cleaned up and without the wild look in her brown eyes, she might come across as elegant, graceful...like a seasoned ballet dancer. "Miss..."

At the sound of his voice she screamed painfully, and a startled Sam stepped backward giving her more space. The last thing he needed was another crazed woman attacking him. But instead of lurching forward, she crumbled to the ground. Her legs splayed out and she covered her face with her dirty hands. He could hear her mumbling something through her anguished cries. He looked back at Justin and Kathy, and Justin was holding his wife protectively. Sam shrugged and moved a little closer to try to hear what she was saying. It was almost like she was saying 'gone...gone' over and over again.

Here goes nothing. He prepared himself for another scream. "Miss, are you alright?"

She became silent and he knew she was watching him through her fingers. After a moment she dropped her hands into her lap and then smiled. "They are all gone. All gone."

Sam frowned. "Who is gone?"

She laughed and stood up. "Everyone!" And then she started twirling in the street. Her yellow dressed floated up around her like the petals of a flower. Her bare feet, although cut, dirty and bruised, danced across the wet asphalt with style. It was like watching a manic version of Swan Lake. Yep...a dancer. A loon-ass dancer. Sam tried to be sympathetic. He wanted to believe she wasn't always like this, but sympathy battled against fear. If Ms. Loon was correct, there wouldn't be any help for them to find. But if she was here, dancing in the street, then surely there had to be others in town too. There had to be.

Sympathy lost. Her dancing was irritating him. He motioned for Justin and Kathy to join him. "Come on! We don't have time for this shit."

Ms. Loon stopped dancing and surprised him by giving him the finger. Sam shook his head and started to walk a wide arch around her, but this time she did lurch towards him and grabbed his upper arm. Sam knew right away it wasn't with the intention of hurting him. Her long graceful fingers weren't digging into his bicep, but they were holding him tightly. "Miss..."

"I'm sorry. But you can't go into town. Everyone is gone! Please stay with me! Don't leave me!" She wasn't laughing anymore, instead there were tears.

Justin and Kathy had joined him. "Sam, we need to get going. We need to get somewhere safe."

Ms. Loon brightened. "Safe! I know where is safe! Please come with me!" She let go of Sam's arm and began prancing in the direction they were going.

Justin leaned a little closer to Sam, "I don't know about going with her though. How 'safe' is she?"

Sam shrugged. "I don't know, man. But really, what choice do we have? Look around, it is getting darker. I don't know about you, but I don't want to be out here when the lights go out. And if what she says is true, that everyone is gone, but somehow she managed to survive, maybe staying with her is the best thing."

She stopped and looked back at them, and motioned for them to come with her once more. She waited until they were with her before she started again. "I was restless last night so I went for a walk. I generally walk to the edge of town and then back. I was just about done when all this screaming started. Although...screaming isn't quite the word for it. It was much more terrible than that. But then people were screaming too. It was awful!"

Sam could hear the scream in his memory and it made him shudder. He didn't want to remember that sound, but he was thankful he didn't hear people with it. Well, except for Abby's. He almost asked Ms. Loon to stop talking, to stop taking him back to last night, but then he also thought it was important to know what she knew.

"At first, I didn't know what was going on. Cars were crashing, people were running out of their homes and the stores like they were being chased. At first I couldn't see what was chasing them, but then I did. They are hard to see, you know? They are part of the darkness. And people are so afraid of the dark when you really think about it. It isn't something they understand."

Ms. Loon stopped and looked at them. They were in front of an old metal warehouse. The windows were broken and the main door was ajar. The white paint was cracked and rusted. Sam sighed; another place for ghosts. It looked like the last place to consider safe, but Ms. Loon was visibly proud of it and she beamed. "We're here!"

"No way, Sam." Justin groaned. Kathy just stood there in her own little world.

"Oh I know it doesn't look like much, but it is safe. Oh yes! Very safe. Once I figured out what was going on, and the fact you couldn't really see those shadow things, I thought it would be best to just hide and stay put. This was the closest thing to me at the time, so I went in here."

She pulled the door open and motioned them in. Sam crossed the threshold and surveyed their surroundings. It was a large square room, but extremely dim. Really nowhere to hide, which was good and bad,

Sam supposed. The creatures couldn't be lurking behind anything, but remembering the bushes from last night, Sam realized that they couldn't be either.

But Justin told them that light holds them off. Their only chance was to create light. There were holes in the ceiling for smoke to escape and Sam still had matches in his pocket from Lucky's. If they gathered some wood scraps and started a bon-fire they might be able to survive the night. But how did she do it? How did she keep them away? He asked her.

Ms. Loon pranced over to a large pipe with a grate over the front of it. She lifted it up and pointed inside. It was dark and damp, and he imagined it to be a terribly tight fit for a man his size. But perhaps for a slender, long, flexible body, she could curl up inside there. That would explain why she was so dirty. He suddenly felt bad for calling her Ms. Loon. She was resourceful if nothing else. "What is your name?"

She smiled, "Jillian."

"I'm Sam. The couple outside are Justin and Kathy."

"Correction. The couple inside are Justin and Kathy." Justin was standing in the middle of the large room with an armload of wood scraps. He had apparently picked up on Sam's wave lengths. "We don't have a lot of time, Sam. Let's get us some light going." He dropped the wood and headed out for more with Kathy at his heels.

Chapter Twenty

Madison and Ethan

W hen she was finally finished getting everything she thought they would need for the night, it was getting difficult to see. The shadows were creeping around every corner and pooling on the floor like spilt ink. The fingers of each shadow seem to be reaching for her, trying to catch her around her ankles. Madison picked up her speed to the point that she was jogging down the aisle. Behind her the clicking noise raced to keep up with her. She was too frightened to look behind her to make sure it was just the dog.

The souvenir store was close. A soft light radiated from the small space. As she pushed the cart across the threshold, the light embraced her like a long, lost lover. It felt clean and pure compared to the darkness, and she smiled at the feeling of being safe.

"Took you long enough."

Ethan was sitting on the counter. He had begun to push some of the shelves off to one side, trying to make room for them to stretch out. He jumped off the counter and walked over to the entrance. In his hand was a long metal hook, obviously meant to pull down the gate.

Madison put her hand on his shoulder. "Wait a sec. We have to get the dog in here."

"Madison..."

"Please, Ethan." He could hear the desperation in her voice.

"Well, get him in here. If I recall, you were the one who gave the deadline. We had to be all closed in and safe before it got dark."

"Shut up, Ethan." He stomped his way back to the counter and sat down.

Madison reached for a dog food bowl and opened a bag of food. She poured some into the bowl and placed in at the other side of the room. The dog must have heard the food falling into the dish because it peered around the door, ears perked. Madison went and stood by the counter. Ethan eyed her skeptically. "That's it? That is how you are going to get the dog in here."

She gave him a dirty look. "You know, if it wasn't for you in the first place, that dog would already trust us."

He opened his mouth to say something but clamped it shut. He knew she was right.

The dog watched them warily, but took a few steps into the store. "Okay, Ethan when he gets in a little more, you just bring that gate down, okay."

The dog apparently decided that the food was much more important than its own safety and ran the rest of the way to the bowl. The sound of crunching kibble filled the room. The dog briefly raised his head when the gate crashed down to the floor and Ethan secured it with the locks, then his head disappeared into the bowl again.

Ethan looked at the full cart and raised his eyebrows. "I didn't think you would choose to go shopping tonight. Didn't I just send you out for candles?"

She walked over to the supplies that she had gathered and started to hand him things. "Well...I thought you'd want a pillow, and a sleeping bag. And then I remembered that I needed to get stuff for the dog, and I did get the candles."

Ethan took the pillows that she had handed to him and slid down the counter's short wall. He took one of plastic covers off a pillow and then held it to his face. All Madison could hear was a muffled scream. "Are you okay? Are you still mad at me?"

He took the pillow away from his face and looked at her. He seemed to have aged several years over the course of the day. His handsome face was long and drawn. The blood on his forehead from the explosion had dried and crusted over, his hair was matted to his head, and it seemed like his frown lines were more prominent than ever. "I'm not mad at you, Madison." He sighed warily. "I never was."

She slid down next to him. "Then why are you acting like you're mad?"

"Jesus, Madi. Look around you, and then ask that question. I can't even begin to explain all this to myself and it is a little frustrating."

"I'm sorry."

He took her hand and stroked it with his thumb. "Don't be. I'm sorry if I took it out on you. It is just for a minute there I thought I'd lost you. And maybe I'm being a selfish bastard, but I was terrified of being alone here."

His voice had softened. Madison was seeing a whole new side to her husband. He has always been her rock, someone who was calm and reassuring when she broke down, which was more often than she cared to admit. Like a true lover of puzzles, he took her broken pieces, her insecurities and fears, and patiently and carefully helped create a wholeness in her. But now she was realizing he was no less vulnerable than she was. He was as scared and as confused as she was. He was human after all.

Across the room the dog had finished its meal. He had put himself in the corner and circled a spot in the floor before dropping to the ground. He let out a heavy sigh and licked his chops before closing his eyes. Apparently he figured if they were going to hurt him, they would have done it already. In any case, he was giving in to exhaustion.

Madison laid her head on Ethan's shoulder. "Are you hungry?"

"No. Actually I think the dog has the right idea. I think I should try to go to sleep."

She looked up and him and blinked hard. "Really? It is kind of early, and do you think you could honestly go to sleep?"

"Well...it's been a long day wouldn't you say?"

"Yeah, but still. I don't think I can sleep, not with everything that has happened."

He was quiet for a moment. The candle light flickered across his features. She could see he was thinking. "I guess, I'm just hoping to go to sleep, wake up tomorrow morning in our bed, make love to you, go to work..." He chuckled quietly. "Isn't that crazy? I never thought I would want to go to work so badly."

Madison stared at the dog that was curled up in the corner, snoring loudly. She could now see that he was actually a she, and around her neck was a collar and tags. If the dog ever let her, she'd have to check and see if it had a name.

"Yep, I just want to wake up tomorrow and know that this was all a bad dream." He was talking more to himself than to her so she didn't respond. He stood up and took the sleeping bags out of the cart, and then arranged the candles around the room. "We'll keep a few lit for the night."

After zipping the sleeping bags together, he put the pillows down and got in the makeshift bed. "Can you believe how much it's cooled off, Madi? Yesterday I was sure that I would melt and tonight I actually think I'll be sleeping under the covers tonight." He patted the space next to him.

Her clothes hadn't completely dried. It would be a death sentence to sleep in them. "Yeah, it is actually kind of cold." She took off her clothes and Ethan followed her example. They draped them over the counter to dry. Madison then slipped under the top layer and pushed herself next to Ethan. He wrapped his arms around her and pulled her as close to him as he could. Together their bodies made incredible warmth, and she sighed contently.

Behind her Ethan was already snoring softly, and she smiled. For the past several years she had teased him about his ability to forget the day and go to sleep. Apparently surviving the apocalypse was no exception. It would seem he fell asleep as soon as his head hit the pillow.

The apocalypse. Was it truly the end? If so, it was nothing like she thought it would be. Where was the fire and brimstone? God riding down on his white horse? And if this was the apocalypse, were they in Hell, for it surely wasn't heaven? Heaven would not scare her in this way, and heaven would not leave her feeling empty, at least everything she thought she knew about heaven told her it wouldn't. But if they were in Hell, surely they couldn't be the only ones. Right?

Madison yawned.

Then again, maybe Ethan was right. Hopefully Ethan was right. It had to be a dream, a really bad dream, but whose? Did it even matter? Tomorrow they would wake up and laugh about it, and go on with their lives.

Just a dream.

That's all.

Nothing more.

She was more tired that she thought. She fell asleep.

Chapter Twenty-One

Madison and Ethan

The bed felt hard, and where was the whining coming from?

Madison tried to open her eyes as they strained to adjust even to the minimal light coming from the candles. As the images came to her, she suddenly realized where she was. Instead of feeling the familiar softness of their double-pillow top bed, she was lying on a thin layer of carpet that covered a cold concrete floor. Instead of the welcoming smell of lavender and vanilla lotion that she smeared on before bed, she was suddenly hit with most unpleasant smell of wet dog. Not even the scented candles could cover it up.

Dog. The dog was hunched over in the corner, whining loudly, and shivering. Although it was colder than ever, she didn't think it was that cold. The dog was definitely scared. Of them?

She turned her head and saw Ethan sitting straight up. She started to sit up herself, but Ethan put his hand on her shoulder and she knew that he didn't want her to move. "What's going on?"

"Shhhhhhhhh. Listen."

At first she couldn't hear anything, just the dog whining in the corner, but after finally recognizing what he wanted her to hear, she wished she could just block it out. The clicking. Steady, and close, and many more than one.

Now hearing it again, she knew that although it was very similar to the dog's nails hitting the tile, it wasn't the same noise at all. It was much more ominous. Simply hearing it caused shivers to run down her spine, and she pulled the sleeping bag tighter around her.

"Do you hear it?" He was whispering, and she could see his hand was holding tightly onto the baseball bat.

All she could do was nod. She was so scared she wanted to pee.

"What the hell is that? I've never heard anything like that before."

"It's them. It has to be."

"Them?" Ethan slowly got up and quietly pulled his shorts on. He grabbed a candle and walked closer to the gate that separated them from the rest of the store.

"Ethan, no!"

He didn't even acknowledge her plea. Instead he stood just inches from thick wire. Anything could reach in and get a handful of him. He slowly waved the candle back and forth, squinting into the darkness beyond them. Madison buried her head into her bent knees. If anything did get a hold of him, she didn't want to see it happen.

"Madi, I don't see anything. Where is that coming from?"

She turned her head towards him and sobbed. "Ethan, please! Come back!" All of her attempts to whisper failed. She was crying out in desperation, she couldn't help it.

He turned his back on the gloom and looked at her. Tears were streaming down her face like two tiny, rapid moving rivers. Her hair was tossed and in tangles, and in the candle light her naked skin glowed. She was beautiful. Suddenly finding out where the noise was coming from didn't matter nearly as much as going to her and comforting her. He had never seen her so scared.

No more than a step later, the clicking stopped altogether. The silence startled him and again he turned to face the dark. Then all at once, SuperMart came under attack. Madison let out an involuntary scream that could barely be heard over the clashing and crashing of them against metal, wood, concrete and glass. Ethan fell backwards into some shelving that contained shot glasses with miscellaneous Montana symbols. His collision only mingled with the sounds of the assault taking place on the building.

"Ethan!" It no longer mattered if she was shouting or not. She knew that she was barely heard over the noise, and whatever they were, they already knew Ethan and she were there.

Ethan tried to thrash his way out of the tangle of shelving, not caring as he scratched his bare chest and arms. Madison was already up and pulling her shirt and shorts on. They were still damp. No time had passed between falling asleep and all-out war.

She dashed over to Ethan and helped him up, and they ran over to the dog's corner. They all crouched and huddled together, trying to be invisible.

Silence. It all stopped at the very same second. Not even clicking could be heard. Even the dog stopped whining.

They both slowly stood up and listened. Ethan looked at her and smiled. "They can't get in! None of that was from inside the store." He felt some kind of victory at being able to keep their attackers out.

He took her hand and they slowly walked toward the gate. They stepped over broken glass and shelving. The candles flickered quietly.

The last thing Madison wanted to do was get near that gate, but she let him lead her. It was true that it was able to keep them out so far, after what seemed like an army of thousands tried to fight their way in, and she wanted to believe that this so-called fortress would continue to stand strong. However, there was a small part of her that thought that they weren't truly trying to get in; that they weren't giving it all they had. She remembered the cars with doors ripped from their frames. Glass and thin metal gates should be no match for them. The more she thought it about it, the more she truly believed that they were simply sending a message. What that message was though was beyond her comprehension.

At the gate, they peered into the darkness, but it remained as quiet and still as a tomb. They shared a smile, but she didn't share his confidence.

Then the scream happened. It wasn't an ordinary scream that came from a human throat, but it exhibited very human emotions. Frustration and anger. In unison they cried out, in a high pitched, agonized chorus that made Madison and Ethan cover their ears. She wanted to go back to the corner, she wanted to go back to sleep. She still held on to the hope that it was just a dream.

She looked up to the heavens in prayer, and began to ask God to please make the noise stop, but instead something caught her eye. God must have read her thoughts because the scream did stop, but she couldn't pull her eyes away from the sight. She nudged Ethan and pointed to a nearby skylight, and together they stared at two glowing red eyes that glared back at them.

"What is that, Ethan?" She was back to whispering.

He shook his head. "I don't know. A cat?"

"You know damn well that isn't a cat."

"No. It's not a cat."

The red eyes narrowed for a moment, but they glowed brighter than red hot coals. Madison was thankful that she couldn't see anything more than its eyes. The eyes were enough.

It continued to stare them down for what seemed like eternity before it finally jumped away from the sky-light and away from their sight.

They stood at the gate for a few minutes longer, before walking back to the counter and sliding down its face. They sat in silence before Ethan finally looked at her. He had new scratches on his stomach from the fall, but nothing serious. "That thing hated us. It was pissed off. It wanted to kill us, but it couldn't get in."

"I know."

"What the fuck was it?"

"I don't know." He was swearing a lot lately.

"How many were out there? I mean we just saw that one."

"I know."

"And it was big. I could tell just from looking at those eyes. How the hell did it get on the God damn roof?"

"I don't know." She was almost numb. As much as she wanted to say something more meaningful to him, she had no answers.

He was shaking his head, arguing with whatever conversation he was holding with himself. "I just can't believe this happening."

"I know exactly what you mean." She pulled her knees up and hugged them, but she couldn't stop shaking.

Ethan put his arm around her. "Are you cold?"

"That and then some."

He bit his bottom lip, and leaned over to bring the sleeping bags up and around them. "Yeah, I'm cold too. And...scared shitless."

The dog slowly approached them and settled herself at their feet. The excess sleeping bags had to have been more comfortable than the hard floor for her, but Madison also sensed that the dog had forgiven them for the bat incident.

She laid her head on Ethan's lap and closed her eyes. He tried to stroke her hair, but his fingers kept getting caught in the tangles. His stomach slightly shook as he quietly chuckled. She tried to smile, she tried to see the humor in all of it, but she couldn't. Instead a heavy sigh escaped her.

Ethan leaned down and kissed her forehead. "That's right, you rest." But they both knew that rest wouldn't come. At least not this night. Maybe not ever.

Chapter Twenty-Two

Sam, Kathy and Justin

Any closer and they would singe the hair off of their arms but it was a risk they were willing to take. All around them were strange sounds that reminded Sam of one of his ex-girlfriends drumming her long fingernails on the countertops. It drove him crazy then, and now it was just terrifying. He couldn't see them, but he knew they were there, and they were patient. It would just take a moment for any of them to step far enough away from the large fire they had built, to step away from the light for the shadows to come up and swallow them whole.

Kathy and Justin stood on the opposite side of the flames; Justin again with the standard protective arm around his wife, Jillian was rocking on her heels to the left of him. The natural shadows mingled with the unnatural that moved only feet away from them creating a dark river, but Sam thanked God for a woman named Alice who told Justin about the secret of the light. It could be the one thing that kept them alive tonight.

"Sam?" Justin was whispering barely loud enough for Sam to hear him over the clicks, "What are they doing?"

"Waiting would be my best guess."

A whimper came from his left and Jillian was still rocking and she was hugging herself. "Jillian? Jillian?" Sam edged around the fire, feeling like he was developing a sunburn across his entire backside. When he reached her he hesitated but then put his arm around her shoulders, laughing internally once he realized that Justin was providing the model for the gesture. "Jillian, you've got to calm down."

Instead of calming down, she sobbed loudly. The unnatural shadows seemed to become excited by this noise so he tried to hush her and pulled her closer to him. She smelled coppery, like a hand that held pennies tightly for a few minutes. "Sam! They are everywhere! We need to hide! I need to get to the pipe!"

He turned her by the shoulders and forced her to look at him, "Now you listen, Jillian." His voice was a low grumble, "We need to stay right here. As long as we are in the light, they aren't coming. Running from the fire to hide in your pipe would be the worst idea. You'll die!"

The word 'die' came out a little louder than he anticipated and it was laced with the trembling of a scared man. And the creatures picked up on that and let out their war cry that immediately dropped Sam's hands away from Jillian's shoulders and they went to his ears to try to stop the feeling of his blood curdling from the cold, soulless sound of their screams. Across the fire, Justin and Kathy had dropped to the ground where they attempted to cover each other's head as if they were being bombarded by grenades. Maybe they were even hoping for it as an alternative.

To his left, Jillian had stopped rocking and her arms were at her sides but they were tight with visible muscles and her fists were clenched to the point that Sam was sure her fingernails were cutting into her palms. Sam glanced at her face and her eyes were sealed tightly closed, and her mouth was gaped open. Sam realized that she was screaming too, similar to the scream she gave when he first spoke to her, but for the life of him he couldn't hear her over the creatures and she just looked like a stiff corpse with a silent scream. She looked like Lisa the last time he saw her.

He wanted to reach for her, to offer some type of comfort to her, but he couldn't pry his hands away from his ears. But when he saw her eyes fly open, like a solution suddenly came to a long standing problem, and he saw her jump forward like a gazelle, he immediately reached for her to try to bring her back. His ears instantly protested, but he ignored the pain. And he felt the fabric of her yellow dress brush against his fingertips as she leapt right out of his grasp.

For a moment he strongly considered going after her and playing hero, but he could already see the night swarming around her. One minute he could see the yellow dress in the dark, the next he couldn't. The shadows stopped screaming and took her over very quickly. But unlike Abby, Jillian took it quietly and with dignity. She was silent and although Sam knew she was in pain and terrified, he also sensed relief coming from her. Maybe she knew she couldn't handle staying next to this fire all night, or any other night. Maybe she knew she couldn't spend the rest of life scared of the dark. Sam even questioned if he would be able to. But he wasn't going to just throw himself to them, at least not yet. He had to know if Sandra was okay before he gave up.

They must have been finished with Jillian because the dark river started moving around them again. "Where is Jillian?"

Sam looked to the other side of the fire, and through the flames he could see Justin helping Kathy to her feet, but the other man's eyes bore into him. Sam could only shake his head sadly.

"What, Sam. How could they...the light..."

"She lost it, Justin! They started screaming and she jumped right into them."

Justin threw his hands in the air and gave a sarcastic laugh. "And a big man like you couldn't hold a frail thing like her back? You should have been able to protect her, man!"

"You know, fuck you. I tried!"

"Yeah. I'm sure you did!"

"Shut up!"

Both men fell silent, startled by Kathy. She stood between them, not far from where Jillian had been. The fire reflected deep into her eyes and she alternated her glance between them. Justin took a step towards her, "Kath, what did you say?"

She put her hands on her hips. "I said shut up. Don't you see what you are doing?" She put her arms out to indicating that they needed to look around them, Boo the teddy bear hanging from one hand.

He was so grateful to hear the sound of her voice, Justin wanted to run over and hug her but instead he turned and finally took notice that the creatures were still. They had stopped circling them, but now hundreds of bright red globes stared at them.

Kathy clutched the teddy bear to her chest and lowered her voice considerably. "Don't you see? They are responding to your yelling? It seems like all your fighting has strengthened them, made them focus on us. So, for the love of God, shut up!"

Justin stood there with his mouth open and Sam could tell he wanted to walk over to her, but he couldn't. Maybe in the last twenty-four hours he had grown accustomed to her silence and allowing him to lead the way, and of all the moments for her to come out and take charge, Sam didn't think Justin was quite prepared for it. Instead of reaching out to her, Justin looked over to Sam and shrugged. "I'm sorry, Sam. I didn't see what happened. I'm sure you did all you could. I shouldn't have accused you of anything less."

Sam sighed and looked up to the many holes in the ceiling and watched as tiny snowflakes made their way in only to evaporate from the heat of their fire before making it to the ground. "No worries, man. Let's just get through the night without killing each other, shall we."

"Sure." Justin shivered against the fire as the red eyes stared into him. "We'll leave that part to them."

Chapter Twenty-Three

Madison and Ethan

August 8th

T he colors of the store had not yet begun to emerge. Everything was a dull gray in the early morning light, but at least it wasn't dark.

The hours of the previous night seemed to creep along like a stealthy predator. Maybe the creatures themselves were the night, kept at bay by the power of candle light. However, neither of them trusted that strength of those lonely, little flames. They spent the night tense and waiting for the creatures with red eyes to return.

As soon as they could see the clothes on the racks and food in the aisles they blew out the candles and raised the gate. But still they hesitated to leave their sanctuary, and continued to stand in the doorway for several minutes. The dog however ran into the store to explore.

Ethan held her hand tightly in one hand, and the bat in the other. "So what do you think?"

"Well, I think the dog wouldn't have gone out there if it wasn't safe."

"Yeah, I think so too. She's the one who let me know they were here last night. She's a good dog."

"I told you so." She playfully nudged his side and smiled at him.

The dog was running through the front fruit aisles, following the scent of something that it picked up. Madison wondered how out of fifty thousand smells a dog would be able to choose just one. And what was so special about that one smell that a dog would chose to follow just it in the first place?

The color was coming into the store. What once looked like a flat, old, black and white photograph now was coming alive with vibrancy. It was almost like an artist had taken a brush and in one swipe gave yellow to the bananas, red to the apples, purple and green to the grapes, and orange to the oranges.

Madison suddenly realized that the rainbow of color not only represented morning, but it also reminded her that they hadn't eaten in almost a day. The SuperMart produce section had never looked better, and her stomach not only growled, but it roared at the mere thought of eating.

She looked at Ethan and she wasn't sure if he was doing it consciously, but he was licking his lips as he too stared at the food.

"So, are you even a little hungry?"

He flashed her a million dollar smile, "I thought you'd never ask."

However, neither of them took a step into the main store. The fact that the dog felt it was safe enough to venture out wasn't enough to convince either of them. Madison gnawed on her bottom lip, but it was a poor substitute for the food that was only yards away. "Do you think it is safe?"

The dog had run back to them. She stood only feet away, her tail was wagging, her ears were perked, and her head was cocked. It was almost as if she was saying, "Come on! It's okay!"

Ethan sighed, "I don't know."

"Well, we didn't see any of them yesterday during the day. So maybe they hate the light?" The one in her closet seemed to at least.

"Yeah, that's a good point, but..."

"Ethan, I trust the dog, and I'm hungry. Let's just do it. If something happens, we'll just have to run back. We should be able to hear them if they come in, and we will still be close."

"You're right. Let's go."

They didn't try to second guess their decision. Like school children after the last bell, of the last day of school, they raced into the store. Madison reached for a handful of grapes, and Ethan was breaking into a tangerine before they even considered that they had an entire grocery store and all its contents to feast on.

Ethan was happily chewing away on his juicy fruit when he looked up and stopped mid-chew. "Oh my God. Madi, look!"

Ethan was pointing to the remaining, intact front door. Through the two glass doors, Madison could see the parking lot lake that formed during the storm, except it was no longer a lake. It had turned into a thick layer of dirty ice with abandoned cars and trucks dotting its smooth surface. On top of everything was a good inch of snow.

They slowly walked towards the door. The snow was falling from a bright-white sky in large flakes that swirled and danced in the wind. It was the closest thing to a blizzard that they had seen in area in years. It is the only blizzard they've seen in the summer.

"Unbelievable," she whispered. She was cold, but she thought it was from being in her wet clothes. Never in a million years did she think it would be snowing. Not in early August.

"Yeah. A day ago we were dying from heat stroke, and now we are going to freeze to death."

She socked him in the arm. "That is sooooo not funny, Ethan."

"I know it isn't. Nothing about this is funny. Madison, this whole thing is crazy. Freaky heat, freaky storm, freaky creatures, now freaky snow. I can't take much more freaky."

She rubbed her hands up and down her bare arms. As soon as they were done eating, and she was nowhere done eating, she was going to try to find some warm clothes. She knew warm clothes, winter coats and gloves were probably going to be scarce with the timing of the freaky summer winter storm, but anything would be that what she had on. She also needed to find a way to clean up, and a place to go to the bathroom. Worrying about the snow was the last thing on her list. She turned away from the weather and started to walk back into the grocery store.

"Where are you going, Madi?"

Madison stopped in the middle of the main aisle, "I don't care about the snow right now. I'm hungry, I'm dirty, I'm cold, and I've got to pee. Where am I supposed to do that?"

"The bathroom?"

"Are there any windows in the bathroom? Any light?"

"No, but I checked them out last night, they were okay."

"What if one got in last night? That room is going to be pitch black, and if they really don't like the light, that is going to be the perfect place to hide."

Ethan walked into the souvenir store and came back with a couple of lit candles. "I don't think one got in. If one did, you'd think it would have already come after us last night. Why wait, you know?"

They had already begun to walk down the store to the nearest bathroom. "Still."

"Listen, I'll go in with you, and we'll have the candles. Maybe later we could find something else to light the bathrooms up better, but I don't think we have anything to worry about though."

After taking turns going to the bathroom, and guarding the stall door, they went back to eating a large breakfast of fruit and pastries. They brought all their food back to the souvenir store and sat on the sleeping bags. They ate in silence, almost refusing to acknowledge the events of the last couple of days. It wasn't until they were full and lacking the distraction of food that they were able to even address it.

"It looks like we're going to be here awhile."

Madison took a sip from her water and nodded. "Yeah, I was really hoping to wake up and have this all be a dream. No such luck, I guess."

"Well on the bright side of things we should have plenty of supplies to last us awhile. I think we'll even be able to keep some of the perishable food good for a while, especially if we use the snow to keep them cold."

"In the worst situation possible, yeah, that's good news."

Ethan took a couple of grapes off the vine and popped them into his mouth. "But I think we still need a plan."

"About what?"

"Well, I think we should maybe spend the day getting cleaned up for one, ummm...maybe make our little living space a little more livable. Go around the store and see what we can use. Maybe find some warmer clothes."

"Hmmm. An unlimited shopping spree? Just what I always wanted!"

Her over-the-top enthusiasm made Ethan smile. "We'll I doubt this was what you had in mind, but here you go. The store is all yours."

"Maybe we should put some water and food in here, just in case we get stuck in here for a while."

"Yeah, that's a good idea. And maybe some guns. For some reason I don't think the bat is going to cut it if it came down to it."

Madison yawned. She had always been the kind of person that required a good eight hour night's sleep, and apparently the last couple nights of not having any sleep at all was catching up with her.

Ethan caught her yawn and copied her loudly. "Maybe we should get some sleep today too."

"We might end up sleeping during the day all the time, especially if those things try to get in every night."

They both fell silent, remembering the large red eyes that stared at them with such rage and hate. The last thing either of them wanted to do was to meet one them up close and personal. Their ultimate goal was keep them out, even if that meant they were to become nocturnal themselves.

"You know what's crazy?" Ethan was staring off into the store.

Madison laid back on the sleeping bags and closed her eyes. She definitely could fall asleep if given the opportunity. "Hmmmmm?"

"We opened the gate, what, an hour ago?"

"Yeah, something like that."

"And we did it pretty much at dawn, right?"

"Yeah, as soon as it was light out."

"Did it seem like the night was longer than normal to you?"

She was about to answer that the night seemed to have lasted forever because they were awake, and they were desperate for daylight. But it did feel much later than early morning. In fact, it felt like it was more like noon. But it couldn't be noon. The sun just rose.

He seemed to know what she was thinking; their daylight was limited, and that there were some things they needed to do before the sun set. Whenever that was. Maybe they only had an hour, maybe four, maybe ten. In any case, he would feel a lot better if they had some of their preparations done, if not all of them. Like she said before, if they needed to stay in the souvenir store for whatever reason, he wanted to be ready.

Ethan held out his hand, and she let him help her up. "I know you're tired, but we'll rest soon."

She smiled at him weakly, "I know. I'll feel a whole lot better once I can get cleaned up, and put some warmer clothes on. Being this cold and dirty is just draining."

At first, they weren't sure how they were going to get cleaned up. They knew that their water was limited to what the store had in bottles, so they used baby wipes to wipe their skin clean of the mud and blood. However they sacrificed a gallon of water to rid their hair of the filth. Ethan suggested that from then on they would either have to keep their hair clean or go melt some of the snow. The drinking water was now off limits, except to drink.

Madison suddenly lit up as they were putting antibiotic ointment and bandages on their cuts, "You know what? We could also melt snow to keep the toilets running."

"That's a great idea."

She smiled, "I know."

He laughed, "You are positively glowing with modesty."

"Do I detect sarcasm?"

Ethan gave her his best offended look and then laughed. It was good to hear him laugh.

After combing their hair, Madison secured hers in a loose ponytail and they went and found some clothes. They best they could find this time of year was jeans and a couple of long-sleeved shirts. They broke open packages of socks and underwear and found some dry shoes. Then it was time to get to work.

"Madi, how about this? The first thing I'm going to do is clear out most of those shelves in our new home and make some room. I'll keep a couple of them in there for storage or whatever, but while I'm doing that, how about you go do some grocery shopping. Get whatever you think we are going to need."

"What about things like milk and yogurt?"

"Yeah, I'll get some coolers since we still have ice. That stuff isn't going to last forever, so we might as well enjoy it now."

"We should find a propane stove so we could have some hot food sometime."

"Yeah, but we'll use that sparingly. We are going to have to get use to eating some things cold. But hey, cold Spaghettios were a way of life when I was in college. Anyway, just make sure to get lots of water. Just fill up some carts and we'll unpack them once we are locked up for the night."

"Okay."

*****

Madison spent the next couple of hours filling up cart after cart of food and drink. She knew that they had a least a couple of weeks to enjoy the milk, yogurts, and cheeses before they went bad. So she filled up a cart of just those items. She also grabbed some deli meat and salads. As cold as it was, she didn't think they would rot nearly as fast as the dairy.

She stocked up on canned fruits and veggies, soups, tuna, and chili. Cereals, power bars, granola, and dried fruit also topped her list. She grabbed juices, pops, and gallons and gallons of water. She couldn't help herself when she put beer, wine coolers, cookies, pop, chocolate bars, and chips into the cart. Breads, pastries, fresh fruit and veggies she took in moderation. It was only a matter of time before those items would disappear into moldville.

By the time she was done, Ethan had already started to stack their provisions on the shelves. There were several coolers that were filled with ice that he must have gotten from the ice machine. "Do you want some help?"

He looked at her as if he was feeling guilty. "I know I said we would start unpacking once it got dark, but we need the room. All these carts aren't going to fit in here."

"Well, that's fine. Do you want help anyway?"

He shook his head. "No, you still have more shopping to do."

Madison sighed heavily. "You've got to be kidding." She scanned over her inventory. "I can't imagine that I forgot anything."

"Oh you didn't, when it came to food." He smiled at her. "I was thinking of things like a can opener, plates, spoons, garbage bags...things like that."

Madison frowned and dragged her feet back to the cart row. She looked back as she pulled a cart from the supply, "You know there was a time I would have enjoyed this, but you made it work!" She hollered back. She couldn't see his reaction but she could hear him quietly chuckle.

"Just think of it like you were buying a whole household but without the electronics."

She brought her cart in front of the store. "Do you want a lawn mower then?"

"Whatever, just don't forget the can opener."

"Love you too, ass."

Chapter Twenty-Four

Sam, Kathy and Justin

August 8th

Justin was really starting to doubt their traveling companion. There was something about Sam that he didn't necessarily trust. He had told them he was a policeman from Washington State, returning from vacation in Texas. But there was something else he couldn't quite put his finger on, a gnawing suspicion that Sam wasn't telling the whole truth. And the fact that he simply let Jillian throw herself to the wolves, so the speak, didn't help improve his opinion of Sam. Granted he didn't see it happen, but he wouldn't put it past him based on first impressions.

In some ways, Justin thought they would be better off moving on without Sam. And even though there were some advantages to having a second pair of eyes, Kathy seemed to be coming back. She hadn't said anything since her outburst during his argument with Sam, but he knew she was coming back to him. Slowly but surely. She could, no she would be his second set of eyes.

Justin felt Kathy move against him and he sighed with relief. It was good that she was no longer comatose, walking around like she was in a dream. Having her be aware would be so much better for them both. They were sitting on the dirt floor with their backs to each other for support waiting for their fire to die. The flames weren't nearly as high and even from their sitting position, Justin could see Sam on the other side dozing. It was a restless sleep, full of turns and whimpers. Justin suspected it was more than the shadows that disturbed his sleep. Sam was a haunted man.

The warehouse was starting to lighten up. He could see all the way to the far walls in a dull gray haze. The one side of his body was warm from the fire and on the other he could feel a distinct cold. Snowflakes fell through the roof all night, but up until that moment their size had not impressed him nearly as much. These flakes were easily the size of his thumb print. As soon as he was sure there was enough light, they would leave this place in search of better shelter, hopefully without Sam.

Sam suddenly sat up, panting. He looked around and forced himself to catch his breath, but then his eyes settled on his far wall. And Justin watched as Sam smiled. He glanced around Sam's massive body to see what he was smiling about and frowned when he realized there was nothing there. And he watched as Sam stood up, never taking is eyes or smile off of that spot on the wall. "Hello, Abby."

Justin's frown deepened. And he stood up, almost causing Kathy to fall over. "Sam? You okay, buddy?

Either Sam didn't hear him or he chose to ignore him. "Abby. God, I'm so glad to see you!"

"Sam, who are you talking to?"

He nodded, and shook his head a few times. "So everyone is gone?"

"No? There are survivors?"

"What about Sandra?"

Sam listened for a moment, and then bowed his head and sobbed. "Yes, I understand."

Justin had had enough. He was more convinced than ever that they needed to get away from Sam, but he also had enough human decency to make sure Sam had a plan of his own. He walked around the edge of their now hot coals. The fire wasn't necessarily putting off any protective light at this point, but Justin still felt better staying near to it. When he reached Sam, he put his hand on his massive shoulder, and Sam instant jerked away. "Sam. What is going on?"

Without even looking at Justin, Sam responded, "Abby says we can't stay here."

"Well yeah, I kind of wanted to talk to you about that. Kathy and I were thinking...wait. Who the hell is Abby? Isn't she the girl you watched die the other night?"

Sam looked at him like he had grown another head, "She is an angel, Justin."

"An angel?"

"Well, two nights ago she was a girl, and then those things killed her, and now she is an angel."

Justin again put his hand on Sam's shoulder. It seemed almost like a risky move but he couldn't think of anything better to do at that moment. "Okay. We've been through a lot the past couple of days, but Sam, I didn't see anyone. You weren't talking to anyone..."

He jerked away again. "That is because she is MY angel. Despite everything that has happened, she is here just for me to make sure I get out of this." He hung his head low, "But what's the point, everyone is gone."

Justin instantly felt sick. This wasn't the first time he heard this. They heard it from Jillian, but she was crazy, and now he was hearing it from a man who talked to angels. The most mature and logical side of him told him not to pay any attention to the rants of the crazed and traumatized. But then there was also the side of him that believed Sam and Jillian and he knew that side was taking over as the bile rose in his throat. "Everyone, Sam?"

"Except two. There are others, but not in Helena....now that Jillian is gone to. What happened here is just the start of it, Justin."

"Only two?" Justin swallowed hard; trying not to throw up. "Did this Abby say where these two people are?"

"SuperMart."

"You've got to be kidding me." But Justin saw a bright side to situation. If he remembered right, SuperMart was on the other side of town. He hoped Sam was wrong, and that they would run into people on the way there, but if they got there without seeing anyone, SuperMart would be a good place to set up camp if they could lock it down securely. If two other people were there, then so be it. If it was empty, well all the better for the three of them. There would be enough supplies and food and water to last them until they could figure out what to do with themselves.

Justin looked to where Kathy was sitting, but she wasn't there anymore. Instead she had ventured out to the door. It was daylight, but she was shivering in the doorway. "Unbelievable."

"What? What's wrong?"

Justin and Sam stepped away from their coals and joined her at the door. A cold wind blew across the white landscape. It had snowed all night and it showed. It was going to be a long walk to SuperMart, but it was the best option for them. Kathy stepped out, her red hair whipping across her face, and the snow covered the top of her hiking boots. "I don't think we have a lot of time. We should get going." She started walking away from the warehouse just as the red coals turned ash gray with Sam and Justin following behind her.

Chapter Twenty-Five

Madison and Ethan

Several hours later, Madison was about to drop dead. She had visited every department in the store and had brought back everything from clothes, to baby wipes, to bedding and kitchen supplies; medicines, personal hygiene products, dog toys, brush, and a large dog bed, even board games to pass the time. And buckets, just in case, God forbid, they couldn't leave the room to go to the bathroom.

Every time she returned with a cart, her disdain for shopping only increased. She wanted so much to tell him it was his turn to shop, but she knew that it really was going to have to be team effort to get through this. Plus he was so busy, and he was actually making their little space look pretty cozy. He helped her a couple of time with some larger items; a futon, a small table and a couple of chairs, a dresser, even a recliner. The last things he went out for were a tool kit, nails and screws, a few guns and ammunition, and hunting knives. Personally she was hoping never to get close enough to stab someone, or something.

Madison returned with the last cart load she was planning on getting. It was full of more candles and lighters, a propane stove, propane bottles, oil lamps, a wall mirror, and some fake plants. Ethan questioned her when he saw the waxy greenery.

"Well, I thought it would make it a little more homey."

He raised his eyebrows. "Homey?"

"I figured if this is where we have to be for a while, I'm going to enjoy looking at it at least."

"You know, it was a good idea." He kissed her forehead. The sun was just begging to set. "Have you seen outside lately?"

"No."

Ethan grabbed her hand and led her around the corner to the main door. The snow had accumulated up to a foot on top of the frozen parking lot lake, and was falling harder than ever. The sky was no longer a bright white. Instead it was a dark shade of gray that held all the warmth of a corpse. The world around them was dark, white, and cold. And it was completely obvious that the sun was beginning to set already. It was confirmed that the days were indeed getting shorter. It was going to be a long night.

He was standing behind her, hugging her close. "You see. Those fake plants are about all the green we are going to be seeing for a long time."

"I don't want to look at this anymore. It's depressing."

"Yeah, I know what you mean. Let's go back. I think the dog already settled down on the bed you brought her."

"You definitely don't have to ask me twice. Let's pull the gate down, make up the futon, and get some sleep. We can tackle the piles of stuff any time."

"I'm on it."

They covered the futon bed in red and green flannel sheets and topped them with the sleeping bags and a couple of heavy blankets. The thermometer Madison had brought in read a cool twenty degrees.

They figured they had at least two hours before darkness completely set in and the creatures would show up. They held onto the hope that they wouldn't show up at all, and they could catch up on some sleep, but they also knew that they could do it tomorrow if need be.

It didn't matter that the air was cold. They buried themselves underneath the layers of heavy fabric, and pressed into each other's body, taking in all the heat they could. It was plenty, and they drifted off into a deep, dreamless slumber.

It didn't seem like much time had passed, however, when Madison opened her eyes and found herself submerged in darkness. She pushed the blankets off of her head and saw that it was minutes away from being completely dark. Madison lay there, staring at the tiled ceiling.

She wasn't completely sure what had disturbed her in the first place. She felt so tired, she was sure she could have slept through anything.

Sighing heavily she turned on her side, facing the gate. The dog was standing there, staring off into the store. Her tail was swishing back and forth. Something had caught her attention.

At first, fear spilled into her body, causing her to start to shake. Maybe the creatures had arrived, but the dog was acting the complete opposite than the night before. She wasn't cowering in the corner; she didn't seem afraid at all. Rather she seemed quite excited.

Madison listened to the night air, straining to hear the distinct clicking sounds that seemed to accompany the creatures, but all she could hear was the cold wind outside. The dog looked back at her, and seemed to smile before turning back to the store. "If you have to go to the bathroom, you're out of luck, pup, at least until the morning. There is no way in Hell I'm opening that gate before then."

The dog started to whine, but it didn't seem to be out of fear. Instead the mutt began to prance.

"What's going on?"

Madison turned to see Ethan trying to sit up, still groggy from sleep. "I don't know what's got into her. Something is happening."

Instantly he became alert. "Are they back?"

"I don't think so. She isn't scared."

The dog trotted over to their bed and then back to the gate. "That I see."

"I told her if she had to go to the bathroom, she was out of luck."

Ethan smiled and laid back down and stretched. "That's funny, but if she does shit in here, you are cleaning it up."

"Yeah, we'll see." Madison began to relax and rested her head on the pillow. The shadows were making their way into corners of the room, but kept at bay by the few strategically placed candles. She was just beginning to close her eyes again when the dog suddenly launched herself into the middle of the bed. Her front paws landing directly onto Madison's chest, causing her to gasp for air.

Ethan jumped out of bed and tried to grab for the dog's collar. "Damn dog! I'm going to..."

Madison pushed the dog off of her and swung her legs over the side of the futon. Her chest was a little on the sore side where the dog had landed, and she sat there trying to rub out the tenderness. The wind must have gotten stronger because it started to rattle the gate at the entrance where they had broken all the glass.

The dog avoided Ethan's hands and jumped off the bed, returning to their own gate and immediately began barking. Off in the distance the dog was answered by an urgent call for help. There was someone at the gate. Someone was rattling the gate. Not the wind. A person.

"Oh my God, Ethan! Did you hear that? Someone is out there!"

Ethan was already raising their barricade, and running down the front aisle. The closer they got, there could hear three separate voices, two men and a woman, that were very close to sounding panicked. They obviously knew about the creatures, and darkness was already upon them. Yet, Ethan and Madison didn't even think twice about their own safety, being out in the store where there was a chance a creature could be lurking. The prospect of seeing other people outweighed any concern for their own well-being.

Being that they ran out in only their stocking feet, Madison and Ethan slid on the tile as they tried to stop at the gate in a scene that closely resembled a young Tom Cruise in his underwear. Any other time it may have been humorous.

The woman was in tears, "Hurry! Let us in!"

Ethan and Madison saved their questions until later, and immediately set to work at unlatching the giant gate.

All three of them were talking at once, urging them to work faster and harder. Madison was close to snapping back that they were going as fast as they could. But she also more than understood their fear.

"Do you hear that?"

Ethan and Madison lifted their heads and found the sound. The creatures had arrived.

"Oh my God! They're here!"

"Open the gate! Open the gate!" They started shaking the gate, almost trying to claw their way through.

"Damn it! Stop moving it!" Ethan tried to hold onto the pins and they shook it repeatedly out of his hands. He finally grasped the last one, "Get ready to come underneath!" He raised the gate up about three feet, thinking it would be easy to slam back down if need be.

The woman was nearly pushed through opening by the two men. Madison looked up just in time to see what looked like a million red bulbs racing up on them. She knew they were the eyes of hell. She couldn't see anything beyond the hate and rage in their depths and it was all directed towards them. "Hurry!"

One of the men rolled his way into the store and the other started to crawl underneath, but suddenly he was jerked back into a mass of black. Ethan didn't even wait to see if he would come back again. The creatures were too close, close enough to touch, and from what he could see the man simply disappeared into the night. Ethan slammed the gate down and pushed the pins in. The shadows on the other side eyed them with disdain, but did not fight the barricade.

The woman screamed and tried to pull the gate back up. "Justin! NOOOOOOO!"

The man who made it through pulled her away from the gate. "Kathy, it is too late! He's gone!"

Kathy pulled herself free of his embrace, and turned to Ethan. "Open the God Damn gate!"

"You know I can't do that. We can't risk the chance of one of them getting in." He started stepping backwards, away from the gate and the hysterical woman. "We should go...get away from the gate." He started back to the store. "Follow me."

She looked back through the gate. The creatures were virtually invisible, except for the angry eyes, but their dark bodies made the night look like it had a current. "But he could still be alive!" She ran past Madison and the man to Ethan. "You bastard! What if he is okay?"

Ethan stopped and looked at her. Her eyes were big and were begging him. He realized that he had not actually seen what the creatures do once they get a hold of a person, so there was a part of him that wanted to believe that there was indeed a chance that he was still alive. But after everything he had seen, and the fact that the three of them were the first people he had seen in two days, he knew that he it would be wrong to give her false hope. "You know, and I know he isn't."

"But he has to be!" All at once she crumbled to the floor like someone hit her in the stomach with a sledgehammer. She let out the most painful sob that Madison had ever heard. And tears began to flow out of her eyes like a dam had broken. Madison noticed for the first time that she was clutching a teddy bear.

The man who came in with her squatted down and picked her up, cradling her like she was a tiny baby. "He was her husband." He almost seemed without emotion, but Madison knew that whatever they had gone through was enough to drain him of that luxury. He nodded to Ethan. "Lead the way man."

They began a slow walk back to their sanctuary. Madison hung her head. The way he said that the man "was" her husband made it much more real, much more final, and much more terrifying than actually seeing him dragged off into a swarm of demons. She briefly imagined being in Kathy's shoes, and her heart broke into thousands of excruciating sharp shards. She would be lost without Ethan. She didn't know how Kathy would be able to survive this.

Chapter Twenty-Six

Madison wrapped a blanket around Kathy's shaking shoulders and offered her some water, but Kathy didn't acknowledge her presence. She couldn't blame her for that. In between shoveling Chef Boyardee raviolis directly from the can to his mouth, the large black man had explained in the past few days, Kathy had not only lost her son and now her husband. No doubt she was traumatized. "What about food, honey? Are you hungry? You should eat." Kathy only pulled the teddy bear closer to her.

"It is such a shame too. We just got her back." He wiped his mouth on his forearm and then took a long drink from a gallon of water.

Ethan had just returned from venturing out into the store. He dropped a pile of clothes in front of Sam. "These should fit." He sat down on their futon directly across from him, "What do you mean you just got her back?"

Sam set his empty can down at his feet and then stared at his hands as his fingers danced with each other. "Well, I never met their son. Apparently he was killed at this house in the hills. Understandably she is devastated. But from the moment I met her she has been like that." He cocked his head in Kathy's general direction. "She is just in her own, sad little world, and then this morning she spoke for the first time."

Madison sat next to her husband. "What did she say?"

Sam shook his head and shrugged, "Well, Justin and I weren't exactly seeing eye to eye at the moment. I was pretty close to slugging the guy, but she told us to shut up, and something about them responding to anger and fear. I mean now that I think it about it, it makes sense, cuz the angrier the two of us got, the more excited they seemed to get."

Madison kneeled next to the pile of clothes and removed what was intended for Kathy. "If you two don't mind, I'd like to help her change into some dry clothes."

"Come on, Sam, you can get changed in the main store."

The men got up and walked around the corner, but not before Sam gave one last glance to Kathy. He sighed heavily and then continued to follow Ethan.

Madison kneeled next to Kathy and smiled sweetly. "Okay, we should get you changed. If you need my help, I will help you." Kathy didn't respond, so Madison gently removed the blanket from around her shoulders. She then reached for the teddy bear but Kathy clutched even harder to it. "It is just for a minute, Kathy. Just long enough to get you changed. We don't want you to get sick." To her credit, Kathy loosed her grip even if she didn't acknowledge her in any other way.

Madison removed the teddy bear from Kathy's lap like it was a delicate family heirloom, and took a long look at its sweet face. "This must have belonged to your son." She saw the tears well up in Kathy's eyes. "I'm so sorry. I didn't mean to bring up unpleasant memories."

"Boo."

Madison blinked. "I'm sorry?"

"Wyatt named the bear Boo. He got it when he was a baby, and would just laugh and laugh every time we played peek-a-boo with the bear. And before we knew it, he was asking for Boo."

"That's a sweet story." Madison set the bear down beside her and helped Kathy out of her shirt, but as the shirt cleared her head, the tears were flowing freely.

"Oh my God!" She wailed. "They are both gone! What am I supposed to do without them?"

Madison looked at the woman sitting next to her in her bra and wet shorts, and then pulled her in to a hug, and smoothed her hair. "I know. I know. I can't imagine what you are going through. You have every right to be upset."

Kathy jerked her body away for her embrace and looked at her coldly. "Upset? You think I'm upset? I just lost everything that mattered, and you think I am simply upset?"

Madison sat back on her heals, "Kathy, I'm sorry. It was a poor choice of words..."

She laughed sarcastically. A laugh that made Madison very uncomfortable. "A poor choice of words? Yeah. I would say so." The tears and sadness suddenly had disappeared from her eyes, but were replaced with resentment and anger. She stood up and started pacing in their small space. "You get to keep your husband, and you get to go on a shopping spree to make yourself a nice secure home while I watch monsters literally suck the life right out of my little boy and drag my husband to his death, and listen to innocent people being ripped apart limb by limb and you have the nerve to say I'm have a right to be upset as if the right was even being doubted. You stupid bitch..." Her voice started cracking with emotion. "I'm not upset. I'm devastated. I am overwhelmed with grief. I have lost every reason to live, and I hate that I'm still here!"

Madison hadn't realized that Kathy was forcing her to walk backwards until her back hit the wall. Kathy was leaning into her, and there was nowhere for her to go. She could feel her hot breath in addition to the chill coming off her skin. "Kathy, I'm so sorry. I didn't mean anything by it!"

Kathy bared her teeth in a wicked smile and put her arms on both sides of Madison's head. If Madison didn't know better, she would think Kathy was a vampire as she leaned her head closer to her. But then suddenly a pair of large black hands were on Kathy's shoulders and were pulling her back. Madison watched as Kathy seemed to deflate right in front of her. All her angry, if not evil, energy seemed to leave her as she allowed Sam to put her back in her chair.

He helped her into the dry shirt and handed Boo back to her, which she immediately clutched to her breast. He turned accusing eyes towards Madison. "What did you say to her?"

Madison stepped away from the wall to rid herself of the feeling of being trapped and turned her back to the main store...there was more room to run if need be. She didn't like the way Sam was looking at her and as he took a step towards her, she took one more step away and crossed her arms across her chest, instinctively protecting her heart. At the moment her heart was overwhelmed with emotion. Not only was she growing more and more uneasy of their "houseguests," she felt a deep sadness for their loss and her heart ached for them. But sadness and fear conveyed vulnerability, and she didn't want him to know that she was vulnerable.

"Nothing. I swear."

"I see. Well I want you to understand something. I'm all she's got left, and she's all I got left. If you hurt her, you hurt me. And trust me. You don't want to hurt me. Someone hurt me before this all went down...and well she didn't have to worry about no damn shadow creatures."

He looked back to Kathy and then returned his leering stare to Madison. "I sure in the hell have nothing else to live for than her now. So it really wouldn't faze me to rid her of you if you start causing problems."

Madison's blood went cold, but it froze when Sam took three long strides towards her. Her plan of using the store as an escape if the need arose froze right along with her blood. She couldn't move as Sam leaned in close to her and inhaled deeply from her hair. Then his lips were close to her ear and she trembled. She could hear a quiet snicker as he took pleasure in knowing that she was indeed vulnerable. She failed; he knew she was afraid. "I kind of like it here, you know. It's warm. There's plenty of food and water. It's safe. And the scenery, well I'm not going to complain." His breath was hot against her ear, and when his lip intentionally brushed against her ear lobe, she jumped, but still could not get away from him. He chuckled again and finally took a step away from her. "So how about we keep this little talk just between us. I think it would be a very bad idea to bring Ethan into our secret." His smile was brilliantly white as he walked back and pulled his chair close to Kathy and sat down. It reminded Madison of a great white shark.

Madison remained glued to her spot in a state of shock. He silently sat next to Kathy, absently rubbing absent Kathy's shoulder. He tapped his foot to his own silent rhythm. Madison could not imagine how he could just sit there so calm and cool while she was standing there reliving his threats that happened only seconds ago. Mr. Hyde was gone, and sweet, mild-mannered Dr. Jekyll sat before her, but she didn't trust it.

She had momentarily forgotten about the monsters outside, and was only concentrating on the monster in front of her. She had forgotten about her back being towards the dark and when an arm curved around her waist she screamed and turned to fight her assailant and managed to punch him squarely in jaw before she realized that he was her husband.

"Whoa! Whoa! Madi! It's me! It's me!"

She immediately put herself in his arms and to his credit he forgivingly and protectively put them around her. "I'm sorry I scared you. My God, you are shaking. Are you okay?"

Somehow he managed to turn her around and she could see Sam over the shoulder of her husband. He wasn't smiling anymore, but was watching them with the eyes of the wolf. Funny how she kept comparing him to animals. To hunters. To killers. She swallowed hard. "I'm sorry I hit you. You just startled me. And I'm just cold, and scared. Very, very scared." At least she was honest about that part.

Chapter Twenty-Seven

Madison hadn't really let Ethan get more than a few feet from her side, and as he held her close in the confines of their sleeping bag, she forced his arms even tighter around her. If he sensed something beyond what she told him was wrong, he didn't let on. Instead he snored loudly into her ear.

Sam and Kathy were using camping cots that were set up on the other side of their small space. Madison knew that neither of them were asleep. Kathy probably wasn't capable of closing her eyes and letting her mind rest long enough to fall asleep. She imagined instead that she was replaying old family movies in her mind over and over.

And Sam was staring at her in the dark. She was sure of it. And she was sure he was smiling. And whispering to himself? She frowned and adjusted her head so that she could use both ears, but she was still struggling to hear what he was saying, so she sat up a little as quietly as she could and without disturbing Ethan much. He simply moaned and then turned over to his other side. His movement momentarily silenced Sam, but after a minute she could hear him again, and much clearer.

"I know."

"Abby, I don't know what's come over me."

"I can't help it."

"What's the point? It isn't like there are any laws left. It is every man for himself. The only person I need to answer to is me."

"Abby, no. I need you."

"Come back!"

"Abby?"

"Abby?"

Madison lowered herself to her pillow again and pulled the blankets tight around her, but she could not stop shaking. She tried so hard to justify their actions; their intimidation and the dangerous aura that surrounded them were simply natural responses to unspeakable trauma. At least that is what she tried to tell herself.

However, as the minutes passed her sympathy was melting away and was being replaced by an intense realization that not only would they have to survive the shadows, they would have to survive Sam and Kathy. Of all the people that could have showed up at their gate, they ended up letting monsters in while keeping shadows out.

It was true time seemed to have sped up, but every moment they were in her presence was painfully slow. It was being aware that the Grim Reaper was on your heels, but never knowing when it was going to be your last breath.

*****

Sam stared at a space formally occupied by an angel. That particular corner seemed darker in the absence of her light. "Abby?"

Across the room, he could hear Madison. He knew she was awake and that she was listening but he did not care. He was pretty sure that he had her exactly where he wanted her...well not quite, having her beneath him would be best. Ethan would need to get out of the picture eventually, but for now that wasn't his main concern.

"Abby? Please?"

She wasn't coming back. He could beg and plead for her, but she was beyond his reach now. He was given the wonderful gift of Abby and he threw it out along with his sense of humanity. But humanity didn't seem to apply anymore. What consequences where there now?

Sam could finally admit to himself that he had always had urges. He imagined that every living person had urges. People wanted to be selfish by nature. They wanted to take the easy road and have instant gratification. They didn't want to work hard, and more times than not they would suppress the urge to tell their boss to go to hell and would instead smile and ask them how the weekend at the resort was? Did they catch any fish?

Why? Because there were consequences. Tell your boss off? You don't get to keep your job. Don't have a job? You can't pay your bills. Can't pay your bills? You lose your house…and so on.

People chose to be fake and to live the lives they thought they had to live. They honored their parents and loved their neighbors. They were gracious, forgiving, charitable and faithful because they believed it bought them one-way tickets to heaven. But Sam figured Heaven wasn't an option for him anymore…for any of them really. Sam figured they were already in Hell, and what kind of consequences could there be in a place where sin was so strongly encouraged? Rewarded even.

So, killing Lisa was the start of him not really giving a shit anymore about consequences. Well maybe he did at first, and that is why he ran, but little did he know he was running right into the arms of Hell, and Abby was Heaven's last effort to bring him back. Heaven failed. And once Abby realized that, she left. Of course Sam would miss her, but not giving a shit anymore really had its perks. Sam suddenly felt free, without the weight of suppression, and it was more fun. A lot more fun.

"Good night, Madi."

Across the room he could hear the sharp intake of breath, and Sam smiled like the cat that swallowed the canary.

Chapter Twenty-Eight

"Ethan, they need to go."

"Go where, Madison? We can't just send them out there. The roads aren't even passable by foot anymore, and even if they could walk through it, they would never make it to safety in time. There is only a couple hours of daylight now..."

"We haven't been attacked since they came, so maybe they've moved on."

Ethan pulled the zipper on his parka higher, and took another sip of coffee, letting the warmth slowly travel down his throat. "Uh uh. I'm convinced they are just watching and waiting for us to do something stupid. Like going out there..."

"Ethan. Please..."

"What is going on? Why do you want them to leave?"

"Shhh...keep your voice down, okay?" Madison looked out into the store and could see Sam and Kathy picking through what was left of the fruit. Most of it had gone bad, or had froze. Fresh food was now a thing of the past. "I just can't deal with them. Kathy is...and Sam is so.... Look, I just think that they should make their own way now. We can make sure they go with plenty of supplies."

"I'm sorry you feel that way, honey, but we can't just send them away. It would be...I don't know...inhumane of us. I couldn't sleep, let alone live with wondering if they made it or not."

Madison sighed heavily. They had been with them for almost a week now, sharing their food, their space, and making Madison nervous. She barely slept. She was always on guard. She barely talked, afraid to say the wrong thing and set one of them off. She avoided being alone with either of them at all costs. And she knew that Ethan had to be wondering why she had suddenly become so clingy. He had to be wishing by now that she would just give him a little space.

"Okay. I can see your point." Not really. "But, maybe we could at least separate ourselves from them? I mean it is a big store, and we know those things aren't getting in, can't they just find their own little corner of the store? I just want some space."

Ethan chuckled. "Oh...I see. You're horny."

Madison gave him a firm but loving shove and he fell backwards on their bed with his hands up in mock defense. "Ethan!"

"Okay! Okay! I'll see what I can do, Madi. Sam and I will figure it out."

"What are we going to figure out, Ethan?"

Ethan and Madison both looked up. Sam was leaning against the door jamb to what they all now referred to as their apartment. They were so startled by his silent approach that neither of them answered right away and Ethan scrambled to sit up.

Sam took a bite from probably the last apple and smiled, "Well? What are we figuring out?"

Madison immediately adverted her eyes away from him, but Ethan wasn't at all threatened. "Hey there, Sam! We were just talking that we were kind of missing our privacy and we thought that maybe you and Kathy might want to consider setting up in another part of the store. There are plenty of supplies here for all of us, and it might be better for all of us to be neighbors rather than roommates."

Sam pushed away from the wall but kept his smile. Madison wondered why Ethan didn't find that smile nearly as menacing as she did. "Is that so?"

"Well yeah, man. I mean, you two are far less likely to get tired of us if we had at least a few feet separating us, right?

"Yeah, well, I thought we were becoming one big happy family. But, you know, I get it. You guys are married and probably want to fuck once in a while."

Ethan flinched. "Come on, Sam. It isn't like that. We are just trying to think of what is best for everyone."

"Yeah. No, no worries. I get it, man. The mute and I will just set up a cozy little place in the tire center or something. Speaking of Kathy, have you guys seen her? I kinda lost track of her there for a minute."

Ethan shook his head.

"Madison? You seen her?"

Madison briefly met eyes with Sam and then quickly found something else to look at while shaking her head.

"Huh. Well, I guess I'm going to go find Kathy and tell her the great news of our eviction."

Ethan sighed heavily. "Yeah, okay. Well, when you find her, you guys come back and we'll eat. We'll worry about the move tomorrow." Sam didn't answer and walked away angrily.

Madison stepped up behind Ethan and wrapped her arms around his waist while he watched Sam stomp off. "That went well."

Ethan snorted. "Yeah...I guess you can say that."

Chapter Twenty-Nine

Ten minutes later Ethan and Madison had just started their daily card game when Sam returned alone. He looked nervous to Madison and that gave her a sense of satisfaction, but then she felt shame. No matter how scared of him she was, she knew she should never take joy in someone else's discomfort. Doing so would be going against everything she ever stood for.

She also sensed a change in Ethan. Maybe he got just a glimpse of Sam's true nature with his reaction to the move request, and he now avoided Sam's eyes right along with Madison. Maybe he finally realized that if he did make eye contact he was opening himself up to evil.

Madison never wanted to believe that people could be evil. They may have bad moments in their life, but Madison chose to believe that people were mostly good. Maybe she was naïve. And Sam was showing her the light.

Ethan played his hand, while Sam paced. "What's going on, Sam?"

Sam stopped pacing long enough to look annoyed that it took a few moments for them to acknowledge him, "I can't find Kathy."

Both Ethan and Madison stopped what they were doing and looked at him in search of sincerity. "What?" They both asked.

"I can't find Kathy! What the hell is wrong with you two? Get up and help me look for her!"

They had every reason to worry about Kathy. She retreated into the deepest and darkest parts of herself and no amount of coaxing from any of them could touch her there. She carried the stuffed animal with her everywhere she went as if it was a part of her body. They tried to take the bear from her once, and she screamed as if they had amputated a limb. So they had given it back to her as the only source of comfort they could provide her.

Kathy slept most of the time, didn't speak and ate only when the hunger pains became too intense. But she did cry. She would cry alone and in the cot next to Sam's during restless nights. She would cry while she bathed and while she ate, and Madison was pretty sure she cried in her sleep. But she never made a sound. Not a whimper. It was the most silent agony, and she was going through it alone.

For the first few days Sam and Ethan took turns watching over her, concerned about her mental stability, but Madison knew they were all starting to slack off, falling into a routine. Hell, they even thought that Kathy was coming into her own routine. Wake up. Cry. Sleep. Mourn. Cry some more. Sleep. Eat. Sleep. Cry. Sleep and repeat. In Kathy's case, falling out of routine was definitely a bad thing.

Ethan was talking to Sam and then he turned to face her. "We are each going to start on one end of the store, the sides and the back and work our way to the middle. One of us is bound to come across her."

Madison instantly felt her stomach knot up. She didn't want to be anywhere alone and vulnerable. She glanced at Sam, but he had already started down the hall towards the pet care isles. "Ethan, can I please just come with you?"

Ethan sighed, and Madison sensed some slight annoyance with her. "What is going on with you, Madi?"

She bit her lip, "Nothing, I just...things just don't feel right. I really don't want to be alone out there."

He cupped her chin and forced her to make eye contact with him, "You are going to be fine. There is still plenty of light," He smiled, "and if it makes you feel any better, you can take your trusty baseball bat. Right now our main concern should be Kathy and making sure she is okay."

Madison weakly returned his smile and bowed her head. Ethan retrieved the bat from the wall and handed it to her. "You start at the back of the store and we'll meet back here before it gets dark, okay?"

She swallowed hard. The lump in her throat stayed, making it harder to breathe. "Okay." She watched him trot down to the rotted frozen meat. She whistled for her closest friend. Once she felt comfortable enough and trusted her enough, she had finally let Madison get close enough to look at her collar and tags and Madison learned that their four legged companion's name was Hope. How appropriate that Hope survived the shadows. "Come on, Hope. I guess it is just you and me. Do you think that maybe you could play Lassie for a minute and find Kathy?"

To her credit, Hope started prancing and headed off into the store. "Lead the way, Hope. Lead the way."

Chapter Thirty

She could hear them calling her name. Even though they were close, they sounded far away to her. Their voices were muffled by the fog in her head. Every now and then a light would show on the clouds of her mind and she would remember she was still living. She was reminded that she still had a heart beat; she still had flowing blood, and a soul. But that light always dimmed quickly and she always went back to feeling numb. She imagined herself as a ghost on one side of eternity while her husband and beautiful baby boy stood just on the other side. But she was trapped in her human body, in what was left of the living world, powerless to join them until she broke through.

The light always kept her from taking any drastic measures, but like the days they were surviving in, that light was fading a little more every day. Hope was fading, and she realized that she would never be okay, never feel whole, and never would have the desire to keep going. Now was the perfect opportunity to escape the chains of life.

Kathy had spent the last few days contemplating the best ways to take care of business. At one time she considered doing the other three a favor and burning the building down, but she decided that doing so wouldn't necessarily be fair to them. If they wanted to keep living in hell, who was she to stop them? When they were ready they would each do it in their own way. It was only a matter of time.

She considered opening the gates and offering herself to the shadows. She knew they were still out there. Sometimes when she couldn't sleep, she would watch them. They no longer attacked the building, they had no need to. The shadows knew that eventually they would all go crazy and they would have their chance. For now they just waited.

Ultimately Kathy decided that wasn't the right way to go either. She would not let them have the privilege of taking her body. They may have already taken her heart by stealing her son and husband, but she wasn't going to offer them anything more.

So she started exploring all the other popular ways to take your own life. She considered the pharmacy and putting herself to sleep with a toxic cocktail of bleach and aspirin. She considered the sporting good department with its guns, knives, ropes, and fire starters. They all seemed painful, slow or messy. No. None of them would do. Her plan was something else. Something special. And could it really be considered suicide if she wasn't the one to pull the trigger? In the end it wouldn't be like suicide at all.

*****

Madison held the bat in front of her, holding its thick wooden base so tightly it seemed to become an extension of her arm. She rounded each corner apprehensively, not so much concerned about the shadows. If she was being completely honest, she would rather encounter one of them over her roommates.

She thought about what she would do if she actually encountered Kathy, or even worse Sam. Kathy was dangerous because of her grief. She was resentful and angry just from the fact that she lived and lost everything. But as dangerous as Kathy could be, she thought she might actually have a chance to defend herself. A blow from the bat would at least immobilize her long enough that Madison could get away.

Running into Sam would be another matter entirely. She suspected he was very angry with her right now. He probably thought that it was her idea to evict them from the apartment. Of course, he would be right, but it was not a good thing for him to know that. She wondered if Kathy's disappearance wasn't just to buy them a little time in the apartment. Or maybe it was just a ploy to get Madison alone and her time was up.

If that was the case then the bat would be pointless. She could hit him and he would smile and just keep coming. Sam was a big man who embodied strength itself. If he wanted to hurt her, he could and would do it and there would be nothing she could do to stop him.

The bat would not be enough. She needed something with a little more power. Something stronger. Something special. She wasn't sure what she could do to protect herself until she found herself face to face with SuperMart's limited gun selection.

Madison looked through the glass display at the few hand guns that rested there. She contemplated whether or not she could actually shoot someone, but decided that if it came to her life or Sam's, she would have no problem with ending his. And she knew that she would not just wound him by shooting him in the knee or shoulder. No, she would shoot to kill and never give him another opportunity to frighten, intimidate, or threaten her again.

After a quick look around, she took the butt of her bat and smashed the glass.

*****

Sam heard the crash of glass but didn't care. He was pretty confident it wasn't a skylight. So whatever it was, it was far enough away that it didn't concern him at that moment. He had enough to think about, enough to plan. It was time to downsize their little family. Kathy was just becoming too much of a liability, too much of a distraction, and Ethan…well Ethan was a cool enough guy; downright kind even. But unfortunately for Ethan, he was also protecting the one thing Sam wanted to get to. It really was too bad, but he had to go.

He did feel a little sorry for Kathy. He wanted to take care of her, and he thought that if he did, he would also have control of her. But Kathy couldn't be controlled. She was ruled by emotion, and had no fear of consequence. He chuckled because he realized just how alike they were. But with this knowledge of no consequences came great power and Sam knew that only one of them could have power.

Sam wanted to be the first to find her, and he wanted to kill her, partially to put her out of her misery, partially to just rid himself of her. He would make it look like an accident, or even better a suicide. That would be believable. They all knew that she wasn't stable. No one would doubt that she would kill herself.

It was such a shame too. Kathy was beautiful. He had considered keeping her around just as something pretty to look at, and eventually touch, but when he looked into her eyes, he didn't see the vacant stare that everyone else saw. Sam knew that Kathy was thinking and planning. What? He didn't know. But he didn't trust it. Kathy was probably unstable enough to kill him while he slept. He would take care of her before the opportunity presented itself to her.

Ethan would be a little harder to deal with. Sam really didn't have anything against the guy, but there could only be one alpha male. He didn't need or want anyone else telling him what to do, when to do it, and where to live. And he didn't need anyone standing between him and Madison.

He supposed a few weeks ago, if he passed Madison on the street, he probably would pass by her without a second thought. That's not to say that she was unattractive. She was short, which made him feel big, and she had the types of curves he could appreciate, but honestly it was her eyes. They were bright, yet deep pools of green and they captivated him. He would happily drown in their depths given the opportunity to just stare into them. And now that the selection of women was limited, he would have to go with the sane, beautiful yet average girl, rather than the mute insane model.

Sam suddenly realized that Madison was alone in the store. She hadn't left Ethan's side since their last little talk and he knew she had a big hand in getting him kicked out the apartment. Now Sam was torn between finding Kathy and finding Madison just to remind her who was in control. The more scared of him she was, the better.

Maybe he would just let fate take control just this once. Whoever he ran into first would be the lucky girl.

*****

Ethan jumped at the sound of the glass explosion. Explosion may have been an exaggeration because the sound lasted for a fraction of a second, but at the same time it seemed to linger in the air. He stopped to listen but then continued on once he was confident that it wasn't from the shadows coming through a skylight. He was sure that it was from within the store.

He didn't like the feeling he had. Even before the shattering of the glass he was feeling uneasy. He didn't like that Kathy was missing. He didn't like how quickly the light was fading. He didn't like that Madison was on her own. Ethan understood that they separated out of necessity, but Madison was carrying something extra on her shoulders lately. The confidence and independence that started to shine through her at the beginning of this ordeal faded with the arrival of Sam and Kathy.

Ethan had tried to talk to her, but she would dismiss the conversation with one hand and cling to him with the other. He didn't know what had happened, but he knew that something did. And Sam's outburst about the move only convinced him that whatever had happened between Sam and Madison wasn't good.

He called Kathy's name again and glanced at the skylight over his head. He was greeted with a set of red eyes. He frowned deeply. The shadows hadn't bothered them since the night Justin died. And the most interesting thing was that it still wasn't completely dark outside. This concerned Ethan. It was indeed getting dark, but Ethan could see the outline of the shadow in a way he had never been able to before. It was the shape of man. A large, bloated by death man, but a man just the same. He didn't have any describable features except for the glowing red eyes, but Ethan imagined that if he had mouth, it would be smiling at him at that moment.

Ethan suddenly had an urgency to locate Madison. If he found Kathy and Sam along the way, so be it, but Madison was his number one priority. He wanted to get her back to the apartment and lock the gate behind them. In the pit of his stomach, he felt that it was going to be a very bad night. With one last look at the overhead shadow, he rounded the chip aisle and headed towards the middle of the store, feeling its hate on his back the whole time.

*****

The metal of the gun cooled her fingertips as she traced its outline. She bit her bottom lip as she looked around again. The chill from the metal had entered into her heart and she shivered, but still she picked it up and felt its weight in her hand. It felt heavy to her, but she wasn't entirely convinced it was because the gun itself was heavy. It was because she was heavy with guilt. She felt dirty just holding a gun. She knew what were her intentions were. And no matter what the circumstances were behind using the gun, Madison would never feel right about it.

Even so, she sighed as she started to search for bullets. A girl has to do what a girl has to do to survive.

*****

Kathy smiled. It was something she hadn't done for over a week and the sensation of feeling the corners of her lips and her cheeks moving up felt strange and unfamiliar. She shook it away feeling like she was betraying the memory of Wyatt and Justin, and continued to watch Madison examine the gun from her hiding place. As Madison moved away from the gun counter, Kathy stalked her like a cat stalks a mouse. When the time was right; when Madison was ready, Kathy would pounce.

She involuntarily smiled again, but didn't fight it. Within the hour, she would see her family again. How could she resist the urge to smile?

Chapter Thirty-One

Madison set the bat down at her feet and held the gun in front of her. She kept her back close to the shelves. "Kathy?" She suddenly realized that she had been whispering instead of calling out. Maybe it was because she had a feeling that she was being watched. Hope had left her on some doggy errand, and Madison was really starting to wish for the extra set of eyes and ears. Cold sweat was dripping down her back and she shivered.

"Kathy?"

She took a deep breath and wiped the sweat out of her eyes and rounded the corner only to literally run into someone. Startled, she cried out she took a step back and looked up. Kathy was smiling at her.

"Hello, Madison."

"Oh my God! Kathy! We've been looking everywhere for you." The sigh of relief that was about to escape from her lungs was caught in her throat, delayed by a continued feeling of unease. Not only did Kathy talk to her, she was smiling. Madison had never seen Kathy smile before, but somehow she doubted that even in her happiest of moments did Kathy ever smile like this. It was sad, yet cunning at the same time. It showed too many of her perfect white teeth.

"Really? Oh well, you found me!" She held her hands out playfully. She started to slowly circle Madison. "You know, I don't think I ever told you that the night this all started, I was going to leave Justin. I had found out that he had been having an affair with some bitch named Amanda."

"I'm so sorry." She wanted to be sincerely sympathetic, but it was hard when Kathy was smiling as she talked about her husband's infidelity.

"We were arguing on the side of a God forsaken country road when Wyatt disappeared. So off into the woods we went and ended up at

Grandma's house." She giggled. "And then that bitch had the nerve to tell us that it was our fault the shadows came. Hell of a night. Really."

"What do you mean it was your fault?"

"She told us that all of our hate and anger woke it up. What a crock of shit, huh?" She suddenly frowned. "So essentially it is my fault that Wyatt and Justin are dead, at least according to her." One of her never-ending supply of tears trickled down her cheek and she swiftly swiped it away and shook her head, "Like I said, crock of shit."

Madison kept her eyes on her as Kathy continued to circle her. She held the gun at her side, really not wanting to have to hurt Kathy, and wanting to keep her talking in hopes that Ethan would come. "What else did she say?"

"Well...I kind of withdrew myself from the situation once Wyatt was gone, but I remember her saying something about staying in the light." She laughed. It was a beautiful and magical sound that Madison was sure at one point was the delight of everyone around her. "Kind of funny, huh, when you think about it. If the shadows are everything bad...hate, anger, fear...how do you fight those things but with love. And what is love? Light. Get it?"

Madison shook her head. "How can the shadows be hate, anger or fear? Those are abstract things. They aren't something you can see, or touch. They don't have physical forms, and we've seen the shadows."

Kathy stopped circling her, and cocked her head. "Are you sure? I mean think about the world before the shadows came. Turn on the news, and all of those things would manifest right before our eyes. We saw hate, and fear, and anger every damn day, and we did nothing about it." She shook her head again. "But you know none of that matters at this point, don't you?"

"Why not?"

"Well, honey, despite everything that Justin did, I still love him. I want to be with him again, and God knows that I miss Wyatt. I am no longer hateful, angry or afraid. The shadows no longer have control of me. I have control now. And I know we will be a family again."

Madison's grip tightening around the gun. She looked into Kathy eyes, trying to predetermine her next move. "Kathy, I know everything seems dark right now..."

Kathy stopped and raised a finger to her, "And getting darker every day. Haven't you noticed? Soon there will not any light but the light you produce and eventually you will either run out of ways to make light or they will adapt. They will get stronger, Madison. You know how I know?"

"How?"

"Let's just entertain the thought that Alice was right, and honestly, I think she was. Let's just pretend for a minute that anger and hate and fear are what caused this. Our marital spat and our little boy's fear of his family falling apart woke up some ancient spirit that none of us were capable of understanding. And what do we do to things we don't understand?"

This was starting to make sense to Madison and a light went on behind her eyes, "We fear it. We mistrust it."

"Typically yes. Exactly. Typically it takes an incredibly strong person to stand up to the things we don't understand and fear in an effort to understand. Most of us are not strong enough. And our fear spreads from one person to the next like a virus. Hate is contagious. It usually starts with one and everyone else goes along with it because they are just too scared to question it."

"Yeah, I understand. It makes sense."

"You think you understand, but I've seen these things up close. The more scared we are...the angrier we are at each other...the more excited they get. They get stronger. They feed off of the ugliest of our human nature, and in their presence there is plenty of ugliness to go around."

Madison frowned. She didn't want Kathy to keep talking anymore. She didn't like the direction she was going. But she had to admit, it was making more sense than she wanted it to. Common sense had no place in a nightmare. "What are you saying, Kathy?"

She smiled again. "Don't you see? They are the virus. And those of us who have our defenses down, who are too scared to stand up to it, are overcome by it. And so the virus spreads."

"Wait a minute! Are you saying that all those shadows are....are...people?" She shook her head in denial.

"People who have essentially been overcome by everything ugly about being human. And when the lights finally do go out...you all are going to be too afraid and too confused about what to do next, the virus will find its way in here because your defenses will be down and you will do something stupid. I mean, that is exactly what they are waiting for. And I know they don't have long to wait."

Madison bit her bottom lip, trying to absorb everything that Kathy just said. It was heavy and difficult to swallow. It was just too much to process all at once. But one thing stood out to her. Kathy had said "you all." She looked up and noticed that Kathy was closer to her. "What are you doing?"

The sad smile was back. "I'm sorry, Madison. I've done a lot thinking lately and I cannot live in a world without light or my family."

*****

Sam had to give her credit; she was smart. Everything she said made sense to him. Her theory explained where all the people went, and why when the shadows attacked, there was no sign of them afterwards. It was because the victims became them. But that would mean his visions of Abby were all wrong. If she became something, then she wasn't dead. How could he be seeing her as an angel if she still roamed about alive as a shadow? But were shadows alive? Maybe her soul, defeated by her fear became the angel and the rest of her, engulfed by ugly emotions became the shadow? But did it even matter? Abby abandoned him…

He crouched low on the cold floor and inched a little closer. In the remaining light of the day, he could see something glint in Madison's hand. With realization, he smiled. Things were working out exactly the way he wanted them too, and he didn't have to lift a finger. By the end of the night, it would be just Madison and him in their cozy little apartment.

*****

Madison frowned. "I don't understand, Kathy. You are going to be just fine. In time…"

She was interrupted by a sound coming from deep within Kathy's throat. It was almost like a growl that was getting louder by the second. She took another step back just as the growl erupted into a primal scream. Madison finally had an opening and turned on her heal and started running through one of the main arteries of SuperMart. "Ethan! Ethan! Oh god, Ethan, help me!

Behind her, she could hear the swift footsteps of Kathy giving chase. Madison did not stop, and did not turn around but pushed herself even harder to run faster. She had a feeling that her life depended on it. "Ethan, help me!"

Suddenly she was hit hard on the back of her knees as Kathy threw her body forward, knocking her to the ground. She landed hard on her stomach, knocking the breath out her. The gun in her hand went skidding across the floor, stopping only a few feet from her. She tried to get up in time to reach it, but Kathy was climbing up her body until she was straddling her back. Madison screamed as Kathy took a fist full of her long brown hair in her hands and started pulling.

As Madison struggled, Kathy pushed her face hard into the floor. Blood instantly burst from her nose and between her eyes. It pooled directly below her face as it was brought up and then smashed forward again. The world went dark for a split second until she realized that Kathy had lifted some of her weight off her back, almost intentionally, and she realized that she would be able to toss her off of her back wild bronco style.

Madison rolled to the side that brought her closer to the gun and Kathy fell off her. That gave just the amount of time for Madison to scurry over to the gun and point it at Kathy. Kathy was on all fours, panting and still growling from her throat.

Madison wiped the blood out of her eyes with her sleeve, but the warm thick liquid continued to stream down. It blurred her vision, but slowly she rose to her feet while keeping the gun on Kathy.

"Madison?!"

His voice instantly gave her relief. "Ethan! Over here!" He was close. Thank God.

Kathy rose to her feet and took a step forward.

"Stop right there! Don't come any closer! Why are you doing this?"

Kathy didn't stop. Instead she slowly inched forward. "I told you why."

"Please, Kathy! Just stop! We'll figure this out. I don't want to have to hurt you!" Madison realized that she was crying now, and it mixing with the blood, created a runny, red flood on her face.

"Madison, honey, you are going to have to kill me. No matter what, no matter when, I'm going to keep coming for you."

"Why?!" She stomped her feet in frustration. "Ethan!" She could hear him running towards her and she quickly looked behind her. She tried to smile, but it hurt and then turned back to watch Kathy. When her eyes finally focused forward, it was too late. Kathy had pounced on her once again, knocking Madison backwards. She could barely hear Ethan yelling for them over Kathy's growl and the sound her fingers made through the air as she tried to claw at Madison's face.

She tried to push her off, tried to turn but she was already weakened from the head blows from before. And as Kathy's hands made their way to her throat, the world started getting hazy. She gasped and clawed at Kathy's hands, but couldn't pry them away. She suddenly realized that the gun was between them.

Madison hesitated, hoping that Ethan was close enough he could spare her from what she was thinking, but she couldn't count on his getting there fast enough to keep her from passing out. His running footsteps still sounded miles away. Madison closed her eyes and as the pressure on her throat increased, so did her finger pressure on the trigger.

Madison didn't hear the shot, but suddenly Kathy collapsed on her chest, her hands now loosened from her throat. Something warm was seeping through the clothes between them and Kathy was getting heavier by the second. Her face was near to Madison's cheek and she could feel her breath against her skin. It was shallow, and hot. And just as Ethan reached them and grabbed Kathy's shoulders to lift her off, Madison swore she heard Kathy say her last words.

"Thank you."

Chapter Thirty-Two

Madison was against the end shelving unit with her knees drawn up to her chest. She had her face buried in the crease, and could smell the rich copper smell from her blood soaked shirt. Some of it was her blood. Most of it was Kathy's. With great, painful effort, she raised her head and looked at Ethan. He was kneeling over Kathy with his fingers to her throat. "Is she...is she..." She croaked.

Ethan looked over to Madison and slowly nodded.

Madison heart shattered and she sobbed. "Oh, God!" She started rocking herself, still holding the gun across her knees.

Ethan stood just as Sam jogged up. He was panting, "I was in back looking for Kathy when I heard the shot. What the hell happened?"

Ethan tilted his head behind him and Sam peered around him. "Oh my, God! Kathy!" He took one look at Madison's bloodied face and his eyes began accusing her, "What the hell did you do?" He stepped towards her and Madison attempted to scramble away.

"She came after me! I had no choice! She wouldn't stop!"

Ethan stepped between him and put his hand on Sam's chest. "Hey, now, Sam. There is no need for that. All she did was protect herself! I saw the whole thing happen. Kathy attacked her! Look at her face!"

Sam swiped Ethan's hand off of him. "Of course you would say that! She is your damn wife!" Sam kneeled next to Kathy's body and brushed a strand of hair off of her cheek. And then he looked back at Madison as Ethan helped her to her feet. "And I know how badly you wanted us gone. So, what now? You going to kill me too?"

Ethan protectively put Madison behind him. "It didn't happen like that, Sam! We all knew she was crazy with grief!"

Madison's voice was weak, "She said she wanted to be with her family."

Sam threw his hands in the air. "Ahhh, well in that case, you should be feeling really good about yourself. You did her a great favor, didn't you? Do you want a pat on the back or something? For fuck's sake, just call it what it is! Murder!"

"No!" They were starting to draw a crowd. In every visible skylight, they could see the shadows. They seemed to be pulsating with excitement and energy. And Madison remembered Kathy's words about how they fed off of the ugliest parts of people. Murder was truly ugliness in its purest form. Madison shivered. "We need to calm down. They can feel us. We can go back to the apartment and talk about things, but we need to go now!"

Sam swept his hand over Kathy's body. A dark pool had formed around her back. "And what? Leave her here?"

Ethan took Madison's hand and slowly led her back to the front of the store. "We are going to have to deal with her later...when there is more light." He looked back at Sam who hesitated to follow, "You need to come with us, Sam. I need to talk to you about something else too. It is about them."

*****

Sam looked up at eyes that stared back without blinking and slightly smiled as he followed behind. He made sure to walk slowly and with his head down so that if by chance they did look back, they would see just how devastated he was. Completely heartbroken.

Poor, poor Kathy. How perfect it all went. Here he was planning on killing Kathy himself, but sweet little Madison took care of the dirty work. Yeah, he was a little worried when Kathy started to bash Madison's head into the linoleum. And for a moment, he considered intervening. He didn't think Madison actually had it in her to pull the trigger, but God love her, she pulled through for him. He had to choke back a giggle of delight.

And Kathy...she was a genius. Forcing Madison to kill her? It was just too good! Sam couldn't see Kathy sitting in some corner, cutting her wrist. She had to have had a bigger plan. She had to have known that by having Madison shoot her that they were going to start turning on each other, and maybe by doing so, she was doing them a big favor.

They would just kill each other off until there was only one. And one didn't stand a chance against the shadows.

Sam looked back up at the shadows. There was a group of them at every skylight. He tried to look past their bright eyes to see if there truly were people behind the darkness. If they were people, they were too far taken by the "virus," as Kathy called it, to be recognized as people anymore. Their humanity disappeared behind their ugly human nature.

Sam frowned. He knew that he had set free all of his ugly impulses. He didn't even try to hold them back, and moment by moment, his humanity was being overtaken. He didn't really care at this point because he knew that if he didn't take care of himself then he would become a victim. It was every man for himself now. And he would be damned if he let one of those things take over him. He was not going to become a shadow, no matter how dark his soul became.

As he reached the apartment, he stopped in the threshold to watch Madison strip off her blood stained shirt. Her back was to him and her skin glowed in the candlelight as the room filled up with the smell of instant hazelnut coffee. To the right of him, someone cleared his throat and Sam met eyes with Ethan. Instantly, Madison covered up her bra with her arms, and even in the dim light he could see her blush; maybe out of embarrassment, maybe out of fear.

"Sam, pull up a chair. Do you want some coffee?"

Madison quickly pulled a clean shirt over her head. Sam tried to hide his disappointment. "No, man. I'm good." He pulled a metal folding chair closer to Ethan and watched as Madison retreated to the other side of the room.

Ethan held his coffee in his hands, letting the warmth seep through the glass and into his skin. He was staring into the darkness of his cup when he finally spoke. "I saw them."

"You saw who?"

Ethan lifted his eyes. "Them. The shadows. They were out early tonight and I saw one."

Sam shrugged. "Okay. We've all seen them."

"No, we haven't. We've seen their eyes. Nothing more. But tonight, I saw one for what it was. It was a person."

Sam wanted to tell him that this was all old news. Kathy had known long before him. But he couldn't without revealing that he had been watching and he let Madison kill Kathy without doing anything to stop it. So, he would let Ethan have his great moment of revelation and play along. Sam leaned forward in mock captivation, "Really? When? How could you tell?"

Ethan leaned in, trying to keep the conversation private. "When we were looking for...Kathy...I looked up and there was one standing directly over me. I could see all of it. It wasn't blending into the dark like they normally do because it wasn't even dark yet."

Sam looked into his hands. "And you could tell it was a man?"

"Yeah...but no. I couldn't tell that it was a man, but I could tell it was human. A really big human."

"What, big like me?"

"No. Bigger. I mean, it was huge, but it had arms and legs and a torso. It was standing erect like a man, but it didn't have a face...except for those eyes."

"Wow. I can't believe it!" He leaned back in his chair and folded his arms while mentally patting himself on the back. Ethan was buying his act. Sam was impressed with his own acting abilities. Obviously he had gone into the wrong line of work.

"Believe it. But you know, that isn't what concerns me most. The fact that they were out before dark, that changes everything, doesn't it?"

"Maybe. But then again, they haven't attacked us, so maybe it doesn't matter."

"No. It matters." Both men looked up to Madison hugging herself. Neither of them had noticed that she had joined them in the circle. "It matters. They are adapting. And if you think about it, they haven't had to adapt much. We are lucky to have even an hour of full light each day. At this rate, they will be out there all the time." She started crying.

Ethan stood up and hugged her while quietly hushing her. Sam rolled his eyes. All he needed was the last female to be weepy.

"Shhhhh. Madi, it is okay. You've gone through a lot today."

She pushed away from him. "You don't understand. They haven't attacked us because they have gotten smarter. They are just waiting for us to screw up! To make a mistake!"

"Like what kind of mistake, Madison? They can't get in, and none of us are stupid enough to go out. So what could possibly happen?"

Madison stared at them for a moment before shrugging. "I don't know. Kathy said they were like a virus, and viruses spread. What make us think we are immune?"

Sam stood up and studied the store for a moment. He turned back to them and shrugged. "Because we are in here, and they aren't."

Chapter Thirty-Three

Madison sat cross-legged on the bed and stared out into the store. Sam and Ethan had left at first light to take Kathy's body into the back store room. She was alone with Hope, and she was cold. Although she knew part of it was due to the fact they now lived in a world that was almost void of the light and warmth of the sun, and a landscape that was covered in deep frigid snow, she knew part of the chill she was experiencing was coming from within her. She had taken someone's life. And when Kathy took her last living breath, a part of Madison had died right along with her. Yeah, it was cold outside. But death was so much colder. She shivered as she felt the deep chill creep into her bones. She tightened the blanket around her shoulders and pulled her knees up as the light began to fade. Within an hour, she had watched the sun rise and set.

Hope was whimpering from her doggy pillow, so Madison encouraged her to join her in the bed. Instead the dog ignored her and began to pace. Her behavior was making Madison extremely uncomfortable. In the past, when the dog acted strangely, monsters entered into her life... of both the shadow and human varieties. "Come, Hope. Come on. You are starting to scare me."

Just then, there was a deep rumble from under her bed, almost like a giant beast growling. Madison jumped to her knees, almost scared to look, but Hope crawled under the bed with her tail between her legs. From within the store, the shelves were swaying and the earth moved below them. All the cans they had stockpiled in the apartment fell off the shelves and joined in the symphony of chaotic noises coming from the store's interior.

Madison was frozen. It occurred to her that they were having an earthquake, but every drill she had ever had in school, every instruction on how to stay alive escaped her memory. She was on all fours and the bed beneath her swayed in a sickening attempt to replicate a carnival ride.

She could hear the guys yelling. And she could see them running towards her. "It's coming down!" Wait. Was that what she was hearing them say? No. No. She refused to believe that fate would be so cruel to add that nail to their coffins. Nonetheless, fate laughed at her with a sickening snapping sound and she watched in horror as a major supportive beam plummeted to the floor behind them. That was followed by skylights shattering and being transformed into glittery rain as they crashed to the floor.

Somehow she had found her way to her feet and she staggered to the gate. "Come on! Hurry!"

They were almost to the apartment when there was a deafening cracking sound from above them, and a major portion of the ceiling came down in front of her eyes. She ducked into a fetal position on the floor and shielded her face from the dust cloud that followed. And even as the world stopped shaking, she was slow to stand up or even look out for fear of what she would see. She hesitantly raised her head from her chest and slowly stood up. Once she realized she was holding her breath, her first exhale came out as a gasp.

Snow was swirling and mixing with particles of dust creating a dirty storm cloud above a mountain of rubble. Madison took unsteady steps towards the destruction, frantically searching for Ethan and Sam. She wanted to call out to them, but her voice only croaked. She looked above and was horrified to see that the store was open to the night. They were now open to *them*.

Madison quickly scanned every direction in search of the red eyed monsters. Once she was confident that they were not stalking her, but knowing that they could be attacking them at any moment, she was inspired to start moving. She just didn't know where to start. The scene before her was daunting.

Finally her voice found her, so she called out as she started digging with her hands. She didn't feel the shards of glass slicing into skin, or when she broke most of her thumb nail off. She just had to find Ethan. "Ethan! Ethan! Answer me!"

To her left, she heard groaning and she rushed to start digging. Within a few moments she found a hand that was attached to an arm, but it wasn't Ethan's. She continued to dig, hoping to find Ethan close by. Sam was almost uncovered when she found Ethan's arm. He didn't squeeze her hand when she grasped it. He was so cold. "Ethan, baby, I'm coming. Ethan!"

Sam was pulling himself out, obviously in pain. He groaned. "Madison...we got to get in....they'll be....they are coming." He collapsed. "Madison. Please! Help me!"

"I have to get Ethan out!" She almost had his arm uncovered. He still wasn't moving. She lifted a heavy piece of concrete off of him and realized that is where Ethan ended. Meat hung from his upper bicep in heavy flaps from where it separated from the rest of his body. She stared at the motionless part of her husband as the scream built up into her lungs. And once it reached her throat, it just went on and on. She collapsed to her knees even as the scream continued. And when she could scream no longer, she sobbed. "No! No! No!"

"Madison. Madison! He's gone. I'm sorry...but we got to go. We can't be out here."

She just sat there on her knees, staring at her husband's wedding ring as Sam pulled himself across the floor towards the apartment. He froze when the screaming started again, only this time he knew it was not Madison screaming. Sam knew the scream all too well, and yet it chilled his blood and stopped his heart as if it was the first time.

He turned and grimaced so that he could look back at Madison and look for the shadows at the same time. Bracing his weight on his hands he could now see why his leg was paining him so badly. About two inches below his knee, his own bloody bone was poking through his jeans. He collapsed onto his back and took some deep breaths. He raised back up and could see the first of the red eyes in the distance.

"Madison! They are here! Come on!"

She acted as though she didn't even hear them screaming. Shit! This was not the time for her to be pulling a Kathy. She was supposed to be stronger than that. Madison may very well be the last woman on earth, and she was not going to disappear into herself the way Kathy did. He wouldn't let her. He picked up a small piece of rubble and forcefully threw it at her back. She immediately jumped and shook her head as if breaking from her trance. She suddenly seemed to notice that the creatures were coming upon them and she quickly stood up and started towards the apartment, but then stopped and turned back to Ethan's arm.

"Madison, no!" Sam was already back to pulling himself towards the apartment. Madison ignored him and reached for Ethan's hand. She hesitated but then grasped his ring finger and pulled the titanium band off. She kissed the hand before running back to Sam.

"Madison, please help me!"

Madison looked down at the man lying on the ground with his leg bone sticking out. His breathing was labored from his efforts to get back to the apartment. She thought for a moment of all the times he terrorized her, and now she had the power to keep him alive or leave him for the shadows. Madison looked back and saw that the shadows were just on the other side of the rubble. They would be on them in a matter of moments.

"Please, Madison. We are so close. Please! Please!"

Maybe it was the desperation in his voice, or maybe it was that the last thing she wanted was to be like him. She would not abandon everything she stood for. She would not let Sam have that kind of control over her. Besides, Ethan would never have wanted her to take revenge on someone. Revenge was so ugly.

She took hold of Sam around his shoulders and started dragging him. He did his best to help her by pushing off with his good leg. He was heavy and it was awkward, but as the shadows crested the top of the rubble, they had made their way across the threshold. She roughly dropped Sam and he groaned. The shadows were almost within an arm's reach when the gate crashed down to the floor. After quickly securing the gate, she stood up straight and was met with the darkest of dark. Slowly she raised her eyes until she was met with the eyes of the demon before her. And there were hundreds more behind this one.

They made no attempt to break through the gate, but they made no move to leave either. The shadows brought a whole new kind of cold with them. Madison wanted to take a step back. She wanted to put distance between her and the frozen hate they saturated the air with.

But she couldn't. Every muscle in her body protested with instincts to just run away. Instead she stared into its eyes.

"Madison!"

Madison closed her eyes, willing herself to be someplace else. Somewhere warm and safe. And when she opened her eyes, for a moment it seemed like her wish was granted. She was no longer in the apartment. Instead she was in a dark, cramped space. She reached her hands up and could feel clothes hanging in front of her. She realized she was in her closet back at home. The feeling she had could only be described as revisiting a distant memory, one that was fuzzy at the edges but still very clear. It was like a vivid dream.

She also realized that not only was she in the back of the closet but she was also standing in the doorway searching for something. As the details of the dream emerged, she discovered that it truly was a memory, only this time, she was seeing it from the outside. She was seeing it from another perspective.

Madison recalled the feeling she had the day she went looking for a backpack; the day they left their home. She remembered feeling like she wasn't alone, and that she was being watched. The memories of the sound, the quiet clicking in the back of the closet, and the snake flooded her mind. And then it hit her! She was seeing herself from the perspective of the shadow. She had been with this shadow before, since the very first day. It was there! Hiding in her closet! And she felt it! And it remembered her.

"Madison!"

She closed her eyes, and opened them again to the red eyes in front of her, standing on the other side of the apartment's gate. Its eyes narrowed and Madison nodded in a silent confirmation that they had met once before. She finally was able to take a step back. But as she did, something grabbed her ankle hard and she jumped away from its grasp.

"Jesus Christ, Sam! You scared the hell out of me!" She fell back on the bed. She had completely forgotten about Sam.

"I'm sorry." His voice was weak and tired. "I just need help. My leg."

Madison looked down at his leg and could see his bone pushing through his pants. It made her sick to her stomach as she remember Ethan's separated arm, but for Sam, she would not show him sympathy...weakness. "That must hurt."

He gritted his teeth in a painful smile. "Yeah. You have no idea."

Madison nodded. She did have an idea, because her heart was broken. But there would not be any medicine for her. She went over to where they kept their small stock of medical supplies. Everything was scattered on the floor, but she was able to locate a bottle of antibiotics and an Ace bandage.

She wasn't exactly sure how to treat a broken leg, but she imagined she would have to put the bone back into his body. That also should prove to be excruciating for him, and in a way that she found disturbing, the prospect of Sam experiencing more pain was very satisfying to her. She sat down next to him and unbuttoned his pants.

"Hardly the time for that, Madison." Madison rolled her eyes, only half believing he was joking. Outside the Shadows were moving, exploring a new territory that was once the inside of SuperMart.

"We need to take your pants off so that I can push your bone back in."

"Seriously?"

"Do you have another suggestion? Would you like me to call a doctor?"

"Shit."

"Yeah. Tell me about it." She leaned back on her heels and studied his leg. "It might be easier for me to cut them off. We should avoid moving you as much as possible until you are stabilized. I'm going to go look for some scissors. I think we brought in a pair."

As she started gathering other things she thought she would need; towels, water, a broom handle to tie his leg to...her thoughts turned to Ethan, and how she couldn't save him. The first tear that fell took away all of her ambition to help the evil man only feet away and she just bowed her head over the cans and bottles that littered the floor. And at the moment, she decided she could really use a hug, so she pulled the supplies she was carrying into a tight embrace and sobbed.

"Madison?"

The last thing she wanted was to hear his voice. All she wanted to do was keep thinking of Ethan, and every moment they had ever shared over the years. She wanted to focus on the way his eyes smiled when he was truly happy, or the way he looked as he watched her walk down the aisle on their wedding day. She wanted to remember his silly imitations of Yoda, Stitch, and the Pillsbury Dough Boy. She shook her head, trying to shake out the sound of Sam's intrusive voice.

"Madison, please! I know how upset you are about Ethan. But there is going to be plenty of time to mourn. Please, help me! I can't do this by myself!"

Madison lifted her head, but didn't look at him. She used the back of her hand to wipe away the tears and bite her bottom lip. Then she took a few deep breaths that burned her lungs. It was colder in the apartment than it had ever been. They were now open to the elements. Their chances of surviving were plummeting by the minute.

But she wasn't just going to lie down and give up. Ethan would want her to keep fighting until the very end. She turned with her supplies in hand and returned to Sam and kneeled at his side. She arranged everything around her and without a word started cutting Sam's pants away from him. And although she wouldn't make eye contact with him, she knew that he was studying her face, "Thank you for doing this. I know it isn't easy for you."

Focusing on cutting the bloody denim around the bone, she sighed. "Don't thank me. A part of me would rather sit back on that bed and watch you bleed to death."

He twitched, obviously jarred and possibly nervous of the fact she held shears in her hand. "Wow. Ok. Then why are you helping me?"

She stopped cutting and looked him square in the eyes. "Because... I'm not you."

"You think you are better than me?" He had an air of defensiveness.

She returned to her cutting. "I think you are not in a position to be arguing with me right now." She squeezed the handle for the last time at the end of the pant leg, and it fell away from his leg. The once shiny silver blades of the scissors now were streaked with blood. "Now comes the hard part."

Sam lifted his head and examined his thigh before he let it fall back down to the floor in exasperation. She rolled up one of her towels and asked him to lift his head again and she placed it under his neck. She could see in his eyes that he thought she was doing it out of kindness, but in reality, she didn't want him throwing his head around and causing a head injury in addition to what she already had to deal with. She took a bottle of hydrogen peroxide and unscrewed the cap. "This is probably going to burn," and she began to pour the liquid onto his wound.

It was hard to hear the sizzle and fizzing of his skin over the moaning and groaning he was making. He was trying his hardest not to yell out, but there was still time for that. Madison restrained a smile from her lips. "Now comes very possibly the hardest part."

He was breathing hard and there were tears in the corner of his eyes. He knew this was going to hurt. She rolled up a smaller towel and held it to his lips. "Here...bite down on this." He took the towel and put it between his teeth and started taking deep breaths through his nose.

Madison was holding her own breath as she reached for the bone. She knew the quicker it was done, the better. "Just like pulling off a Band-Aid."

Sam's eyes look confused for a moment and then a second later they widened in agony. Sweat instantly appeared on his forehead and he screamed through clinched teeth. Outside the gate, the shadows pulsated, excited by the negative energy Sam was giving off. Madison tried to ignore Sam and everything else as she went to work on stitching Sam's skin back together.

But then the gate started shaking, and Madison scrambled away from Sam. The shadows were throwing themselves at the gate, trying to break it down. "Why are they doing that? They've never tried to break in!"

Sam ripped the towel out of his teeth and a variety of cuss words exploded from his mouth. This only encouraged the shadows to ram the gate that much harder. Madison remembered how Kathy had said that the shadows feed off of their pain, fear and anger. She looked at

Sam, and knew he was experiencing all of it at once, and looked at the shadows being motivated to devour it.

She inched her way back to Sam and took his thrashing head into her hands to hold him still. She put her face near him, and although she was upside down to him, she did her best to look him in the eyes. "You need to calm down."

"It hurts so bad!"

Her voice was barely a whisper. "I know it does. I still have to close you up, so there is still going to be some pain, but I can't do it with them rattling the cage. And if you don't calm down, they are going to get in here and that is it!" Sam nodded and took a couple of calming deep breaths.

Once she was confident that he was calm, she took her eyes away from him and looked at the shadows just a few feet from them. They were no longer trying to come through the gate, but they watched her with a combination of interest and disdain.

Then, even though she was tempted to drop his head back down to the towel on the floor, she gently guided it back, determined to keep him calm and serene, and then went back to work sewing his leg back together. To his credit, he only grimaced, but he kept quiet, and the shadows went along on their shadow business. Madison couldn't help but wonder to herself, with no other people to torment, what did they do all day?

Chapter Thirty-Four

After stitching Sam up, and dumping more hydrogen peroxide for good measure, she had brought him a pillow and a couple of blankets, and he had immediately fallen asleep on the floor. He was snoring loud enough to keep her awake if she been able to sleep in the first place. Instead she sat cross legged on the bed and alternated her eyes from Ethan's ring that she rolled from one finger to the next to the spot on the mountain of rubble in the store. If she looked hard enough she thought could almost see his arm.

She was beyond the ability to cry. Her body, her heart, and her soul were numb. With Ethan, she thought there was a chance to survive. But now that he was gone, she was no longer confident. Even before the shadows, she doubted she would be able to survive without him. He was her best friend, her rock, her light, her reason for living. Trying to come up with a new reason was proving to be beyond challenging.

Hope tried to comfort her. She never really strayed more than a few feet from her, and in these moments of quiet, she would lay her furry head on Madison's leg and look up at her with big brown eyes. Madison scratched behind Hope's ears, and sighed. "At least I have you."

Madison looked over to sleeping Sam. He wasn't so bad when he was injured. He seemed half-way human. But his leg and the monster within him would heal. And then it would just be the two of them. He would not be her new reason to live. If anything, he would be the death of her. In the meantime, she would be a decent human being and bring him back to health. Even if it meant the end of her.

She turned her focus back on the wedding band in her hand and closed her eyes. The metal was warming in her palm and she closed her fingers around it. As she did, the warmth from the metal warmed her hand, and the sensation flowed through her blood and traveled up her arm and straight to her heart. Her eyes flew open as a new kind of energy filled the air.

On the other side of the gate, all eyes were on her. The shadows felt the new energy too, and they didn't like it. There was a strange new sound coming from them. The only word Madison could use to describe it was moaning. It was so strange to hear when they had only made war cries in the past. The moaning almost sounded like fear to Madison.

Madison frowned in confusion. She stood up slowly and walked to the gate. The shadows on the other side retreated away several yards. "Strange," she whispered.

Madison shook her head in denial. She had to be exhausted and delirious with grief. Slowly she walked backwards until the back of her knees touched the bed and sat down. The shadows on the other side were watching her every move. She shook her head again and closed her eyes and laid back. She told herself all she needed was sleep. And maybe when she woke up she would find that this had all been a dream. It was the same hope, no...the same desperate prayer she had every time she went to sleep since the blackout. If God had a heart at all, this time the results would be different than every time she woke up since the lights went out.

*****

"Madison?"

The voice seemed so far away, so she ignored it and kept her eyes closed. It seemed like only a couple of hours had passed since her eyes were open and everything still seemed too fresh. Not quite dream state yet. She wasn't ready to face reality. Instead she focused on the warmth that was still in her hand but now had spread its way all the way down to her toes.

"Madison, wake up."

"Why are you whispering?" She still didn't want to open her eyes.

"Because....because something has happened. Wake up." His voice was different. There was a tone of awe and amazement and a little shock.

"I am awake." She pulled the covers up over her head to block the light. She froze in confusion. Wait. Light? Bright light? She slowly pulled the covers down and blinked at the sunlight streaming through the gate. She sat up and looked around, more confused than last night. Sam had pulled himself up to a sitting position against a wall. But he wasn't looking at her. He was staring out into the store, where they could now see Ethan's arm clear as day. The shadows were nowhere to be seen.

"Sam, what is going on?" She was now whispering herself. It was almost like they feared that the sound of their voices would break the spell.

He closed his eyes, bathing in the light. "I don't know."

Madison pushed the covers off and walked to gate. She scanned the destruction.

"They aren't here. They won't come out in the light."

She couldn't believe him. She couldn't even believe her own eyes. "How is there light?"

"I don't know. But can you complain about it? It is sunlight." In front of the gate, small droplets of water were dripping from the jagged edges of what was left of their ceiling. There was a certain degree of warmth in the air.

She shook her head. "I'm dreaming."

"I don't think so. But if you are, you can keep it going."

She realized she had been clenching her fists so tightly that her fingernails were cutting into her. She opened her hands and examined the ring that Ethan's wedding band had imprinted in her flesh. Madison stared at the circle and then went searching for a piece of string or thread.

"What are you doing, Madison?"

"I'm going to look for a something I can use as a necklace, and I guess while I am at it I will straighten up some. By the way, how's your leg?"

He was looking at her with confusion. His head was cocked to the side and his mouth slightly open. "You are going to clean up now? Madison, there is sunlight to be enjoyed! How long has it been since we've been in the sun?"

She stopped and bit her bottom lip. It hurt, another point for reality. "Entirely too long. But I'm not entirely convinced I'm not dreaming either."

"What?" He readjusted himself against the wall the best he could. "First of all, so what if you are? You could at least stop to enjoy a very good dream. And second, I doubt we are sharing a dream. Cuz, let me tell you, if I was doing any dreaming right now, I would be dancing instead of sitting here against a damn wall."

She lifted a section of shelving back to a standing position and began placing the items that were not broken on the shelves. "Maybe we aren't dreaming the same dream. This is my dream and I'm just dreaming of you saying all this. Trying to create logic and reason in a very unreasonable place." She found a spool of black thread and fashioned a necklace out of Ethan's ring. Once the metal hit her chest, her heart was instantly warmed.

"I don't believe it. No. This is real. Something is different. I can feel it. They can feel it."

She paused and then continued carefully placing cans of fruit on top of each other. "They were acting strangely last night."

Sam burrowed his forehead. Tight wrinkles appeared in his dark skin. "What do you mean?"

"I don't know. I was sitting on the bed, just thinking, playing with Ethan's ring, and they started...groaning. Almost whimpering or whining. I don't know how to explain it, really. But they started to back away from the gate. They watched me the whole time as they... they... retreated."

"They retreated? Maybe you were dreaming then?"

Madison shrugged. "Maybe. And maybe I still am."

Sam watched as she continued to stack cans for a few minutes. He could do little more than watch and he was irritated that all of his plans for her were falling apart. "So what were you thinking about?"

Madison stopped what she was doing and tried to remember what she was thinking about. As her memory returned, she smiled and turned around to face him. "Honestly I was thinking about you."

Sam smiled back. She could see him basking in misidentified flattery. "Were you now?"

She walked over to him and kneeled beside him. "Yes. I was thinking just how easy it would be to let you die." Sam's smile slowly faded and something that resembled worry flashed in his eyes. "But that would be wrong...inhumane. No doubt, had it been me with the broken body, you would have left me to die. But I'm not you. Despite everything you have done to me you can be confident that I will help you heal."

"You bitch." Madison stood up and walked away from him to return to cleaning the apartment. "You think you are so much better than me? You don't know anything about me!"

She ignored him. "Look at me when I'm talking to you! Answer me!" Sam then erupted into a vulgar, adult-sized temper tantrum. But Madison continued to ignore him. She was no longer intimidated and confident that he couldn't touch her for some time. For now, she was safe. For now at least.

Chapter Thirty-Five

For the next few hours, Madison kept her distance from him. Every time she came within a few feet of him he would call her a bitch or a cunt or tell her how lucky she was he couldn't get up and beat her ass, but Madison took herself to another place where she could not hear any of his insults. She was in a place where she was safe, at peace, and warm. There was a fire in her heart and she was comforted and protected by it.

As the sun began to set, Sam's anger passed and he just eyed her with mild disdain. Madison almost had the apartment back to its former glory and was going about setting up candles. Maybe the shadows were gone for the day, but they would be back once the sun was gone. As her own shadow passed over him, he offered her small smile. "Madison? I'm thirsty. Can I have some water?"

Without a word, she retrieved a gallon of water and set it down a few feet from him. He looked at the water and then looked at her. When she didn't move to give him the water, he sighed. "I'm sorry."

Madison raised her eyebrows and tilted her head to the side. "For what?"

"Damn it, woman!" He softened his tone as she took a step back. "What I mean is, why do we have to rehash everything? I said I was sorry, and I am. Please, may I have some water?"

The thought of making him beg briefly entered her mind. As it did, the ring around her neck seemed to grow warmer and she put her hands around it. It reminded her that to get through this and remain true to herself, she had to treat the situation and Sam with warmth. She found the broom handle and pushed the water to him. He quickly snatched it up and took a long drink as he watched her.

The sun was down and Madison still felt like they needed more light. She turned and looked out the gate. Several feet from the cold metal, a lone shadow faced her. The shadow's red eyes were wide and bright, and if they were any other color than red, they might have appeared innocent to Madison.

Madison took a step forward, and the shadow moved back a foot. Madison smiled triumphantly and quickly finished the distance to the gate. And then right before her eyes the shadow collapsed. Madison froze. "What?" She whispered.

"What? What just happened?" Sam was trying to peer around her.

"It just collapsed, Sam."

"What?"

She looked back at him. "It collapsed." She turned to the dark lump on the floor. The red eyes were gone, but something was happening to it. The shadow was quivering. Madison looked around to find the other shadows, but they were nowhere to be seen. She walked to the where she could release the door and put her hand on the pin.

"Madison! What are you doing?"

"I've got to know what is going on with it. It is like an electric current is going through it."

"No. You can't go out there! Are you crazy? You'll be killed!"

"I think I'm going to be okay. I will lock it behind me so you will be safe."

"You've got to be fucking kidding me, Madison! You go out there and die and then I'm screwed in here. I forbid it!"

Madison shrugged in defiance and pulled the pin.

"Madison!"

She ignored him again and raised the gate enough that she could slip through the bottom. He was still yelling at her even as she closed the gate behind her. "Shhh. Do you want the rest of them to come? Be quiet." In the dim light, she could see him snap his mouth closed, but he continued to watch her as she slowly approached the shadow on the floor. She stepped over mangled ceiling tiles and twisted beams. Shards of glass crunched beneath her shoes, but everything else was silent.

She was within a couple of feet of the shadow and could see that the electric quivering was actually more like a flowing. The shadow's black body was flowing underneath a thin transparent skin. She kneeled down and reached out. She could barely hear the sound of

Sam telling her to stop over the thumping of her own heart. However, Madison hesitated her hand an inch away from its skin, but after a moment of consideration, she made contact.

Its skin reminded her of a balloon, cold, thin and rubbery. She could feel its thick, oil black "blood" flowing beneath her fingertips. But why did it collapse?

"Is it alive?" Sam had pulled himself   to the gate, obviously with considerable effort. Even in this light, she could see beads of sweat on his forehead.

"Yes. I think so."

"Well, kill it! One less shadow would be doing the world a favor!"

She looked at Sam and then back at the shadow. Even if she wanted to, she wasn't sure how to kill a shadow. And she wondered if she even wanted to at this point. Something was changing. All around them, the energy in the air had changed. Things did not seem as bleak, cold, and lonely as they had a mere twenty-four hours ago.

Madison reached into her pants pocket and pulled out a pocket knife that she had started carrying with her. Mostly to protect herself from Sam and Kathy, but now she was starting to consider its usefulness for the shadow. She opened the knife.

The blade must have caught some light because the glint of the metal immediately caught Sam's attention. "Yeah. That's right. Stab the bastard."

"Be quiet for a minute and let me think."

"What's to think about? You don't get an opportunity like this every day."

"I know. I don't think I want to kill it."

"Have you lost your mind? First you go out there, and now you won't kill the one thing that has been trying to kill you this whole time? What is the problem?"

"Do you think they are still in there?"

Sam sighed and leaned his forehead against the gate. "Is who still in there?"

"The people. Kathy said they are just people who let hate and fear overtake them."

"I don't know. I think they are gone."

Madison bit her lip and rubbed her fingers again the knife's handle. "I think they are just trapped. They don't know how to let go."

"Maybe. And what are you going to do about it?"

"Free them."

Sam closed his eyes and shook his head. "It is too late for that, Madi. Just come back in here if you can't kill it."

"Don't call me that."

He looked confused. "Call you what?"

"Madi." She kneeled down to the shadow again and brought the knife close to its skin. Sam started encouraging her to start stabbing and slicing, but instead she merely poked it with the tip. She stood up and watched as thick, black fluid slowly flowed from the hole the same way water would have left a water balloon with a pin prick. There was so much fluid, and as it started to pool and as it stretched towards her feet, she took some steps back. Not knowing what the liquid was, she didn't want to have any contact with it.

"Madison, maybe you should come back in here."

"Not yet."

"You are just going to sit and watch it bleed out, huh?"

She shook her head. "I don't think it is blood, Sam."

He snorted. "You're the expert now? You know everything about shadows? Just get your ass back in here."

The shadow was nearly deflated, and Madison's breath caught in her throat as a new shape began to form beneath the skin. It began with her noticing a shoulder, hip and legs, and as the last of the fluid drained there was a face of a girl. "Sam!" She half whispered, half screamed.

"What?"

She looked at him and he had his back to her and was leaning against the gate. "Look, damn it!" She stepped around the pool of black and leaned over the girl. The skin seemed to be tight around her small form. She couldn't imagine being able to breathe through it so she started tearing it away from the girl's face. Its skin had felt firm and flexible to her touch when she first reached for it. Now it felt sticky and slimy, and the texture instantly reminded Madison of decay. She held back the urge to gag.

"Is it alive?" His voice held a tone of reluctant hope. He wanted to believe that a human was not only in the shadow but that it also lived despite the shadow.

"It is a girl." She could finally make human skin to human skin contact and she put her fingers to the girl's throat. A pulse was there, strong and steady. "Yes!"

"Oh my God! Get her in here!"

Madison quickly grabbed the girl under her arms and dragged her to the gate. Sam moved away from the gate so that Madison could push it up. As soon as there was an opening, Madison brought her and the girl through and then pinned the gate down.

"Bring her over here. Let's get some water...maybe that will help revive her."

She again dragged the girl over to Sam and then collapsed to the ground, trying to catch her breath. She watched as Sam reached for the gallon of water from his sitting position and then brought it to the girl, and then she watched as he froze. The gallon of water suddenly seemed too heavy for his hand and he dropped both the water and his arm to the ground.

"Sam, what is the matter?"

He was shaking his head. "It can't be. She died. I know she did. She was an angel!"

"What are you talking about?"

"Her name is Abby. I'm looking at a dead girl, Madison. She was an angel. She was an angel!"

Chapter Thirty-Six

The pretty blonde was still and quiet under the covers. Through the night, Madison constantly got up and checked on her, and watched as her chest rose and fell with every breath. The rest of the time, she spent in her chair, quietly thinking and quietly observing.

The darkness was fading again and the light was beginning to penetrate the gaps in the roof. There were steady streams of water through other holes as the snow melted from the roof. The store was sopping wet. And Sam was in a corner on the other side of the apartment, shaking.

He never was able to elaborate on how he knew the girl. He was terrified of her and quickly retreated to his corner. All she knew is that Sam was convinced that this girl had died the first night. That he had watched her die a horrific and painful death and that there was no way she could be here now.

Madison got up again and as she passed the girl, she checked on her and then she went to Sam. He warily watched her approach him and then his eyes went immediately back to the bed. She followed his eyes and then shook her head, "What's going on, Sam? I don't think she is going to jump from the bed and attack you. Look at her. She is comatose."

He also shook his head. "No, Madi," she thought she would let the nickname slide this time in his fragile state of mind, "she is dead. I watched her die. No one can scream like that and live and not only that..." he broke off, almost looking embarrassed.

"Is this the same Abby you were talking to that night?"

"That night? Oh...yeah. She was angry with me because of the way I was behaving."

"Can you really blame her?"

"Abby died. She had to have because she was an angel. She helped me escape the shadows. She saved me from the storm. She directed me here. There is no way she could be here now!"

"Well, then perhaps you are mistaken. Maybe that girl isn't Abby."

Sam seemed to consider it for a moment but then he made up his mind. "No. I would know her anywhere. That is Abby."

"But you said it was impossible."

"I know what I said. It is impossible! I don't know how she is here, but that is Abby."

"Okay, it is Abby..."

"Who's there?" A new weak voice broke into their conversation. Both Madison and Sam froze at the sound until Madison realized it was coming from the bed. She slowly approached the bed with her hands out in front of her. She wasn't sure if it was to let "Abby" know that she would not hurt her or if it was to protect herself should "Abby" attack her.

She was coming from behind her and she didn't think the girl realized it because she was looking side to side searching for her. As she rounded the corner of the bed, the light from the store hit the girl's face. Madison could see where Sam might have taken her for an angel. Despite being covered in black residue, she could see the flawless skin, the pert little nose, and the luminous blonde hair. And as the girl made eye contact with her, her already large, grey blue eyes widened even more in fear. She attempted to scramble away from Madison, but she was weak and could only scoot a fraction of an inch away.

"Who are you? Where am I?"

"No, no! It is okay. We mean you no harm."

She looked worried and looked around. "We?"

"I'm Madison, and the man over there with a broken leg is Sam." She thought that maybe telling the girl that Sam was injured might make her feel a little safer. It sure made her feel safer.

"Abby, it is okay." Sam didn't sound all that convinced that the situation was indeed 'okay' but she had to give him kudos for trying.

The girl looked back at Sam, "How did you know my name?"

Madison sat on the edge of the bed and the girl scooted another fraction away. "Wait. You really are Abby?"

"Of course she is! I tried to tell you."

"Let the girl speak, Sam. Are you Abby?"

The girl nodded, and as much as Madison wanted to believe it was mere coincidence, she couldn't ignore the uncanniness of it. "You are the same girl that Sam has been talking to all this time?"

"I....I don't know what you are talking about."

"Of course you do! Madison, I'm not crazy! She was an angel!"

"Abby, what is the last thing you remember?"

"Ummmm...I remember being at home, and then there was this terrible scream. That's all really. Everything after that is....blank. Well, except I keep thinking of the color red."

"I watched you die, Abby!"

"I'm not dead! Am I dead? No...I'm not dead!" Her eyes seemed to glaze over with a fever of panic.

"You're not dead. Sam, leave her alone. Let's get you cleaned up, and then we can bring you up to speed. Are you hungry? Thirsty?"

Abby nodded. Madison hung a sheet around the bed so that she could have some privacy while she used baby wipes to clean herself and put clean, dry and warm clothes on. Madison helped wash her hair and then settled her back into bed. As she prepared some food for them, she started telling her about the shadows with red eyes, and everything that has happened since.

"You were inside of it, Abby. And here you are alive, despite what Sam wants to believe." She heard him grunt. She could see him struggling with wanting to believe what he saw and carried with him over the past few weeks, and what was in front of him now. "Kathy knew. She said they were people trapped by hate and fear." Madison felt the air in her body leave her hard. "She was right."

She handed Sam and Abby each a bowl of soup. Sam set his down beside him, completely uninterested, and Abby immediately took hungry gulps of the warm liquid. She finished the bowl and then blushed with embarrassed at her understandable lack of manners, she wiped her mouth on the back of her hand. "Sorry. I guess I was more than a little hungry."

"It is okay. I understand. Would you like some more?" She handed Abby her own bowl which she immediately began devouring. "I can't imagine you got a lot of nourishment inside of it."

Abby shook her head. "I don't really remember being inside of it. Although, it seems like I was always eating, but I was never satisfied. And I remember being extremely cold."

"Well, I suppose if they really are all about fear and hate, I can't imagine they would be filled with warm and fuzzy feelings, can you?"

"No. I guess not. Maybe that's why it snowed?"

"Because the world lacked warm and fuzzy feelings, it snowed? I like that."

Abby smiled. It was beautiful and warm. Outside of the apartment, the sun was high in the sky, and the SuperMart parking lot was becoming a slushy lake. Warm and fuzzy was making a comeback.

Madison suddenly felt overwhelmed with internal conflict and sat beside Abby and put her head in her hands. What to do? What to do? Was it possible to get back to the way things were before the shadows? If one person could be taken back from darkness could others be saved as well? But maybe Abby was the exception. What if the only reason is because somewhere deep inside she wanted to be saved and that made the shadow vulnerable? How many gave up on hope and accepted their new dark existence? How many people were more like Sam and less like Abby?

She jumped as a small, delicate hand squeezed her shoulder and she looked up to see Abby's concern. She tried to force a smile and patted the hand on her shoulder. "I'm fine. I think I'm just really tired. Maybe we should get some rest and try to come up with a plan tomorrow."

Chapter Thirty-Seven

"Have you lost your mind?" His voice bellowed with disbelief as he stared at Madison with wide eyes filled with fear. "You can't possibly be serious!"

Madison paced the length of the apartment in front him and Abby feeling like maybe for the first time since the power went out, and perhaps even before that, she knew exactly what she was doing.

Abby had gained strength with food and rest and was sitting on the edge of the bed, nervously wringing her hands. "I don't know, it might work. I mean it did work, but there is a lot at stake for a maybe, you know?"

"It won't work!" He was leaning on crutches that Madison was able to find in the rubble of the store and he pointed one of them Madison, leaning heavily on the supporting crutch. "Forget it!"

Madison kept walking, dismissing their doubts in her mind, "No, it will work. I thought about this all night! If they need me to be afraid to win, then I won't be afraid. You saw what happened with Abby's shadow."

He hobbled over to the bed shaking his head furiously and plopped down next to Abby with a grimace. "Being strong had nothing to do with it, Madison! You just need to accept that this is just the way things are now. We are no longer the top of the food chain. They will live, and some will die, and all we can do is keep trying to survive. Going out there and throwing ourselves at them is not surviving. It is suicide."

She stopped pacing and threw her hands up in the air. "The way we are living now? I don't consider it surviving, Sam! All we are doing is waiting to die. Look around! The store is gone, we have nothing but a gate separating us not only from them, but also from the elements. We might survive by doing nothing, but for how long?"

"So, you are going to go out there, get yourself killed, and leave a traumatized girl and a man who can't defend himself alone here to die?"

"I'm not traumatized." Abby was sitting up straight and listening very closely. "Besides, it might work. She stood up to it, and it released me. She can do it again."

"Abby, no! That shadow just died or something. She had nothing to do with it. Damn it, Madison! You cannot do this! There are just too many risks!"

Madison started pacing again. She had already made up her mind, but she was letting Sam's doubts and fear make her question herself. Could she face them all on her own? She would be alone, Sam obviously couldn't, he was filled with all the hate and anger they could need to satisfy them and Abby couldn't because she was weak and had already been taken. No, it would just be her. Maybe....maybe they were right? And as doubts began to concrete themselves in her mind, Ethan's ring warmed the skin on her chest. Her hand pressed it hard into her heart and she could feel him. She knew his spirit was with her. His love was with her. And he was encouraging her. She knew that he would be her strength and that he would get her through this. Ethan's spirit would not mislead her. He would keep her safe no matter what.

"You can't do this, Madison. You can't."

"Sam, just shut up."

*****

Daylight lasted hours. Even longer than the day before. It only made Madison that much more optimistic as the sun began to set. She stood at the gate and watched for the shadows. But all she could see were natural shadows. It didn't make a difference to her. She had a feeling that they wouldn't come to her anymore. They feared her and they knew they would be defeated by their own fear. No. They would wait for her.

She had spent most of the day talking to Abby since Sam now ignored her. But she didn't need him to talk to her to see that he was begging her to reconsider her plan every time her eyes met his. It was interesting to Madison considering how aggressive and ruthless he was when she first came to know him, but now she saw a great weakness in him. He was terrified of being left alone. But knowing that Sam had vulnerability didn't make her dislike him any less.

Abby talked of her family and how she hoped that they would be uncovered. Madison assured her that they would. She wanted to believe that everyone who had been overtaken by the shadows would come out okay. Unfortunately people like Kathy would not be able to come back. She was overtaken, but only by herself. But neither would people like Ethan.

She also realized that there was a chance that the only reason she was able to release Abby is because Abby possessed the desire within to be released. Yes, she was afraid, but there was a purity and innocence and a general goodness about her that made the shadow that possessed her vulnerable. Madison thought most people would be like her, but she also knew she would come across people like Sam, who used the shadows as an excuse to let their own darkness and the demons within themselves be free. They would not have the will or even the desire to fight back, and the shadow would win.

But as she uncovered more people, she hoped to be able to recruit help. If it worked, she could show them there wasn't anything to be afraid of and they could uncover everyone. She hoped she wouldn't have to stand alone long.

The last of the day disappeared behind the horizon and Madison took a deep breath. It was time.

"I wish you would reconsider. This in an insane plan. We need you here."

Abby scowled at him. "Shut up, Sam."

Sam's face fell. "I think I liked you a lot more when you were dead. You weren't such a bitch then."

"Whatever. Madison, listen, I know this will work. It has to. Just stay strong."

Madison nodded and put one hand on the gate and one hand on Ethan's ring. She felt his strong arms around her, giving her strength. She knew she would need it.

As she lifted the gate she heard Sam give one finally plea for her to stay, but she could barely hear it over her own heart. It wasn't fear that was making it pound so hard that she could feel it between her ears, but rather adrenaline. She had faith that good would win over evil, and she was excited to watch it fall one shadow at a time.

However, as she stepped away from the safety of the apartment and made her way into the interior of the store remains, she became very conscious of the absence of a gate. She briefly glanced back and could see Abby and Sam watching her intently. They both seemed frozen with fear but had found each other's hand for comfort. They seemed miles away. She felt very alone in the chaotic destruction of the store. Alone, but not afraid. She reminded herself that she can't be afraid, so she took several deep, calming breaths.

The sun had set and the darkness caressed her skin like unwanted advances. It felt dirty to her, so they had to be close. She found moonlight and searched the darkness for them, then smiled as she caught the first set of red eyes. And the first set was followed by another, and another, and then more. And as the feeling of being alone was replaced by an awareness of being completely surrounded, she stood a strong stance and waited for their next move.

Somewhere in the darkness she could hear Sam and Abby, they were desperately calling her to come back now; Abby obviously had a change of heart about the success of the plan. She could also hear Hope whimper. But even if she wanted to, she would never make it back. The minute they sensed her doubt, they would take her.

Instead she tried to make eye contact with each and every set of eyes. There were so many, and not one of them were impressed with her boldness. Their eyes narrowed and they looked at each other in confusion. Disdain radiated from them, and the air was chilled by their hate. Their glances to each other gave Madison the impression that they were trying to come up with a plan. How do they deal with a human that doesn't run away?

Madison took a deep breath and clinched her fists at her sides. "What are you waiting for?" She was impressed that her demanding question didn't come out shaky. "Come on!"

The shadows continued made no movement towards her, and Madison frowned in confusion and frustration. "You cowards! Come on!"

"There is no need for name calling, dear." The new voice took Madison by surprise and she whirled around and searched for the source. Her eyes scanned the dark mass, and all eyes remained on her, even those of Sam and Abby who had fallen silent. Then she saw her. The woman glided through the shadows as though her feet weren't touching the ground. She appeared to float through them untouched. In fact, they moved away from her.

Even in the darkness, Madison could see the woman's flawless pale skin, the color of the fresh milk, but as she stepped out of the shadows and into the moonlight, the woman took Madison's breath away. Her long, wavy, black hair draped over her shoulders like a satin curtain. Her thick black eyes lashes fluttered against flushed checks, and when she opened her eyes, Madison could clearly see, despite the dim light and distance, the color of lilacs.

The woman was dressed smart, but sexy with a fitted pant suit. She almost looked like she was prepared for a corporate meeting with white pants that hugged her hips and ended at her pointed red heals. The tight jacket buttoned just below her breasts, but that is where the professionalism ended. She wore nothing under the jacket and the outline of perky perfection panged Madison with jealousy. The woman seemed to be aware of the affect she was having on Madison because her immaculate, full red lips parted and she smiled with pleasure.

Around her neck was a silver necklace that coiled around her like a snake with a single ruby eye staring back at her.

"Hello, Madi. Long time, no see." The voice was breathy and seductive. It promised ecstasy with every syllable.

Madison took a step back, not out of fear but because she could feel an unbearable cold coming off of this woman's skin. Hate and cruelty radiated off of her. Madison could feel the pain of millions and it was nauseating. "Do I know you?" She shook her head even as a sense of familiarity panged her. "Who are you?"

The woman frowned, fronting deep offense, "Now I thought our meeting in the closet would have left more of an impression on you."

She was less than an arm's length away now and she leaned in closer. "Remember? I've tasted you."

Madison swallowed the bile rising in her throat as an image of a dark closet at home resurfaced. She wasn't alone there. There was something in the closet with her. A snake. "You were there."

"Oh so you do remember me, but I suppose I may have updated my look since. Easy mistake." She looked around Madison and waved to Sam and Abby, "Hello, you two! So nice to see you again!"

"Who are you?" Madison demanded a second time.

The woman returned her attention to Madison and smiled again. "I'm Eden. These..." she gestured widely to the waiting shadows "...are MY shadows. And you are beginning to royally piss me off, Madi." In an instant, Eden's lilac eyes change to the brilliant red that the shadows were known for. The smile never left. Madison couldn't help herself and she gasped even as the eyes returned to lovely shade of purple.

"Oh calm down, dear. No need for the theatrics, I was just trying to make sure you know exactly what you are dealing with before you do something stupid." She began circling Madison while lazily fingering the snake around her neck. Madison felt alarmingly vulnerable with Eden to her back, so she quickly turned with her while holding onto her own necklace.

"I don't understand..."

"Of course you don't." Eden stopped and looked at her shadows with pride and sighed contently. "Can you feel it? The sadness and misery of each and every soul? Do you see what happens when you let all your petty little human hatreds take over? I don't know about you, but I find it absolutely delicious!"

Madison clinched her fists. "No! This is horrible! Please let them go!"

Eden's hand rose to her chest to demonstrate how much Madison's accusation wounded her, but Madison doubted she would feel a heartbeat there. She then laughed and rolled her eyes. "Oh sweet, naïve, stupid Madi. I've always been here, but I didn't do this. This is not a hostage situation. These people are what they have made themselves. I do not make people fear. I do not make them act in anger or greed or selfishness. Freedom of choice, baby! How long did you think you all could carry on like this and not have real consequences?"

"We are not all like that!"

Eden cocked her head to the side as though she was deep in thought and sighed, "No, not all of you. Not you." She was fiddling with her necklace again and she turned her back to Madison and studied her shadows. "And that is the problem."

Madison looked back at Sam and Abby and they motioned her for her to run while Eden's back was turned towards her. Unease accompanied this woman as she entered, but the tension was building like a multiple round game of Russian roulette; they all felt it.

Madison considered making a break for it. She could sense that she was quickly approaching the point of no return, but running, at the most, would only buy her temporary time. Eden was timeless. Madison knew that she had been there from the beginning; probably from the first sweet, tempting bite of fruit. There was a snake there too. Coincidence? Probably not at this point. She could feel Eden's ancient knowledge of pain and suffering. She *was* pain and suffering. The feeling of the tears of billions surrounded her like a turbulent ocean and it was fracturing her heart more and more by the minute. She was drowning.

They could run to the ends of the earth and for the rest of their lives and they couldn't outrun Eden.

But could they fight her? There were stories that were just as timeless as Eden was; good defeats evil, love conquers all, the white knight wins. They were the stories of redemption, invention, sacrifice and hope. There was always hope.

"Madi..." She sang her name. Madison was distracted and didn't notice that Eden had turned her attention back to her and was studying her with interest. There was a faint smile of amusement but when Madison met her eyes, she saw something else that betrayed her. Eden was concerned. Or angry. Or perhaps both. Seeing that almost made Madison smile herself. There was always hope. "Oh, Madi, I would love to know what you are thinking right now." She put her hands in her pockets and lazily sauntered the short distance between them. The sway in her hips was both alluring and obscene.

Madison crossed her arms in front of her heart, "Honestly I was thinking about hope."

She stopped strutting and a wide smile broke across her face. "Hope?" Eden broke into hysterical laughter.

Madison rose her chin in defiance, "There is always hope!"

"What exactly are you hoping for here, sweetie? Look around! Things are looking pretty bleak. Wouldn't you agree?" She gestured to the destroyed store and the waiting shadows. "In fact, I would go as far as to say things are looking downright hopeless."

"I saved her. There's hope."

Eden stopped smiling and looked back at Abby in the apartment, and then returned her cold stare to Madison. All her amusement had vanished. "Yeah. About that. I kind of have a problem with you killing my shadow." She strode to the nearest shadow and frowned. "You see, I have come to think of them as my children. And like any good mother, it upsets me when my children are killed by worthless cunts who think they are holier than thou."

"I....I don't think that."

"So what's the plan, Madi? You going to save all these people all by yourself? I mean, it is just you. You have a scared little girl and an asshole as back-up." Her smile returned, but it was far from friendly. She put a finger up and seemed to start counting her shadows, before waving it off as too much work. "I just have to give them the word, and that's it. Game over. I win. In the end, I always win."

Madison looked at the darkness looking back at her and strained to see past their hate-filled stares to see the people trapped within them. How many of them were begging for her help? Madison looked at the woman who was holding them captive and found that she didn't hate her, but instead pitied her. To spend eternity surrounded by souls that only feels disdain must be lonely. "I have to at least try."

Eden sighed. "At first your presence here was a mere annoyance, and then you got really interesting. But unfortunately for you, after spending a short five minutes with you, I find you are really quite mundane. I'm getting bored with you and your 'I'm so brave, I'm going to save the world' delusions." Her tone was sarcastic as she mocked Madison's voice.

Madison felt the hot bubbles of fury inside her. If anyone was annoying, it was this woman. How dare she mock her! How dare she mock hope! But she forced herself to take several calming breaths. She can't feed into the hate and anger. It is exactly what Eden wanted her to do, and that is how she would win.

Eden seemed to notice that Madison was controlling her emotions because she frowned with disappointment. She then put her finger on her lips as though she was deep in thought, "I will tell you what, boring Madi. I'm feeling extra generous tonight. How about we give humanity another shot?"

Madison's brow creased and she frowned deeply. "What? What do you mean?"

"I'm saying I'll let them go."

"I thought you said this wasn't a hostage situation."

Eden shrugged, "What can I say? I lied. Sue me. Oh...wait. You can't! I own all your lawyers!" She giggled.

Madison put her hands on her hips with annoyance, "What's the catch?"

"Can't I do something out of the kindness of my heart?" She laughed and then put her arm around Madison's shoulders. "But you're smart. You know better than that. I like that about you." She leaned in close and brushed her lips against Madison's ear lobe. "But I also kinda hate it too."

Madison's skin, and blood froze and burned with Eden's touch. She felt like maggots were crawling on her skin and was revolted. She squirmed out of her embrace and Eden let her arm drop heavy to her side.

"Alright. Enough pleasantries. Let's make a deal."

Madison couldn't shake the feeling of decay off of skin and she was still quivering in disgust. "What do you want?"

"I want you. And Sam. And Abby. Three people for billions! It seems like an excellent deal if I do say so myself."

"Why would you do that?"

"Why question my generosity?"

Madison persisted, "Why would you do that?"

Eden crossed her arms, sighed heavily and rolled her eyes. "Because I can't have you running around saving people from themselves. You people are like fertile soil. Plant seeds of emotion, feed it and it will grow. And I found that the seeds of hate and rage grow really well in these recent time, and my harvest is doing very well." Her eyes suddenly glowed like hot coals and Madison took a step backwards. "But every now and then, an insignificant weed like yourself invades my garden and it has to be plucked from existence before it spreads."

Madison knew now that Eden wanted to take her not because she was an insignificant weed, but because she could plant seeds of something stronger than hate, she could sow hope. "But why Sam and Abby?"

Eden shrugged. "I don't know. Sounded like fun. Besides, seems pretty fair considering I'm giving up my children." She stuck her bottom lip out in a pout.

"You don't need them."

"Maybe not. But I want them."

Madison looked back at Sam and Abby in the apartment. She didn't think they could hear what was being said but they were intently watching the two of them. "I can't decide this for them. I need to talk to them."

"That's out of the question."

Madison bit her lip. It just wasn't right. Abby had just gotten her freedom back. She was sweet and innocent and was forced to learn so much about hate and anger so quickly. Could Madison force her to leave any chance for hope...for happiness, for love, for a future?

And Sam. Sam was practically already a shadow. Even as recent as a day before, he terrified Madison just as much as the shadows did. But Madison sensed he couldn't have always been this way. She sensed there was such a vulnerability in him. He carried his scars in the form of rage, but he deserved as much of a chance at redemption as anyone. As a shadow, with no one to save them, redemption would be denied to him. "What if it was just me? Can't you just take me?"

"Oh for fuck sake, you are so annoying! I said three for many. That's the deal!" Madison thought she saw the snake around Eden's neck move, but Eden's hand wrapped itself around it before she could be sure. The sweet smile she provided Madison was strained, "But you know, I wouldn't blame you if you didn't take it. Not at all." She spoked slowly with bogus empathy. "It is a lot to ask; giving up your life for perfect strangers. People who wouldn't give you a second thought. I mean look at you, you are so ordinary. Who would do it for you? It would be perfectly reasonable if you wanted to spare yourself and your friends. You all deserve a chance at your future. And you have already been through so much already."

Madison smiled back, brightly and sincerely. There it was. The truth. The crack that Madison had been waiting for. Eden was counting on her to be human; to be self-preserving; to be selfish. And maybe she could be, but at what cost? She would be signing the life sentence papers on each and every person trapped in the darkness, perhaps millions of souls.

Eden said they deserved a future, and they did, but how long of one would be provided? How long before the shadows came for them? An hour? A day? A week? A month? Madison considered just the time since the power outage and how sure she was every day would be her last. She was confident that she didn't want to spend the rest of her future thinking the same thing, no matter how long of a future it was. Seriously, quality over quantity applied here.

And why was Abby's, or Sam's, or even her future more important than anyone else's? They all deserved a future, one of second chances, and peace and not having to be scared of the dark. Madison wasn't sure if Eden could be trusted, but she said she would give humanity another shot and if there was the slightest chance for a do-over, it deserved to be taken.

Eden's smile fell and her brow burrowed. "Time's up, Madi. I need your answer now."

Madison closed her eyes and took a deep breath. She found Ethen's ring around her neck and slowly opened her eyes. As she bore into lovely lilac and with strength, faith, hope and love, she answered. "Deal."

Chapter Thirty-Eight

Madison braced herself for Eden's taking. She waited for the assault from the shadows, but instead Eden gave her a simple smile and shook her head. One by one the shadows around them groaned in pain and fell to the ground. Madison turned and watched the quivering dark masses and when she returned her attention back to Eden, Eden sighed dramatically. "So, so close! You just had to ruin my party, didn't you?" Eden's eyes narrowed as she searched Madison's face and then she smiled and winked at her, "Oh well! You people are nothing if not predictable. There's always next time! See you around, Madi." With that she turned and began stepping over her fallen children without any regard. A moment later, she was simply gone.

Madison frowned. "What just happened?" Around her neck Ethan's ring grew warm against her heart. The heat intensified until Madison had to pull it away from her skin and that is when she noticed it had changed. Inside of Ethan's ring, the very symbol of love and hope eternal was the single ruby snake eye from Eden's necklace; the symbol of hate, deception and rage. It suddenly occurred to her that the fact that Ethan's ring encircled Eden's jewel meant that Eden hadn't won. Love won. Madison acted selflessly and made the choice for humanity.

The groans from the shadows had changed as well. They were becoming more and more human sounding. Suddenly Abby's arms were around her, hugging her tightly as she scolded Madison for acting so foolishly, but also congratulating her for the same. She talked a million miles a minute, and her girlish excitement provided Madison a brief, weak smile. She wished she could give more, she wished she could celebrate, but she felt as though she had aged forty years in the last half an hour. She let Abby babble as she watched darkness melt off the backs of their friends and neighbors.

Abby suddenly let her go, and even over the groans of their community, Madison heard Abby's sharp intake of breath as she stared at her. Madison frowned, "What? What is it? What's the matter?"

Abby's large eyes blinked several times, "Your hair....it's beautiful! It's like the light of the moon...."

"What?" Madison pulled her long hair to the front and gasped. Her dirty brown hair was now white, so bright it seemed to give her a halo of light.

"I guess you won't have any trouble staying in the light now." Sam had hobbled over to where Madison was standing, still stunned. "What happened?"

Madison gently put her hand on Abby's shoulder, "Why don't you see if anyone needs any help?" Abby gave her a bright smile before searching for those in need.

Sam reached out and took a lock of hair between his fingers, "It looks good on you. How did she do that to you?"

Second chances or not, she still didn't like the guy and she pulled away from him. Her hair slid through his fingers without resistance. "I don't know."

"Who was she?"

"I don't know. I mean...maybe I do, but..."

Sam leaned heavily on his crutches and shook his head. "Look, I couldn't hear a damn thing that was being said, and I want to know what the hell happened!"

"I....I think that is exactly what happened. I think we just beat hell..."

Sam studied her for a moment, "A month ago, I would have said you were crazy, but now..."

Men, women and children were standing, covered in dark residue that Madison knew could be wiped clean. "I know..."

"So how did you do it though? How did you make all the shadows fall?"

She looked at Sam and paused, unsure of his reaction. But did it even matter at this point? Eden was gone. The shadows were dying... "I offered the three of us in exchange for all of them."

Sam cocked his head as though he didn't hear her correctly the first time. "You did what?" His eyes were narrowed accusingly. "I'm sorry. Did you say you offered us for them?"

Madison had the urge to take a step back. She felt a familiar habit of fear, but instead she squared her shoulders and lifted her chin. If she could stand up to Eden, then surely she could stand against Sam. "Yeah. It is what she wanted. I couldn't ask you though."

"It wasn't your decision to make! I don't know these fucking people! You are talking about MY life here! You want to sacrifice your damn life, you go right on ahead, but I ain't for sale!" They had caught the interest of several people around them, and they began to gather around them.

"Sam, look around! We are still here, and everyone has been saved!"

"But you didn't know that was what was going to happen! Who the hell do you think you are?"

Madison looked at Sam for a moment, suddenly feeling very sorry for him. She had no more words to offer him, but instead turned and walked away. She walked away from Abby and all the people emerging from the darkness. She could hear Sam yelling for her to come back. She could hear him calling her names. She could hear Abby saying her name with concern, but she kept walking until she could no longer hear them.

She waded through the lake of what was once a parking lot and found the hood of the car to learn against. The metal was rusted and cold but she couldn't feel it. She didn't know if she would ever be cold again. There was a pleasant warmth coming from inside her, and on any other day, she might have enjoyed it, might have found comfort in it, but right now all she felt was exhaustion.

Madison was suddenly very aware of the weight of everything that had happened since the blackout; the lost and the found. She thought of Kathy's husband, a man she barely got a glimpse of. He would be among the emergers, and he would be searching for his wife. Madison was panged with regret and remorse that Kathy suffered from a darkness she couldn't be saved from. And she knew exactly what he would be going through when he realized Kathy was gone.

She thought of Ethan. Every cell of her body ached for him, and the tears rolled down her checks hot. Madison found herself angry. It wasn't fair that he died the way he did after fighting so hard to stay in the light. It wasn't fair that he died as such a good man and would never be able to able to emerge. It wasn't fair that she was now sitting on a rusty car hood, alone, being forced to pick up the pieces of what was left of her heart.

Madison looked towards the east and noticed the sun was beginning to rise. Its light reflected off of her tears producing rivers of diamonds on her face. There were streaks of pink and orange that stretched across the sky. There were several times since the blackout that she wondered if she would ever get to see such a sight again, and now it simply took her breath away. Ethan would have loved it. He would have told her it was a gift to witness the start of a new day. It held a promise of new opportunities. He would have told her to dry her tears and believe in better things to come.

Suddenly Abby's face surfaced in her mind. There was such an innocence there, so full of promise and hope. Madison sincerely hoped that the emergers would be like Abby. She hoped that the people who lived in the dark would begin to embrace each day as a child and with every sunrise take the opportunity to reinvent themselves for the better, not only for themselves, but also for the good of mankind. She hoped they all would remember what it was like to feel empty while filled with hate. She hoped they would embrace learning, acceptance, understanding and growth rather than jumping right back into the dark.

She didn't know if it was possible to erase the prejudices that have been passed down from the dawn of man, but she did know that Eden would be waiting if they failed. If Eden believed in hope, her hope was in people like Sam. People who looked for ways to be angry. People who found reasons to hate.

As the sun reached the destroyed store, people covered in leftover shadow stepped out and allowed the light to caress their skin. Its warmth reached into their very beings and chased away any lingering cold. A hush fell over the crowd as everyone just absorbed the light and Madison found herself smiling. She didn't know how much time they had. She didn't know how long they would remember the darkest days in their history before time made the lesson blurry and their past mistakes began to repeat themselves. But for now, they were okay and she could be thankful for that.

A ray of light found Madison and suddenly all eyes were on her. She could see the awe in their faces as sunlight was brilliantly caught in her white hair. She could feel its energy flood her veins and its power was overwhelming. She didn't know whether she cried out in ecstasy or pain but as a small cloud drifted in front of the sun, she collapsed into the water at her feet.

Many of the emergers ran to her aid. They lifted her out of the water and began to lead her back to the store. The story of her standing up to Eden had already been passed around and after witnessing the sunlight, they sang of her praises and called her an angel. Madison could only shake her head weakly and her denials went unheard. She didn't want the responsibility of being their angel! She didn't want white hair that trapped the sun and made her feel like she was going to explode!

She searched the crowd for someone that was actually paying attention; someone that was maybe picking up at how uncomfortable she was. She was met with smiles and thankfulness as they joyously celebrated their "savior." But her eyes stopped at that one face in the crowd that wasn't celebrating. Wasn't smiling. His familiar glare pierced through all of their bodies. Although he was hunched over on his crutches, his shoulders heaved with ugly emotion.

And somewhere in the darkness Eden smiled. "Oh yes, yes, Madison. There is always hope."

The End

H. D. Raye